After the Flood

STACY NOTTLE

silver phoenix

Silver Phoenix
An imprint of Black Phoenix Publishing Collective
1 Lake Street
Crescent Head NSW 2440
www.blackphoenixpublishing.com

Published by Black Phoenix Publishing Collective in 2019.

 A catalogue record for this
book is available from the
National Library of Australia

ISBN: 9780648397236

Typeset in Book Antiqua, Garamond and Helvetica.

Cover design by Andreja Amijettska.

Printed in the United States.

10 9 8 7 6 5 4 3 2 1   19 20 21 22 23 / 1

DEDICATION

I dedicate this book to my dad, Donald Cooney, who passed away in March 2019. This is some of what I said at his funeral.

Dad felt nature. It was as though he could turn down the volume of his senses and allow the beauty of nature to seep right into his soul. Whenever I went out into the bush with him as a child, I would sense the deep connection he had with the Earth. He understood the vast cycles that moved around him while, at the same time, he noticed the tiniest of creatures, the intricacy of a spider's web; the arrangement of a leaf's veins and the slightest change to the way the air felt.

Dad also appreciated the cultural history of the land he inhabited. One day when I was a girl, he stopped the car on this lonely ridge, so he could show me a plant that stored water in its leaves and could be used as a source of hydration if no other water was available. He then proceeded to point out a thousand-year-old roadway that had once been used by aboriginal people, then he showed me where these people had built their campfire, and a story began to emerge from the stark landscape around me. To me, it was all just dirt, rocks and a few straggly plants.

"Half close your eyes," he said. "That will make it easier to see what's really there."

Dad was deeply affected by human endeavour and was a great admirer of any kind of artistic and creative talent. He was fascinated with patterns and symmetry; he loved the collection of things, and he loved the infinite possibility of words. We shared words, Dad and I, giving them to each other as though they were precious gifts. We shared ineffable and whimsy. Pluviophile, woebegone, sonorous and quark …

Dad chose gentleness over violence. This was evident in everything he did — from working with horses and dogs and livestock to being part of a family. He never attempted to strong arm any of us into doing things his way because he believed we had the right to choose for ourselves. He was a gentle man.

Even though Dad held strong opinions on many things, he would never diminish another person's point of view. He respected women. By this, I don't mean that he altered his behaviour because of the expectations of the society he was part of. It was something more deeply genuine than that. To him, women were his equal and he was never intimidated by their strength and independence.

Dad always made me feel like a worthy person. With him, I always felt visible and understood because he never judged me through the filter of his own ego. He never needed me to look a certain way or act a certain way in order to enhance his own status in the world. It wasn't that he didn't see my flaws. He did. But he accepted them as part of who I was, because, to him, I am perfect just the way I am, and he loved me.

A star falls from the sky and into your hands. Then it seeps through your veins and swims inside your blood and becomes every part of you. And then you have to put it back into the sky. And it's the most painful thing you'll ever have to do and that you've ever done. But what's yours is yours. Whether it's up in the sky or here in your hands.

C. JoyBell C.

CHAPTER 1

Leaving his bowl of half-eaten Weet-Bix on the kitchen table, Jamie goes to his sister's bedroom. All week while she's been away having her treatment, he's been mad with excitement about his idea and now that she's home, he can't wait to share it. He doesn't knock like he's supposed to in case she's still asleep but opens the door and peeps inside.

Sophie's already awake, her nose stuck in a book, so he climbs onto the end of her bed.

'Hey, Soph.'

'Hey, little brother.'

While she marks her place with a green frog bookmark, adds the book to the top of the stack on her bedside table, wriggles upright and smooths her ballerina bedspread across her legs, he studies her for signs of the sickness that's supposed to be in her blood. It's hard to tell if she's any different than before.

'What's up?' she asks.

'Well ... um ... err ...'

He's determined to tell her about the idea but it's harder to say the words than he thought. She might laugh and tell him to stop being a baby.

'You know what Mrs Hendy said the other day?' he says, thinking of his School of the Air teacher's cheery, crackly voice travelling all the way from Charleville and into his schoolroom.

'What?' Sophie's already fidgeting like she's not interested in hearing about Mrs Hendy.

'She said you can have anything you want if you're prepared to work really hard for it.' He chews his bottom lip, wondering if it's a mistake to tell her about the idea after all.

But then she says in her kind voice, 'Jamie? It's okay. Tell me.'

'I'm going to try for a superpower.'

They stare at each other while his words hang between them like dust motes on a still day. When the idea was only a thought in his head, it had felt amazing, but the spoken words make him feel embarrassed — like he's being a baby — and he expects she'll burst out laughing any minute. Which is okay because he likes the sound she makes when she laughs.

But instead of laughing, she waits for him to say more.

'Dad says I'm a hard worker and I'm prepared to work really, really hard to have a superpower, Soph. I've been thinking about it for a while now, ever since … um … well … ever since you got sick, except I didn't think a normal boy could have one. I thought you had to be born with it or come from a different planet or something but when Mrs Hendy said the thing about being able to get whatever you want, I … I …'

Sophie pulls strands of blonde hair from her scalp and mats them into a tiny bird's nest in her lap but her eyes never leave his face.

'I can practise on animals first, of course,' he says, 'and when I get really good, I can do it on you.'

'Do what on me?'

'Fix you.'

A smile lightens her face, followed immediately by a frown and he worries he might have upset her.

'The doctor told Mum to stop trying to cure me because it could interfere with my chemotherapy. He said chemotherapy is trying to kill the bad cells and Mum is trying to keep them alive.' She lowers her voice to a whisper. 'He made Mum cry.'

Jamie stares at his sister, trying to understand how Mum's obsession with smelly potions and vitamins has anything to do with him wanting to cure her with a superpower.

'It'll be really cool for you to have a superpower,' she says, her smile returning. 'Only … I think we should leave curing me to the doctors.'

'Oh,' he says, disappointed.

She gets out of bed, the ball of hair falling forgotten to the floor, patters barefoot to her unpacked suitcase that's spewing clothes across the dusty floorboards, digs inside and produces a glossy pink notebook with white dots and a spiral down one edge. More digging uncovers a pink pencil with feathers sprouting from the end. Every time she comes home from the city, she has new stuff. Not that he wants a pink notebook and feather pencil but ... he would like new stuff too.

'Okay,' she says, back on the bed cross-legged and poised to start writing. 'First, we should write down all the superpowers we can think of, then pick the best one for you to start working on.'

'You think I can have more than one?'

'I'm sure you can, but you should concentrate on one at a time.'

With a flourish, she writes *Jamie's List of Superpowers* at the top of the page. Under this, she writes the number one, then looks expectantly at him for the name of the first superpower.

'Um ... well ... fixing sick people is all I thought of.'

'Let's put it first then, even if it isn't the one you decide to do.' She writes *Fixing People*. 'What about number two?'

Jamie scrunches up his face, and tries to think of another idea.

'Flying?' she asks.

'Yeah. Like a bird.' He nods and spreads his arms like wings.

'And three can be dancing like Anna Pavlova. I always wanted to be able to do that.' He looks at the black-and-white prints of an old-time ballerina on her bedroom wall.

'Okay,' he says, unsure.

Sophie laughs. It's a tinkling sound that gives him the prickly feeling of happiness. 'Maybe dancing like Anna Pavlova shouldn't go on *your* list. Unless you want to dance like Anna Pavlova?'

He shakes his head dramatically and grins back at her. 'No way.'

She crosses out number three.

'What then?'

'Seeing in the dark,' he says.

'I like it. What else?'

'Um … being very, very strong.' He clenches his fists and jaw and makes muscle arms.

'What about being super brainy?'

'Or being able to see through walls. Or walk through walls. Or … or being able to get places straight away and not have to sit in the car for ages.'

'Good one,' Sophie says, gazing in thought at the spider webs on the ceiling. 'I think that's called teleportation.'

He watches his sister write in neat cursive, impressed by how quick she is and by how she keeps all her letters the same size; and he admires her talent for knowing big words like teleportation. And invisibility.

The list grows — ability to change the weather, talking to animals, reading people's minds, turning rubbish into gold, breathing fire. Altogether they come up with forty ideas. Some are hilarious, like befuddlement, where you can muddle up a person's thoughts. In the end, they're laughing so hard, they're holding their sides and flopping about on the bed wiping tears from their eyes.

Then Mum is at the door carrying a tray of food and Sophie snaps the notebook closed as if the words inside are a secret. Special words meant only for him and her.

'Sophie has to rest now,' Mum tells Jamie, even though she doesn't seem tired. 'And your father needs you down at the sheepyards to help load the trucks.'

For the first time in ages, Jamie feels happy. It's good having Sophie home. He pulls on his elastic-sided boots and stockman's hat, takes an apple from the bowl on the kitchen table and heads outside.

Month after month, no rain has fallen, and you don't have to go far to see the roos and birds and other dead creatures turning to dust in the paddocks. The grass has shrivelled and lost its grip on the soil, allowing the fine, powdery earth to spiral upward into giant red clouds that dirty the sky and get in your eyes and clothes and food. Even in your bed.

But the drought can't dampen Jamie's mood this morning. Munching his apple, he walks with a swinging stride along the dusty track past the hangar, across the end of the airstrip and down towards the shearing shed. By his side is Woofy. The old dog no longer has to live in the dog yard with Mickey, Dozer, and Hebe because he's the oldest. He gets to live at the house and keep an eye out for snakes.

When they get to the sheepyards, the trucks haven't arrived, so Jamie gets to hang out with Dad while Woofy keeps himself busy sniffing and cocking his leg on things.

'Why're you sending the sheep away on egistering?' he asks.

'Agistment. Because there's not enough for them to eat.'

'You said Moonbroch was the best grazing country in Australia and even when there's no grass, you said the sheep could eat mulga. Couldn't we cut down mulga for them to eat?'

'Yeah. We could.' Dad turns his body away so Jamie can't see his face.

'Then why don't we? Why can't we keep them here and feed them mulga?'

No answer.

'Why not?'

Dad scrapes his rough bush hand across his face. 'I just don't have the heart for cutting scrub anymore, mate,' he says, choking on his words. Then he walks away towards the approaching cloud of dust to greet the first truck driver.

Three days later, a decision is made for Sophie and Mum to
return to the city. He wants to go with them but last time
he went, it hadn't worked out so well. Especially when he'd
bumped over the doctor's skeleton and plastic bones had
fallen all over the floor. So, he doesn't ask to go. Instead, he
loiters solemnly in the background hoping he can get some
more time with Sophie before she leaves because he's
thought of some really funny superpowers he wants to tell
her about. He just doesn't want to tell her in front of Mum
and Dad because it feels too secret. Like something special
between just the two of them.

From beneath the shade of the gidgee tree by the corner
of the hangar, he watches. He doesn't want to get yelled at
for being in anyone's way and he wants to avoid the awk-
wardness of saying goodbye. Sophie sits pale and breathless
in the passenger seat of the Landcruiser, staring straight
ahead. Mum and Dad are still inside the house.

Then he hears the Landcruiser's horn toot and sees Sophie signalling to him. He saunters over.

'I've been thinking about the superpowers,' she says. She
climbs down from the car and is standing in the dirt in front
of him so that his eyes are level with hers. He looks down
at her t-shirt. It's her favourite and she only ever takes it off
for washing. On the front is a picture of an owl's head in
black and white, and he finds it hard to look away from the
owl's enormous eyes.

'Jamie? Do you want to know?' she asks, leaning against
the open door, struggling to get her breath. The kitchen
screen door bangs. Mum is coming.

He looks into his sister's smudgy blue eyes and nods.

'You should start with flying,' she says. 'You can practice
while I'm away.'

Then, to Jamie's great discomfort, she steps close.
Reaches out her arms. Being hugged by his sister is a bit
queer and his natural reaction is to slap her away, but he
doesn't. He allows her to put her arms around him and
squeeze while his own arms hang loosely at his sides.

———

Dad mostly leaves Jamie alone in the house during the day to do his school work while he goes off to do jobs in the shed or the hangar; or down at the sheepyards. There are always jobs to be done on a sheep station, even when there are no sheep, and Jamie would prefer to be doing jobs with Dad than being stuck in the schoolroom alone. Sometimes, he hears the Cessna start up and goes out onto the verandah to watch the small aircraft vanishing into the wide, blue sky. Before Sophie got sick, Jamie used to go in the Cessna with Dad and he liked to look down at the tiny buildings and trees and fences and sheep spread across the vast landscape. But now, Mum says it's too dangerous.

Even when they're together at mealtimes and in the evenings, Dad doesn't say much. He drinks beer with dinner, talks to Mum on the phone at eight o'clock, then falls asleep on the couch in the lounge room.

On the second day of batching with Dad, Jamie decides to get started on learning to fly. He goes into the breezeway that runs the length of the homestead and starts by jumping off the blanket box, then the silky oak table, bending his knees as his feet hit the floor.

Next, he begins jumping from the wobbly, steel-framed fence that borders the house yard. The hard ground below the fence is brutal but he remembers Mrs Hendy's words about being able to do anything if he tries hard enough, so he ignores the pain and keeps on jumping. This is for Sophie. Every day, when Dad is not around, he jumps. Time and time again.

About ten days after Sophie and Mum left for the city, Dad decides to take the old ute out to the back paddock to check on a windmill and he doesn't ask Jamie to come with him. Knowing he'll be left alone for hours, Jamie moves his flying practise to the sheepyards. The outer fences are made from dry, weathered tree trunks which are easier to balance on and decades of sheep hooves have softened the ground around. With a more stable base and a softer landing, Jamie starts to jump further out, and he begins to extend his arms, flapping as he falls.

That night after his eight o'clock phone call, Dad comes into Jamie's room, sits on the edge of his bed and tells him that Sophie and Mum are due home tomorrow. He seems happier and wants to chat.

'So, what've you been learning about in school?' he asks, and Jamie's heart beats a little faster.

'Just stuff.'

'What kind of stuff?'

His footprints are all over the sheepyards and he wonders if Dad has seen them and knows he hasn't been doing school work at all. He should have brushed them over.

'Jamie? What kind of stuff?'

'Just writing and maths and stuff like that.' He forces a wide yawn.

'All that brain work must have tired you out.' Dad smiles for the first time in ages and gets up to leave. 'See you in the morning, mate.'

Jamie worries all the next day about what he'll tell Sophie when she gets home. He's no closer to being able to fly than he was when she left and he doesn't want to let her down, so he's relieved when, at four o'clock, Dad says he's going flying. Jamie needs to go flying too, for real this time. He needs to man up and jump from somewhere really high.

He watches the tiny plane speed down the runway, getting faster and faster, dust clouding about it like a red pillow before it lifts into the air. Once Dad is safely up and away, he surveys the various buildings — homestead, meathouse, shed, hangar — and settles on the hangar. Easy to climb onto. Plenty high enough.

He spends a few minutes hanging out on the semi-circular shaped roof psyching himself up for the jump. He walks the full length of the highest section sounding out each of the giant faded letters painted there —

M.O.O.N.B.R.O.C.H.

It's written like that so that people in aeroplanes can know the name of the station.

Next, he carefully walks sideways down to the corrugated edge of the roof so that his boots don't slip. He sucks in a few big lungfuls of air and courage, then hunches into a squat, extends his arms wide and — jumps. And once again, despite trying so very, very hard and not giving up, he loses his battle with gravity and smashes into the ground at the back of the hangar.

Another failure. It isn't fair. He is so disheartened he doesn't even bother getting back up out of the dirt. Just lays there on his back until Woofy's wet, curious nose forces him to roll onto his side and cover his head with his arms. If only he could cry.

'What the hell? Jamie. Jamie! Are you alright?'

He must have fallen asleep. Or fainted. Dad lifts him, carries him inside and lowers him carefully onto his bed.

'What happened?' Dad says, trying to check him for life-threatening injury and broken bones.

'Nothing.'

He pushes Dad's hands away.

'I don't understand. Why were you lying on the ground like that?'

Jamie remains silent. How can he even begin to try and explain? Dad wouldn't understand.

'Jamie, did you jump from the roof of the hangar?' And again. 'DID YOU JUMP FROM THE ROOF OF THE HANGAR?'

Jamie nods.

'How could you be so stupid?'

Dad pulls Jamie's boots from his feet and tosses them angrily against the wall.

'Don't move out of this room, you hear?'

If Jamie could speak, he would ask Dad how long he has to stay in his room for. He would ask about whether he can come out for dinner. Or to have his bath. Or to brush his teeth. He has to brush his teeth before he goes to bed. But no words will come out.

'YOU HEAR?'

He nods.

'You can stay here until I say it's okay to come out.'

Dad stomps from the room, leaving the door ajar.

Jamie lies on his side on the bed and stares as the shadows on the wall grow longer and more golden, then fade to black. His ears follow the sounds of Dad moving about the house. The sounds stop for a while — Dad is probably outside feeding the dogs and the chooks, then his heavy tread comes back down the hallway to Jamie's bedroom. Jamie closes his eyes and pretends to be asleep while his father is standing at the door. He doesn't want to talk to him, and he doesn't want to look at the knotty tension his father carries about his body like armour. He doesn't understand Dad's grief. He doesn't *want* to understand it.

Mum and Sophie arrive home from the city sometime after dark. He hears the dogs bark, then a vehicle approaching across the flats. In the darkness of his bedroom, he hears two car doors slamming followed by the screen door in the kitchen banging. Then voices. Raised voices. Frightened voices. Footsteps. Mum's shoes clicking down the hallway. Then his bedroom floods with light. He squeezes his eyes closed in order to keep his tears in and the light out.

'Jamie-love. What happened?' Mum sits into the curve of his body and strokes hair from his forehead.

Silence.

'Jamie?'

He shakes his head.

'Dad said you jumped off the roof of the hangar. Why would you do such a thing?'

He curls his small, wounded body against her.

'Jamie-love, it's okay. Just tell me what's going on.'

Maybe she'll understand. About Sophie and everything. Maybe if he can get her to understand, the horrible pressure in his chest will go away.

'I was trying to fly,' he mutters.

'What did you say?'

'I was trying to fly.'

She slouches forward and drops her head into her hands.

'Shit,' she says. 'Shit. Shit. Shit. Shit. Shit.' Then she lifts her head. 'It doesn't matter how much we want some things, they're just not possible. Flying is not possible. You aren't ever going to be able to fly and you're not to try. Ever, ever again. Do you understand?'

She doesn't understand.

'But —'

'No buts, Jamie. It's to stop. No more jumping off things. DO YOU understand?'

He knows if he can learn to fly, Sophie will get well again. He's one hundred percent sure of it and wishes he knew how to explain that to Mum.

'Jamie? Promise me you won't do anything so stupid again,' she repeats.

He swallows. 'I promise.'

'Good. We've got enough to worry about without you banging yourself up,' she says, shaking her head from side to side. 'Now my beautiful, crazy boy, you'd better come out to the kitchen and say hello to your sister. I've bought KFC all the way from the city for our dinner, so let's go heat it up.'

CHAPTER 2

Jamie sees less of his sister and Mum, who spend more time away in the city so Sophie can have treatment. After that one time when Sophie wrote the list of superpowers in her glossy pink notebook with her feather pencil and they laughed until they cried, she hasn't talked to him much. She's kind of drifted away and he no longer has any way to reach her.

Deep inside, he holds on to the belief that if he can do something amazing like flying, then she'll be okay and everything will return to normal. For this reason, he doesn't give up the idea of learning to fly — but he does change his tactic. Instead of jumping off things, he decides to work on being very, very fast. If he can gain enough speed, he should be able to lift off the ground and into the sky — like the Cessna does. Every afternoon, he pulls on his hat and boots, calls Woofy out from his hole under the oleander bush, and they go running in the scrub. Before Sophie started going away all the time, Jamie never took much notice of the old dog other than to give him a quick pat in passing. Now, he and Woofy are best friends and go everywhere together. Jamie's training regime involves sprinting full pelt through the bush until his chest is about to explode and his ribs are in agony, then walking for a bit until his breath recovers, then sprinting again. Over and over until his body is ragged with exhaustion.

But by the time the cold fingers of winter penetrate the homestead, and with his mother's words still in his head — *flying is not possible, you're not ever going to be able to fly* — Jamie's hopes begin to fade and he starts thinking about other superpowers he might try; anything that will help Sophie get better.

The short winter is quickly replaced by a hot, dry spring. Mum and Sophie are staying at Granny Linley's place in the city when one evening, Jamie hears Dad arguing with Mum on the phone.

'Don't be stupid. Of course I can't take him with me.'

...

'I took the job at Condabin because we need the money. You think the doctors are free?'

...

'No. No. It's just that I don't understand why you can't have him with you.'

...

'Jesus. How much trouble can one small boy be?'

...

'I'm not criticising you Sue, but Jamie needs his mother too.'

...

'Yeah. Yeah. Uh huh. Okay. I appreciate it.'

Later, sitting on Jamie's bed, Dad says 'I've got to go away, mate. It's a flying job out at Condabin Station, good money, but don't worry 'cause Granny Linley is driving out tomorrow to take care of you.'

'In the Volvo?' He grins at the thought of his grand-mother driving the ten hours out to Moonbroch in her beat-up, lime green Volvo. Laughing at Granny Linley's car is better than thinking about the fact that neither of his parents wants him with them.

'Yeah. I guess so,' Dad says, and smiles back. 'She'll be able to help you out with schoolwork, and with looking af-ter the dogs and chooks and watering the fruit trees while I'm away. Doesn't that sound like fun?'

Jamie thinks it sounds like more fun than staying with Dad.

The following evening, while they wait for Granny Lin-ley to arrive, Jamie is in the hanger with Dad while he gets the Cessna ready to leave at dawn the next day. Jamie wants to talk to him about Condabin, about what he'll be doing there and when he expects to be back, and about if he thought it would rain soon, but Dad is banging things around and not in the mood for talking. Once, he spins around and bumps right into Jamie and yells at him to stay out of the way.

After that, Jamie goes to stand near the door and starts digging a hole in the earth floor with the toe of his boot. While he's busy staying out of the way, a bat flies through the door, swoops low over his head and causes him to cry out in alarm. Normally he's not scared of bush animals at all, not even snakes, but at the School of the Air camp last year he heard about a girl who had got a bat stuck in her long hair and had needed to get it cut out.

'For crying out loud,' Dad says. 'It won't hurt you.'

'It nearly ran into my head,' Jamie yells back, his face red with anger. 'You didn't see, so you wouldn't know.'

He flops down onto the ground, draws his knees up to his chin and buries his face. Dad comes across, squats by his side, pats his back and says, 'It'll be okay, mate. You'll see.'

'No, it won't.'

'Did you know that bats don't bump into things as a rule?'

Jamie lifts his head and looks at his father, interested more by the change in his tone than by his words. He doesn't like angry, grumpy Dad, who bangs things around and yells at him. He wants to hang out with softly-spoken Dad who talks to him about stuff.

'The bat did nearly hit me.'

Dad smiles. 'Maybe that old fellow had a bit too much nectar because, mostly, bats don't go around bumping into people. You see, they're special little creatures. Did you know they've got a superpower?'

'Really?'

'Yep. It's called echolocation. I don't recall how it works exactly but it's like a special way of being able to see in the dark. And because of this superpower, they can fly around all night and not ever bump into things. Not even small boys' heads.'

Dad ruffles his hair which has gotten long without Mum home to cut it. Jamie lets him. He's too busy thinking about the thing bats have — echo-something.

He starts practising the very next day and every day after that, for six whole weeks. It's not difficult to find time to practise when Granny Linley is in charge. Each afternoon after lunch, she yawns like Jonah's whale and says, 'Just off to get my forty winks,' then lies down on her bed and falls into a coma for about two hours. While the house rattles in time with her thunderous snores, Jamie is meant to be in the schoolroom keeping up with his lessons. But Granny Linley never checks, so instead, he slips quietly out the screen door, careful not to let it bang, and goes out to practise his new superpower.

He walks to the edge of the flats, about a kilometre west of the homestead where the hard, loamy ground gives way to red sand and mulga, then closes his eyes and attempts to walk home. The only plants between him and the house yard are dried out clumps of neverfail grass that stick out of the ground like old fuse wire and isn't usually enough to trip him over. But there are other obstacles too — half-buried, gnarly chunks of timber that have washed there during past floods, cracks that have opened up during the drought like a thousand thirsty mouths, ants' nests, and brown snakes whose venom is the deadliest in the world. Walking over the flats with his eyes closed is hard. But Jamie never expected it would be easy. He doesn't want it to be easy. He wants it to be hard. The harder the better. If he can do something really, really, hard, he might be able to cure Sophie. Then, everything will return to normal.

Jamie sees a lot of death during the year Sophie is sick. Every day, he notices another creature lying in the dust shrinking from the inside out. One day, he and Woofy find a kangaroo down on its side. A fan pattern has formed in the dirt where its feet are hopelessly sweeping against the ground but it's too weak to get up. He doesn't want the kangaroo to die, but even more, he doesn't want it to suffer an agonising death, so he runs home to tell Dad. Dad gets his rifle and they walk together out across the flats.

'It's over here,' Jamie says, pointing out the poor old roo.

'Hold the rifle,' Dad says, passing it to Jamie.

'You want *me* to shoot it?' he says, a slight squeak in his voice, but Dad has scouted around and picked up a solid chunk of wood.

'No. I'll club it. Turn away.'

Dad doesn't want him to watch, but he's curious so takes a few paces backwards and squints his eyes closed, leaving a small slit so he can still see what happens. Dad swings the wood in a short, vertical arc, there's a dull thud as it collides with the roo's head, and then the roo doesn't kick any more. Dad nudges it with his boot a few times to check that it's dead, then drops the wood on the ground next to the roo's bloodied head.

'Why didn't you shoot it?' Jamie asks.

'Didn't want to waste a bullet.'

'Why didn't you hit it with the rifle?'

'Didn't want to break the rifle. Come on. Let's go.'

Jamie half walks and half trots to keep up with Dad's big strides. He's thinking about the way the roo had kept sweeping that big fan shape in the dirt with its legs, and then he starts thinking about Sophie.

But Sophie is only sick. She isn't going to die like the roo. He knows this because she once told him she had things to do with her life.

'What kind of things?' he'd wanted to know.

'First, I'll go to boarding school and make lots of friends and have dancing lessons,' she'd said, twirling about, 'and then I'll go to the Opera House and maybe the Eiffel Tower, which is in Paris, or to New York City,' another twirl, 'and then I'll become a teacher and I'll get married and have four children — two girls called Holly and Anna and two boys called Noah and Tyler. And Tyler's middle name will be James, after you. And we'll live in a big white house with five bedrooms and have a dog who lives inside.'

When they get back to the house, the phone is ringing. It's Mum. Calling to say Sophie has died. Jamie is angry at Mum for saying that. For lying. How can Mum say such a thing? He knows it's not possible. Sophie can't have died because she still has all those things left to do.

If Jamie had known his sister was going to die, he might have done things differently. Tried harder. Said more.

Now it is too late.

After the funeral, lots of people gather at Granny Linley's house in the city. They wear good clothes and talk in hushed voices, and there's lots of hugging and sandwiches. No-one thinks to ask Jamie how he might be feeling. Some people mess his hair or pat his shoulder, but no-one looks him in the eye and asks if he's doing okay. What would he know about feelings and sadness? He's only a little kid.

CHAPTER 3

Cass squints her eyes and tries to get a better look at her father through the tinted glass. It's been a while since she last saw him, and she wants to make sure the man behind the wheel is not just some random stranger. The car does look like the kind Jamie McKenzie would drive — a big, boxy, four-wheel drive with red dust embedded in the creases around the windows and the remains of a tree captured in the roof rack. It looks like a car that belongs in the bush, not double-parked in front of the city apartment block where she lives with her mother. She taps on the glass and her father opens his eyes. He starts to get out of the car then notices he's blocking someone's exit.

'Hi Cass. Quick. Hop in,' he says.

She goes around to the other side of the car, pulls open the door and climbs into the passenger seat, shoving her backpack onto the floor at her feet.

'That's all the luggage you've got?' he says. 'Not much for a week.'

'Eleven days,' she says, reaching for her seatbelt.

Someone honks at them.

'Eleven days?' he says, pulling his oversized car into the Sunday afternoon traffic along Coro Drive.

'Uh-huh.'

'Your mum said it was going to be a week.'

'Huh-uh.'

He frowns. 'Okay. Good. More time for you and me, hey?'

Cass digs her iPhone from the pocket of her shorts, unlocks it with her fingerprint and starts flicking through the apps.

'Eleven days seems like an odd amount of time.'

Sighing, Cass fixes an AirPod into one ear and holds the other like a threat. 'Why not just ask me why you're getting stuck with me, if that's what you want to know?'

When he doesn't respond, Cass continues. 'It's because she needs a break.'

'It's just … it was all pretty sudden,' he says.

'I guess that's the thing with nervous breakdowns. They're not something you can schedule.'

He holds the steering wheel tightly in both hands and glances across at her. 'You think your mother is having a nervous breakdown?'

'No. That's just what she said to get rid of me.'

'You sound like you're mad at her.'

Well. Yes. She *is* mad with her mum for constantly picking fights about the smallest of things. Such as her tiny-bit-messy bedroom or the one dirty dish she left on the floor. Mostly, however, she is mad because she's being made to go stay with *him*.

'I'm sure your mum deserves a break,' he says, 'and I love getting stuck with you for eleven days. We'll find all kinds of fun things to do.'

Cass puts her feet up onto the car's dash and wriggles her purple-painted toenails.

'Such as?'

'Well … um … I haven't planned anything yet. Let's get you home and we can decide together what we're going to do.'

Cass pushes the other AirPod into her ear and turns her attention to the music app on her phone. It's too pitiful listening to him suddenly trying to be her dad after all this time. Next thing, he'll start asking questions about her life and then, worse, he'll try and tell her stuff about himself. Gross. As if she cares anything about him.

She studies him out of the corner of her eye, notices the way he sits slightly forward on his seat, concentrating, as he drives the big car up the ramp that merges with the Western

Freeway. He's like a stranger to her. Why would her mother send her away with a stranger?

When she was little, she would see her father twice a year like clockwork. He would fly down to Brisbane from where he lived in Mt Isa — he once showed her on a map where Mt Isa was — and he would take her places like Dream-world and Australia Zoo; and then, when she was ten, he took her to the coast for a whole week and taught her how to ride a boogie board in the surf. And then … nothing. Not another word. That was two years ago.

Of course, she'd asked her mother about him. Every school holidays. Is Dad coming? And her mother would shake her head and say, not this time. But when? When's he coming? Can't I just call him? The answer was always sorry, but no. She found out how to get into her mother's Face-book account, but he wasn't listed as one of her friends; and she went through the contacts on her phone, but he wasn't there either. It made her crazy that her mother wouldn't say why he didn't come until, in the end, she just stopped asking and accepted that he was gone from her life. And now he was back. Worse, she has discovered that he now lives in Toowoomba. At least when he lived in Mt Isa he had an excuse because it was far away. But *Toowoomba!* Why hadn't he come to see her if he only lived in Toowoomba?

He's more relaxed since he got off the Ipswich Motor-way and onto the road to Toowoomba, she notices. His hands are looser on the wheel and his back is resting against the back of the seat. Behind his silhouette, the country is hilly and green and the afternoon light has begun to soften. He looks over at her and smiles.

She jerks her head down and returns to staring at her phone and he goes back to watching the road ahead, squint-ing into the sun. He drums his fingers on the wheel a few times. Clears his throat. Sighs and rubs his hand across the stubble on his chin. She knows he's confused about her at-titude but what did he expect? It's been *two* years!

The car's braking wakes her. Her head is resting crookedly against the door frame of the four-wheel drive and her neck is stiff. She straightens and peers outside — misty rain, streaky lights, Sunday night traffic.

Her father has stopped at a red light. He's looking at her and there's a weird, far-away expression on his face.

'Where are we?' she asks, pushing her soft blonde hair back so that her blue eyes and round, pretty face are strikingly visible.

'We're in Toowoomba, Soph. Nearly home.'

CHAPTER 4

Cass's father's house is a cute, two-bedroom cottage with a little verandah out the front, another out the back, and lavender bushes growing in the garden.

She lies sideways across the double bed in the spare room and chats online with her friends who are on summer holidays in places way cooler than Toowoomba. Hannah is camping on Straddie, Indi has gone to the Woodford Folk Festival with her cousin, Su-Lin is skiing in Japan, and Sara has gone to Paris with her grandmother. As far as she knows, only one of the girls from school is left in Brisbane this summer — a girl called Winter — who must be kind of povo because she doesn't have an iPhone like everyone else.

Some of the other girls say Winter is just plain weird, but ever since she started at Cass's school a year ago, Cass has been intrigued by her. The thin, dark girl floats from group to group — she doesn't seem to have any particularly close friends and it doesn't seem to bother her. Cass wishes she didn't care so much about what Hannah, Indi, Su-Lin and Sara think of her. She wishes she could just be herself and be friends with whoever she likes, but she knows her friendship group will get upset if she starts hanging around with someone new.

On the last day of school before the summer holidays, Winter had surprised Cass by giving her a hand-written note.

Cass,
Happy holidays. Yay!
Thank you for being my friend this year. Sort of.
Love from Winter

PS — We should do stuff over the holidays.

Feeling guilty about not calling Winter earlier and wanting someone new to listen to her complaints about having to stay with her father in Toowoomba, Cass gets off the bed and retrieves the note from the front pocket of her backpack. Across the bottom, Winter has written an address in Paddington and a phone number. Cass calls the landline number and chews the inside of her cheek while she waits to be connected.

Hello. A man's voice.

'Hello, I —'

This is the Rose residence. James, Geetha, and Winter are not able to take your call right now. Please leave a message after the...

Relieved that it's only a recorded message and she won't have to talk to Winter's dad, she's about to hang up when Winter answers.

'Hello? Winter speaking.'

'Winter? Hi. It's Cass. From school.'

'Cass. CASS. Hi.' She sounds pleased.

'I should have called sooner. Sorry. Are you home? I would ask you over to my place except I'm not home. I've been sent to stay with my father in Toowoomba.'

'I didn't know you have a dad.'

'Well, I don't really have a dad. Most of the time. I hardly ever see him.'

'What's his name?'

'Jamie McKenzie.'

'He lives in Toowoomba?'

'He does now. But he used to live in Mt Isa.'

'Is he nice?'

'How the hell would I know? I haven't seen him for two years.'

'But do *you* like him?'

Cass pauses. Does she like her father? She wants to tell Winter no, she doesn't like him, thus ensuring she gets maximum sympathy. But she can't do it. It feels too disloyal.

'He's alright, I suppose.'

'What's his name and address? Wait. I'll get a pen.'

Cass laughs. 'You crack me up, Winter. What do you want to know that for?'

Winter echoes her laughter. It's a confident, robust sound that doesn't seem to match the scrawny, black-eyed girl she knows from school. 'Sorry. I've been reading Nancy Drew books over the holidays. She's like this girl detective who goes about the place solving mysteries. My Poppy says I'm like a detective myself, or a nosy journalist, because I've got a special notebook that I write information in, just in case I need it later.' She laughs again. 'Anyway, I've got my pen and notebook right here so you might as well give me some details. I want to know everything about this Jamie McKenzie who is masquerading as your parent. His name, address and phone number, his occupation, the number of limbs he has, the length of his nose, and what he eats for breakfast. And give me your phone number too, so I can ring and annoy you whenever I like.'

A huge smile has spread across Cass's face. Winter is so funny. Funny and interesting. Amidst much laughter, she shares details about her father and her current captivity in Toowoomba, which Winter says sounds worse than Kerobokan Prison, whatever that means. Cass describes her father's big, boxy car that has red dirt in all its creases and a whole tree in its roof rack; and she imitates the slow way he talks because, she says, he's a bushie who grew up out west.

After she finishes speaking to Winter and is tucking the note under a little vase on the dressing table, she realises that her father is standing at the bedroom door. Was he listening in to her conversation? The smile slips from her face and her cheeks redden.

'What?' she says.

'I've made us some lunch.'

'Not hungry.' She flops back onto the bed.

'You didn't eat breakfast.'

'Still not hungry. Thanks.'

'Well, you can come and sit at the table please.'

Actually, she *is* a little hungry, so she slides off the bed and saunters out through the pretty lounge room where several framed photographs of strangers, presumably his family and friends, are on display. She'd studied them last night while he was in the shower, curious to see if she was represented amongst the collection. She wasn't. For a moment, her heart had lifted with hope when she'd seen a photo of a blonde girl about her age and she'd picked up the antique white frame for a closer look. But it wasn't a photo of her. It was another girl with a big smile and hair blowing across her face. 'Who the hell is she?' Cass had thought. 'And why does she have my face?' She wants to ask her father about the girl in the photo and about why he'd called her Soph in the car when they first got to Toowoomba, but it's impossible. She's too mad at him. Every time she tries to talk to him, her words tangle in her throat like a giant knot of spaghetti.

She marches into the kitchen and flops down at the table where her father has placed two homemade ham and salad rolls and two glasses of orange juice. A quick press with her index finger switches her phone back on and she places it strategically next to her plate so she can see the screen while she eats.

'Got any idea what you'd like to do while you're here?' he asks, taking a bite of food. She can hear him chewing.

'Cass?'

'What?'

'What do you want to do this week?'

She swipes her phone and takes another bite of food, biting back the urge to remind him that it's eleven days, not a week.

'Cass?'

She swallows. 'Do you want me to talk with my mouth full?'

Her father doesn't answer. He gets up from the table, goes out through the screen door, allowing it to bang be-

hind him, and tromps along the back verandah to the laundry. Cass stops chewing and listens to him opening and
closing cupboard doors, then he comes back into the
kitchen and drops what looks like a ratty old backpack onto
the end of the table.

'Tomorrow, we'll go hiking,' he says. 'It'll be an early
start.'

Cass stops chewing.

'Okay with you?' he asks.

Before she can respond, her phone begins to vibrate. She
stares at her father, unsure whether to answer it while he's
standing over her.

His jaw clenches. 'Answer it.'

'Hello?'

'It's Winter again.'

'Um. Can I call you back? It's not a good time.'

'Because of him?'

'Yep.'

'Well, I'll be quick. It's important. When I told my Poppy
I had a friend who was staying in Toowoomba, he said
would I like to visit you because he has to go up there on
business. Tomorrow. Would that be alright, do you think? I
could come over around three tomorrow afternoon?'

Cass holds the phone away from her face and says to her
father, 'Can I have a friend over tomorrow afternoon?
Please?'

She holds her breath and crosses her fingers under the
table.

And he nods. 'Sounds like a good plan.'

'He said yes,' Cass tells Winter.

'Da de da dum, Winter to the rescue,' Winter replies in a
sing-song voice. 'See you tomorrow.'

Trying to hold back her grin so her father doesn't start
thinking she's happy, she ends the call, puts her phone
down, and takes another bite of her roll.

'We'll leave for our hike early so we're sure to be home
in time for you to see your friend,' her father says.

Cass can't remember the last time she actually got out of bed before the sun was up. Maybe never. She's definitely not a morning person and especially when she's on holidays, but her father doesn't give her a choice. In the middle of the night — 3:30 a.m. according to her phone — he comes into her room, switches on the light which burns great holes in her retinas, tells her to, 'rise and shine, and don't forget your sneakers,' then takes her backpack from the wicker chair and heads out through the lounge room to the kitchen.

'Cass, you up?' he calls a zillion times until she throws off the pillow she's been holding over her head and trots through the kitchen to use the bathroom. In the kitchen, he's jamming all kinds of stuff into her new backpack and his ratty old one — food in clip seal bags, water bottles, sunscreen, insect repellent, hat, rain jackets so musty and smelly she'd rather get wet, first aid kit, maps, torch, compasses, and who knows what else. OMG! Where's he planning on taking her? Will she even make it out alive?

Before long, they're sitting side-by-side in the four-wheel drive. The main street running south from the city is called Ruthven Street and at this hour, only the occasional vehicle scurries past, carrying unknown passengers to unnamed places. Her father drives silently between the arch of Jacaranda trees and on past Kmart Plaza and Harvey Norman. They wait on the boundary of the city under the red glow of traffic lights and then they're winding into darkness. One minute, streets and buildings. The next, nothing. Or hardly anything. Hills hug the road on both sides leaving only a narrow space for them to pass through. The car's headlights give her glimpses into the surrounding country but not enough for her to get an idea of what it's like. She listens to the purr of the motor and thinks at least the car sounds happy to be on the open road at this time of day.

The change is subtle. The road becomes straighter and the land's shape begins to emerge from darkness. There are hills further out to her left, but to the right she begins to see a vast, grassy plain, broken occasionally by a white silo or farm shed. At first, everything is washed with grey, then streaks of mauve and pink appear, and finally the plants and clouds start to turn golden as the yet-to-be-seen sun throws its light into the world.

'Isn't this something?' her father says with quiet restraint. 'You know you're alive when you see a sunrise like this.'

Cass digs into the pocket of her shorts and pulls out her phone, switches it on and begins flicking between apps. She checks the time in Paris.

'Turn it off and put it away.' His voice is harsher than she's ever heard.

Yesterday, after she'd finished talking to Winter the second time, he'd started ranting on about her having way too much screen time and made her promise that this morning, she'd stay off it. And she'd agreed. Kind of.

'I mean it, Cass,' he says.

'I was checking the time,' she replies before slipping the phone out of sight beneath her thigh. 'Old people like you use a watch to tell the time and people like me use a phone. I don't tell you not to look at your watch.'

Her father's jaw is tight and his shoulders tense as they pass a service station on the right, drive a kilometre or two further and take a left turn towards a place called Goomburra.

'So, what's your thing?' he says, his voice strained with the effort of trying to find a way to reach her. Cass frowns. She hates question time.

'You play any sport?' He looks across at her.

'Sometimes. At school. In P.E.'

'What sports do you play? In P.E.'

'Whatever the teacher says.'

'What about a musical instrument? Do you play music? Or dance?'

Cass shakes her head. No. She doesn't do sport or music or dance or model railways or basket weaving or mathematical sequences, and she can see that her not having a thing is making him mad. Maybe if she had a thing, he wouldn't have stayed away for two years.

'I like hanging out with my friends,' she says hopefully.

'I don't think hanging out with your friends counts as an interest,' he replies. 'Do you read books? I used to love reading when I was your age.'

Her hand finds the phone concealed below her leg. She takes it out, turns it on and begins flipping through her apps, all the while watching her father in her peripheral vision. She notices his large-knuckled hand opening his window and feels the warmer outside air roll in. Next, his hand comes down over hers. He grabs the phone and pulls it free. So unexpected is the move that she has no time to protect her very expensive, Christmas-present-from-her-mother, only-contact-with-the-outside-world, soon-going-to-high-school iPhone and she looks up in horror as it goes sailing out the window, traces an arc through the air and lands in a bush growing in the drain on the side of the road.

Her father closes his window and keeps driving. His mouth is tight. His hands are clenched around the steering wheel. White-faced with shock, Cass rotates around and looks out the back window.

'Dad. DAD! Go back. Dad. You've got to go back. Please.'

He keeps driving deeper into the valley. The summer heat and lack of rainfall has burnt the farm grasses brown but here in the valley, the vegetation is green and cattle graze peacefully in the pastures near the creek alongside the occasional group of campers, their campfires creating a smoky eucalyptus haze.

'Are you going back? Dad? It's worth eight hundred dollars.'

Her father stays silent and concentrates on the narrow, gravel road.

'You have no right,' she says, her face red. 'It's against the law to take someone else's property which means you've broken the law and should go to jail. My mother wouldn't let me go with you if she knew you were a criminal. You have to turn the car around. NOW!' She reaches across and grabs the steering wheel, the sudden jolt causing the car to skid sideways. Her father pushes her hand firmly away with his left hand while righting the vehicle with his right.

'Don't be silly, Cass,' he mutters. 'You'll get us both killed.'

'I don't care,' she says. 'I want you dead. I hate you.'

Then she goes silent.

He glances across as she slumps low in her chair, her arms crossed menacingly over her chest, her face set into the meanest of scowls. A tear separates from her eye, runs across her cheek and is angrily wiped away on the back of her hand. Her father swallows hard.

The National Park carpark is empty when they arrive and before any further words are spoken, Cass flings open her door and marches away up the nearest bush track. Her bare legs are scratched by the dense grasses growing along the edges of the creek. She hops across some flat stones in the dry creek bed and vanishes into the forest on the other side. Not once does she look back to see if her father is following.

He snatches their packs from the backseat, locks the car and trots after her, but it's several minutes before he catches sight of her moving ahead through the trees because, despite the state of the outdated, overgrown track, she moves with extraordinary speed and grace.

CHAPTER 5

Willy holds open the door to the ramshackle dump they call home and presses herself against the wall so her mother can hobble past her into the musty interior. As far as she knows, there's no physical reason her mother walks like an old person. Her doctor says she's in okay shape physically. Her blood pressure is good. Her heart is strong. It's the inside of her head that's the problem. She hears voices. She thinks about killing herself all the time. Willy wishes they would make her stay in the hospital permanently, so she didn't have to take care of her.

'We're home, Aggie,' she says, raising her voice so that the woman who comes to help out knows they're back from the hospital. No answer. If only they could afford to pay for a proper carer or even get a volunteer who is reliable and actually does something to help, instead of smoking and doing puzzles all the time. Aggie is so lazy and critical. She's a giant busybody who is always going on about how good it is to help the poor and needy. Makes you a better person, she says. Willy grits her teeth. She takes in a deep lungful of air in an effort to settle her irritation, because she knows that without Aggie, she would be stuck at home permanently.

'Aggie?'

She glances at her Mickey Mouse watch and bites the inside of her cheek. Collecting her mother had taken longer than expected and she needs to get ready to go out. Today is her eighteenth birthday and she's got plans.

'Aggie? Are you here?'

She turns her attention to removing her mother's shoes and settles her into her favourite chair, then goes into the kitchen to lock away the tablets the nurse at the hospital gave her. The frown on the nurse's face had told her everything she already knew — her mother is not well enough to be at home. But the doctor had signed her discharge papers. They probably wanted to free up a bed for one of the other schizos.

On the cluttered kitchen table amongst the unwashed dishes, sauce bottles, crumbs and old newspapers are two items that bring a smile to Willy's face. The first is Aggie's familiar, overstuffed handbag with tasselled edges. Good. She's here somewhere. The second is a gaudily-wrapped birthday present the size of a shoe box. She picks it up and gives it a shake. Doc Martens. Has to be. She's been dropping hints about needing a pair of Docs for weeks and she knows her mother gave Aggie money to get the present.

'Aggie?'

Still no answer. She stomps her foot.

'Mum?' she says, popping her head around the door to the lounge room, 'I'm going down to Onfro's place to get Aggie. Only be a couple of minutes. Okay?'

Willy goes out the back door past the laundry and through the broken picket fence into old Mrs Rossi's small back garden which is wildly overgrown with vegetables and every kind of herb you can imagine. She snaps off a sprig of sweet basil as she passes and inhales the peppery aroma, then glances again at her wristwatch. Her best friend, Ray, will be here any moment and she really has to be ready when he gets here because he hates waiting. Getting him into a bad mood will ruin everything.

Through the next fence is Onfro's place. This is where she's most likely to find Aggie — Onfro is the real reason Aggie volunteers to help take care of her mother. So she has an excuse to be around the neighbourhood. But who'd be interested in a creep like him? Willy had only been fifteen when he'd started calling over and trying to get into her mother's bed. What kind of man takes advantage of a woman like her mother? And when Willy told him to piss off, he'd pushed her against the wall and tried to grope her breasts and she'd had to kick him in the shins in order to

get him off her. At least that's how Willy remembers it. Onfro, of course, has a different memory of what happened —
he had told the police that Willy was a neglected and pro-
miscuous child who needed to be put into foster care. Nothing ever came of it, but she still hates him for trying to have
her put away.

Stepping onto the back landing of Onfro's house, she
leans against the outside wall and peeps through smudgy
glass into the kitchen. Onfro is inside. And Aggie. He's got
her pressed against the kitchen bench and he's going for it.
Screwing her. Pumping and grinding his pelvis against her
like there's no tomorrow. His head is bent back and his
mouth is open. It's disgusting.

Willy has already gotten dressed ready to go out and is
sitting quietly in the lounge room with her mother when
Aggie finally arrives back from Onfro's place. She glances
with distaste at the plump woman's dull, curly brown hair
and at the familiar mole on her chin, at her ridiculous,
brightly-coloured kaftan, the hippy thongs on her feet and
the rings on her toes. At the black polish on her toenails and
the small glass jug clutched in her pudgy hands.

'I just had to go down to Onfro's place and borrow some
milk for my coffee,' she says. 'You really need to do grocery
shopping, Willy. Your mother can't live on air, you know.
And you need to clean this place up. It's a pigsty.'

Normally, Willy would react to Aggie's criticisms by saying that other kids at her school didn't have to shop and
cook and clean and take care of their retarded mothers while
studying for their HSC, to which Aggie would have reacted
by telling her not to call her mother a retard, and a yelling
match would have ensued. But she hasn't got time to fight
today. She's got plans. She's going out. In silence, she follows Aggie into the kitchen.

Aggie points at the large parcel while lighting a cigarette.
'That's for you.'

She neglects to add that the present is from her mother. Despite herself, Willy feels excited to open her only birthday present and carefully separates the tape from the paper with her long fingers. She likes wearing cool stuff — Docs are definitely the coolest — and she's already imagining the feel of the soft leather on her feet. A small warning bell starts to go off inside her head as she spies the random-looking box under the paper, but she holds on to hope until the box is fully open and she can see inside. Plastic sports shoes. White with pink trim. Something you would get from Kmart. Aggie loves to shop at Kmart.

'It's what you need,' Aggie says, puffing on her cigarette and nodding at the box full of ugliness. 'Weren't cheap, either.'

'But I ...' What's the point? She swallows down her disappointment and mutters her thanks. Then Ray arrives and he's hyper-excited about their trip into the city where they'll meet up with some of the others and celebrate her birthday.

'Happy birthday, Willy. Ready to partay?' He gives her a mischievous grin and passes her an elaborately wrapped present.

Inside is a pair of Doc Martens. Black leather with purple laces. Perfect.

'You're a bright girl, Willy,' say Mrs Batzloff, the school counsellor. 'And when a bright girl stops achieving in the middle of her HSC, my experience tells me there's usually a good reason. Is everything okay at home?'

Oh, everything's just hunky dory, thank you, Mrs B. My mother is a crazy schizo who should be locked away permanently in the loony bin. My house is a dump. And... and... my best friend, Ray, made me take drugs so I would have sex with him. I told him I didn't want to take the drugs but he said I was chicken shit if I didn't and then I said I didn't want to have sex with him and he said I was too old to still be a virgin and if I didn't hurry up and have sex, I'd dry up and no man would ever be able to get it in there. After we did it, he said I wasn't very good anyway and I needed to loosen up and stop being boring, and he was sorry he'd wasted all his money buying me such an expensive birthday present. Now he acts like he owns me and expects me to take drugs and let him do it to me whenever he wants.

But she doesn't say any of this to the counsellor. She just sits there staring down at her lap, ignoring the woman everyone refers to as Mrs Fat Slob.

'Willy. You have the power to decide what kind of life you want and what kind of person you will become.'

Willy looks up, startled to think that Mrs Batzloff might have just read her mind.

'Don't let others take that power away from you.'

A short while after completing her HSC, Willy is given an opportunity to get out of Sydney.

Apparently, Aggie has been talking to her daughter, a woman called Moira who works as a bank manager in western Queensland, and apparently, this Moira woman has suggested that Willy might like to come and visit her in the outback. She even suggested that Willy could stay a while and try to get a job in the town.

Willy can only imagine the awful things Aggie has been saying about her. But she doesn't care. She's never been out of Sydney before and she'll do anything to escape her life. She hates her waitressing job and when she's not at work, everyone expects her to be out drinking and partying. Going to clubs. Taking drugs. Ray has started calling her 'my girl' and insisting she do all kinds of horrid sexual things with him that she doesn't want to do. This is not the life she wants, and with her mother back in the hospital, there's no reason to stay. This is her opportunity to escape and if she likes it, she might never come back.

She'll not even tell Ray where she's going. She'll just disappear.

CHAPTER 6

After Sophie's funeral, Jamie, Mum, and Dad return to the station and try to get back to normal. But Jamie soon concludes that there's no such thing as normal anymore.

Mum is angry all the time. Her mouth is tight and crooked and she won't look at him. Dad sits outside drinking beer and even starts sleeping on the verandah, sprawled on top of a saggy shearer's stretcher, sometimes with his boots still on. Woofy moves onto the verandah alongside Dad, positioning himself so that whenever Dad's hand drops over the edge of the stretcher, it falls onto Woofy's head.

Every so often, Mum or Dad remember that Jamie still exists, and they act like everything is okay for a few minutes or an hour before retreating back inside their own misery.

One evening, about a month after the funeral, Mum gets a phone call. Jamie is slouched at the kitchen table waiting for his dinner. His arm is stretched across the wooden tabletop and he has one eye closed while he lines up the salt, pepper and sauce bottles so he can only see the item that's in front, closest to him.

Dad is also at the table, a cold stubby of beer in his big, warm hands. Both Jamie and Dad listen in on Mum's phone call. They both know something else awful has happened because Mum is coiling her hair around her finger.

'I'll leave first thing in the morning,' she says in a stretched voice before hanging up the phone and going back to cutting up salad for dinner.

'What is it?' Dad asks.

Without turning to face him, she says, 'Mum's had a stroke. She's in St Vincent's.'

She doesn't cry.

Jamie doesn't know what a stroke is, but he does know that people who go to the hospital die, and he doesn't want

Granny Linley to die. He scrapes his chair across the floor, stands and bolts out the door, allowing the screen door to bang behind him. No-one comes after him and he doesn't care.

After hugging Woofy on the front verandah for a bit, he goes back around to the kitchen side of the house and is just about to push his way through the screen door and go back inside for his dinner when he hears Mum and Dad arguing.

'What about Jamie?' Dad says.

'You'll have to look after him.'

'Jesus, Sue, you know I've got the job out at Tibberoo. I can ask Jonny Fletcher to come take care of the dogs and chooks while we're away, but we can't leave Jamie with Jonny. If you won't take him, he'll have to go stay with the Curries. Or we can send him to my sister.'

There's a long pause and when Mum speaks again, her voice is all kind of whispery and broken and Jamie has to lean close to hear her words.

'My mother just had a stroke,' she says.

'I'm sorry about your mum. Really, I am. I just don't understand why it's such a big deal you taking Jamie with you. He's your son, for God's sake.'

'He's your son too.'

'You know I can't take him to a muster.'

Jamie has heard this argument before, except this time Granny Linley won't be able to come to the rescue because she's in the hospital with the stroke.

'I can't take him.'

It sounds like Mum is crying.

'You have to, Sue.'

'Please. I can't. You know I can't. What if something goes wrong? What if I have a car accident? What if he gets hurt?'

'What about the Curries, then?'

'No. NO.'

He hears Mum running out of the kitchen into the breezeway, all the way down to her bedroom, and her bedroom door closing.

When Jamie re-enters the kitchen, Dad is wearing his warrior face. He makes vegemite toast for their dinner and, just after nine o'clock, tucks Jamie into bed. The sheets have a gritty texture on account of not having been washed since the last time Granny Linley was on the station and because the red dust keeps blowing into the house and coating everything. Even when you have a bath, the dust gets on your feet from the floor and goes into the bed with you.

Jamie lies in the dark with his eyes open, listening to Mum packing. He knows the clickety-pow of her suitcase catches, the zing of her toiletry bag zipper, the scrape of clothes hangers sliding along the rail. Dad is out in the kitchen talking to someone on the phone. Then, with heavy steps, he goes to the bedroom he once shared with Mum and talks to her in a low, rumbly voice. Jamie thinks about having super-hearing so he can hear what Dad is saying. And then about whether dogs have super-hearing as well as super-smelling. He wonders if Sophie had written super-hearing and super-smelling on the list of superpowers in her pink notebook. And what about talking to animals? Was that on the list?

Next morning, he wakes with a jolt, startled because he doesn't remember falling to sleep. With his bare feet leaving a trail over the dusty floor, he goes to the toilet and then on to Mum's room. She's gone. Her bed is made with the same tight precision she uses every time she goes away. Had she come early to his room and kissed his cheek and told him to be a brave boy and say she would be home soon? Or had he dreamt that?

He climbs onto her patterned bedcover and spreads himself amongst the boats and sea clams and summer flowers, causing a tiny rumple of disorder. The air is filled with the earthy, floral scent of the potions and oils she'd started using after Sophie got sick. He folds his hands behind his head and starts to count the number of squares in the pattern on the ceiling. He thinks about having a superpower where you instantly know the number of things without needing to count them.

'Here you are.'

Dad tries to smile but looks more like the grim reaper, his mouth stretched into a grimace. Why is he trying to smile? Shouldn't he be sad? Because of Mum leaving? Because of Granny Linley? Because of Sophie? Because it won't rain and everything is dying?

'Guess what?' Dad asks with false jolliness.

Jamie stares at the ceiling.

'You know Moira Tanning? Mrs Tanning?' Dad sits on the edge of the bed, messing the cover some more.

'Nope.'

'Yes, you do. The bank manager. She gave you a lollipop last time we were in the bank.'

'Nope.'

'Anyway, she has a girl from Sydney staying with her for a bit and she's agreed to come out to Moonbroch and stay with you while Mum and I are away. Doesn't that sound like fun?'

Jamie frowns. 'Mrs Tanning is going to stay here?'

'No, silly. The girl. She finished school last November and is staying with Mrs Tanning while she decides what to do with her life. And she's happy to stay with you while we're away.'

Jamie rolls onto his stomach and wraps his arms around his head.

'It'll only be a few weeks, mate,' Dad says, patting his shoulder. 'Just while I help with the muster at Tibberoo. I've gotta go, mate.'

Jamie keeps his arms locked over his head.

'Come on out to the kitchen,' Dad says, getting off the bed. 'I'll make us some eggs, and after breakfast Mrs Tanning and the girl will be here. You'll have fun together. I'm sure of it.'

As soon as the dogs broadcast the approaching vehicle, his father and Woofy go out to the gate to greet the visitors. Jamie remains in the kitchen, peering through the screen door. He doesn't want a stranger in his house, pretending to be nice and feeling sorry for him.

Also, he has the hiccups. It's his own fault. He'd been banging his foot against the leg of the kitchen table while he ate his eggs and toast and Dad had yelled at him to stop. He didn't like it when Dad yelled so, in an act of defiance, he'd snatched up the bottle of milk, taken a giant swig, and made a loud burp — but a little had gone down the wrong way. Before Dad could say, 'Jesus Christ,' and blast him some more, the dogs had started barking and Dad had hurried away.

Through the kitchen door, Jamie sees a white Toyota Hilux coming to a halt at the gate, the ball of dust that accompanied it across the flats continuing on into the house. There are two people in the car. Mrs Tanning, who he does remember, gets out of the driver's seat and Woofy rushes forward, his dribbly old mouth agape and his tail wagging furiously.

Hiccup.

Someone gets out of the passenger side of the car but is mostly blocked from view by the car. She takes a moment to look around, then steps forward and shakes his father's hand.

The day after Willy had arrived in the dusty town where Moira Tanning lived, the woman had asked if she'd like to go out to a station and help take care of a young boy for a few weeks, while his parents were away.

On her own.

Her and the child alone in the bush.

The whole idea sounded terrifying. And thrilling. The most exciting thing she'd ever had the chance to do.

'Yes,' she'd said. '*Yes.*'

'You sure?'

She'd never felt more sure about anything in her life. 'Yes.'

'I believe he's become a bit of a handful since his sister died.'

'His sister died? How?'

'Leukaemia. It's been tough on his parents too. Their place is in drought ... and close to bankruptcy, which is why the father has to go away. He called me last night to let me know he'd soon have some money to make a payment on his overdraft because he's got a flying job. But I doubt it'll make much difference. They won't be able to hang on to their land much longer, I'm afraid.'

'What's the little boy's name?'

'His name is Jamie. Jamie McKenzie.'

It is like she's spent her whole life holding her breath and not even known she was doing it. When she steps down from Moira's car into the red dust at Moonbroch Station, the sense of abundance quite overwhelms her. Abundance of space. Abundance of air. She lets go of her breath completely, for the first time in her life, then refills her lungs with a hunger she never even knew she had.

A man with a sad face steps forward to greet her.

'Hello. I'm John McKenzie,' he says, and offers his hand.

'Hello. I'm Will —' Should she say her name is Willy? It's what everyone calls her. But somehow, out here in this vast space, Willy no longer seems like an appropriate name and it occurs to her that this may be her chance to leave that name behind and start with a new one. A better name. For the first time in a long, long while, she starts to feel ... hope.

'Um, hi,' she starts again. 'I'm Willis.'

And she shakes his hand.

Hiccup.

Jamie goes over to the sink and gets himself a half glass of water which he downs in one gulp. Then he squeezes his nostrils closed and holds his breath in an effort to make his hiccups go away.

'BOOOOOOO!' Someone taps him on the back.

'AGGGHHHH!'

'Sorry I scared you,' the girl laughs, 'but it's the best way to get rid of hiccups, you know.'

Jamie's already forgotten about the hiccups. He's too busy staring at the intruder in the kitchen. She's at least as tall as Dad. On her feet are a pair of lace-up black boots with purple laces and she's wearing a short, blue, sleeveless dress. Her fair hair floats half way to her waist and there's a sparkle of mischief in her blue eyes.

'They're gone, hey?' She smiles at him.

'How did you …?' he starts to say, wondering how she'd managed to sneak up on him — he hadn't even heard the screen door open and close — but the query is already forgotten. He's enthralled by the vision of her. Her smile is like a thousand suns and he can no longer think straight. He's never seen a smile like it. It's as if she's brought something wonderful into the kitchen with her and for the first time in a long, long while, Jamie starts to feel … hope. Perhaps even the return of happiness.

'I'm Willis,' she says, taking his hand and shaking it, still smiling. 'You must be Jamie. I just can't believe I'm here in the outback. Sooo excited.'

The screen door squeaks and rattles, and Dad and Mrs Tanning enter.

'Go a cuppa?' Dad asks, and Mrs Tanning shakes her head.

'I can't stay,' she says, dropping Willis's small carry-all on the end of the kitchen table. She looks around the room, drawing Jamie's attention to the egg-smeared breakfast plates, the crumbs, the greasy sheen on the cluttered bench tops, the piles of old newspaper, the empty beer bottles, the fly spatter and cobwebs and dust. She's frowning as if she's worried to leave the clean, pretty girl called Willis in such a dirty place and she promises to call every evening. Then she leaves.

Jamie expects Dad to leave right away too. He expects him to climb into the Cessna, start the motor, accelerate down the runway and disappear into the sky so that he can get to Tibberoo before lunchtime. Not that he wants Dad to go. He wants Dad here, with him. He wants Mum here, too. And Sophie. He wants them all back together like it used to be before Soph got sick, but that's not going to happen, and he can no longer tolerate the unbearable sadness and grief that clings to everyone and everything. So he won't try to stop Dad from leaving. He'll stay home with the stranger who has purple shoelaces and knows the best way to stop the hiccups until Dad gets home in two weeks' time and then, hopefully, Granny Linley will get better, and Mum will come home, and everything will go back to normal. As normal as it is ever going to be.

But Dad is in no hurry to leave. First, he unpacks the boxes of groceries that Mrs Tanning has brought out from town, then he washes the breakfast dishes while Willis wipes. They chat happily together at the sink, him asking about her plans for the future now she's finished school and her telling him about how she'd like to study journalism at university one day and about how she'd like to become a writer. Next, he gives her a tour of the house.

He leads her down the breezeway, carrying her bag, and shows her the guest room where Granny Linley usually sleeps. He waves his hand in the direction of Sophie's closed bedroom door with the little porcelain ballerina attached three quarters the way up and says, 'None of us have been in Sophie's room since … we're not ready and I'll ask that you respect our privacy and not go in there either. Clearing it out is something for us to do together … as a family. When we're ready.'

He glances at Jamie who looks away.

'I understand, Mr McKenzie,' Willis says, her blue eyes wide and serious.

'John. Call me John.'

'I won't go in there, John. I promise. You can trust me.'

He takes her into his office and shows her the list of jobs and phone numbers and 'what to do if' guidelines he has left on the desk, and Willis solemnly nods her head at each instruction. He says she is not allowed to try and kill a snake or ride the motor bikes or drive the old ute, and she says she'll be sure not to do any of those things. He shows her how to use the radio in case the phone line goes out — in case of emergency. He leads her into Jamie's schoolroom and tells her that Jamie has missed a lot of school this last year and, even though it's holidays, she should encourage him to practise his reading and writing every day. Willis looks over at Jamie who is hanging silently in the background and gives him a wink.

Finally, Dad is ready to leave. Together, Jamie, Dad, and Willis walk out past the hangar to the airstrip where the Cessna is loaded and ready for take-off. Dad squats down in front of Jamie and gently holds his shoulders.

'Willis is a city girl,' he says softly. 'She's not used to being in the bush so I'm relying on you to take good care of her. Do you think you can do that for me?'

Jamie nods.

'Good. Then I'll be seeing you in a couple of weeks.'

He reaches forward and pulls Jamie into a rough, tight hug.

Then he stands and faces Willis.

Willis likes Mr John McKenzie. She can tell how terribly sad he is about his daughter dying and how worried he is about leaving his son on the station while he goes away for work. Also, even though he's late leaving for his flying job, he's taken the time to show her around and talk to her. And listen to her. He's asked her questions about herself and paid attention when she answered them.

Now, standing on the edge of the runway, she watches as he hugs Jamie tightly against his chest with one big hand cupped against the back of the small boy's head. After he's done saying goodbye to his son, he stands and looks steadily into her face. His eyes are kind of squinty, like he might start crying at any moment, except she doesn't imagine he's a crying type of man.

'Thank you, Willis. Take good care of him for me.'

'I will. I promise.'

She means it with all her heart.

Together, Willis and Jamie stand beneath a straggly clump of trees and watch as the small plane taxies down the runway, turns, gains speed and finally, in a great cloud of dust, lifts into the air and arcs away to the south.

CHAPTER 7

Cass strides out in front of her father down an ancient for-
estry track that hasn't seen human life for decades. Not
once does she turn back to check that her father is still following. Sometimes she gets so far ahead that it takes a small
miracle for him to keep track of her.

It's her screams that bring them back together. When Jamie arrives by her side, Cass is twisted around trying to get
a closer look at a squirmy black mark on the back of her
calf. He drops the packs and has a look.

'What is it?' Her blue eyes are wide with fear.

'A leech.' He wears the fixed expression of someone trying not to laugh. 'I wouldn't have expected leeches to be
around when it's so dry.'

'Get it off.'

'It won't hurt you.'

'Get it off.'

'Leeches have an anticoagulant in their saliva and if you
pull them off, your leg will bleed. The leech'll drop off by
itself once it's finished feeding.'

'GET IT OFF.'

He reaches down, pinches the little squirmer between his
fingers, and pulls. She shrieks and pulls away.

'Hold still. I don't want to leave the head in.'

She swallows. Her eyes widen even more, but she remains still while he pulls the tiny creature free and flicks it
into the bush. Then he empties out half the contents of his
pack to locate the first aid kit, adds a dob of disinfectant to
the wound and covers it with a plaster before the freely-
flowing blood can reach her sock and shoe.

'There you go,' he says. 'You'll live. How about we have
some breakfast?'

She makes herself comfortable on a log and waits to be
served. She's starving. And thirsty. Her father passes her a

bottle of water then begins to remove items from his pack and spread them out on the ground.

'This tiny fuel stove is called a Trangia,' he says, showing her a blackened, pot-shaped object.

She ignores him and gazes away into the forest. The day is already heating up and the forest makes her feel itchy. She's worried there will be more leeches and the only reason she's stopped is because she wants food.

'I remembered you liked pancakes,' he continues, 'with lemon and maple syrup and banana and fresh blueberries. I hope you still like those things because that's what we've got for our breakfast. And Greek yoghurt.'

'Bacon,' she says.

She's sure he won't have remembered every detail about the last meal they'd shared — in the little café on Hastings Street in Noosa two years ago. But he surprises her by holding up a foil wrapped parcel which he peels open to reveal several pre-cooked strips of crispy bacon, cooked just the way she likes with the fat rendered.

'Munch on these while I cook the pancakes,' he says, tossing her a small Tupperware container filled with mixed nuts. She carefully selects a few cashews and takes a long drink of water. Some birds are chatting in the gumtrees overhead. A pancake begins bubbling in the Trangia's frypan and her father lifts the edges with a spatula, preparing to flip it.

'Once I'm done cooking, I'll boil water so we can have a cup of English Breakfast tea with milk and sugar,' he says. Cass remembers they had that last time too. The shared memories, along with the aroma of caramelizing butter and hot batter, begin to soothe her anger. She feels like smiling. But she can't.

'Who's Soph?' she asks.

He freezes. Her question hangs between them, unanswered, and Cass immediately recognises it as something with the power to open old wounds and cause him pain. The edge of the pancake starts to darken.

'Dad. You need to flip it.'

He does as she says and flips the pancake but it's not a good flip and half of it crumples into a thick, sticky mess.

'How did you find out about Sophie?' he asks eventually.

'From you.'

His forehead creases into a frown.

'You called me Soph in the car when we first got to Too-woomba. I woke up and you called me Soph.'

'I did?' His face is stricken as he tries to remember.

'Who is she?'

He pauses before answering. 'She is ... was ... my sister.'

'I ...' Cass realises that she doesn't know anything about her father's family. She knows he grew up on a station out west because he has mentioned it, but only ever about the land, never about the people.

'What happened to her?'

'She died.'

Her father goes back to preparing the food. He cuts a lemon into quarters with a Swiss Army knife and squeezes the tangy juice over the pancakes, tops them with yoghurt, sliced banana, fresh blueberries, bacon, and maple syrup, then passes a plate to Cass.

'Here you go, love,' he says. Before eating his own, he lifts a pot of water onto the Trangia to boil for tea.

Cass eats the food slowly, deep in thought. About half-way through she says, 'Thanks, Dad,' but it isn't until they're both finished and sipping sweet, milky English Breakfast tea from tin mugs that she brings up the topic of Sophie again.

'Why didn't you ever tell me about her?'

'It was a long time ago and I didn't think you'd be interested.'

He's right. She has always been reluctant to have him talk about himself. But he's been equally unwilling to share stuff with her.

'Will you tell me about her?'

After a pause while he sips his tea, he says, 'Sophie died of leukaemia when she was twelve and I was ten.'

'She was my age when she died?'

He nods.

'What was she like? What did she look like?'

Her father stares at Cass for long seconds, swallows, then says, 'She looked a lot like you. Except, you're taller, I think. Sophie didn't grow much after she got sick.'

'That's why you called me Soph in the car? You got confused because I look like her?'

He puts his mug on the ground and begins scraping dirt from under his nails with the Swiss Army knife. 'I guess you did remind me of her for a moment. Same blonde hair. Same blue eyes. Same pretty face. I must have got confused.'

'I'm really like her?'

'Yes and no. There are differences, too.'

'Such as?'

'It's hard to explain but Sophie always had a kind of vulnerability about her that you don't have. You seem stronger than her. More robust.'

Cass weighs up her father's words, desperately seeking clues as to how he really feels about her. Is being stronger and more robust than his dead sister a good thing or a bad thing?

'There's a photo of her back at the house if you'd like to look at it when we get home,' he says.

'She's the girl in the photo in the lounge room, isn't she?' Cass scuffs at the dirt with her sneaker causing a tiny cloud of dust to rise into the air. 'I thought maybe you had other kids.'

She lifts her head and they stare at each other — blue eyes into blue eyes. And he gives her a tiny smile. 'You're the only one, Cass.'

Then he looks uncomfortable and turns his eyes away and begins to gather together their belongings and put them back into his pack. 'We'd better be getting back to civilisation,' he says. 'You have a friend coming to visit this afternoon, remember.'

Once the packing up is done, Cass pulls her own pack onto her shoulders and they walk out of the clearing the same way they entered it, on the western side, expecting the track they'd been following to be obvious. Except, it isn't. For half an hour, they zigzag around trying to find a path through the forest until they no longer know their way back to the clearing.

'Are we lost?'

'Geographically embarrassed.'

'Huh?'

'Never mind.' He swings his pack down and rummages through it for the map he'd printed off the internet last night — *Hiking Tracks in the Main Range National Park, Goomburra Section* — and spreads it over a fallen tree trunk. Cass watches over his shoulder as he tries to figure out where they might be.

'I think it'll be easier if we go east until we get to the Scenic Rim,' he says, pointing to a heavy line on the map. 'Then we can follow the rim south until we get to a proper hiking trail and follow that back to the carpark. It shouldn't be too far.'

Cass silently follows her father downslope through a gully where he holds some wait-a-while vine aside for her. She likes it when he does thoughtful things for her. And when he remembers things like pancakes. It makes her feel like she means something to him. On the flip side, he *did* stay away for two years, there's no photo of her on the shelf in his lounge room *and* he did throw her phone out the car window. She aches to have the easy relationship she once had with him but she's too wounded to forgive that easily.

The forest above the gully is thick and their progress slow, but eventually they come out onto a rocky shelf and in front of them is nothing but empty space. Cass feels a rush of excitement. It's one of the most incredible sights she's ever seen. She sidles closer to the edge and peers over. Stretching vertically below is an enormous wall of rock that seems to go down forever before vanishing into a sea of trees far below.

'How good is that view?' her father says. 'Shall we rest here for a bit?'

'Have we got time?'

Her father looks at his watch and nods. 'We'll be home in heaps of time for you to see your friend.'

Cass sits close to the edge of the basalt slab, so her legs dangle over. She likes the rush of terror she feels, balanced between the certainty of the ground and the uncertainty of the void in front and below. Her father carefully removes his pack and places it well back from the edge, sits on his backside and shuffles forward like a crab until his feet are over the edge like hers.

She watches his clumsy and cautious approach with a reluctant grin.

'First rule of being near a cliff edge,' he says in his teacher voice, 'is to remove your pack. Did you know that most people who fall over cliffs do so because they don't take their pack off and when they rotate, the weight of the pack carries them right over the edge?'

'You're just scared.'

He grins. 'You got me.'

They sit for a minute in silence and allow themselves to merge with the visual feast before them.

'Do you know how to spell abyss?' she asks.

Her father smiles at her unexpected question.

'I'm not much of a speller so you'd better tell me.'

'A. B. Y. S. S.'

'I'm going to have to believe you. It's a great word.'

'It describes the feeling you get sitting here. Abyssssssss. Sounds like you're falling into nothing. I wonder if it is an onomatopoeia.'

He laughs. 'A what?'

'An onomatopoeia is a word that sounds like a sound. Like splish splash.'

He remains silent, but she can tell he's listening by the way his head is tilted and by the little crinkle on his brow. She continues.

'This place reminds me of my friend who is coming to visit. Her name is Winter.'

'Winter, hey? That's an unusual name.'

'She's an unusual girl.'

'In what way?'

'Well, she would know if abyss is an onomatopoeia or not because she's kind of addicted to big words. And ... she doesn't eat junk food and she doesn't do homework because her parents don't believe in it. And she doesn't have a computer or internet at home, and she doesn't have a mobile phone.'

He cringes. 'Cass, I shouldn't have thrown your phone away. I'm sorry. We'll stop and try to find it on the way home, okay?'

'That's just it. I like not having my phone all the time. It feels good to forget about my friends for a while.' She sighs and stretches out her legs. 'This must be how Winter feels all the time. Kind of free.'

They sit in silence for a few minutes, absorbing the heat, sounds and smells of the bush; feeling the breeze on their faces, taking occasional swigs from their water bottles.

'We'll have to find the phone, though. If I go home without it, Mum will kill me.'

She sighs and reaches back her hands to rest them on the rock behind her; except, her right palm comes down onto something that feels more like firm jelly than hot basalt. Something that moves. It takes one millisecond for her to go from confusion to comprehension and her expression becomes one of extreme terror as she tries to scramble away from the writhing snake.

But there's nowhere to go.

'Careful,' her father says and tries to reach her, but her body is already slipping over the edge. She pivots as she falls and attempts to throw herself forward onto the basalt slab.

One hand grasps the clifftop while she throws the other desperately towards her father. But he's too far away to catch hold. They stare hopelessly at each other as the gravel below her fingers surrenders to gravity and she falls.

CHAPTER 8

Willis reaches down and scratches behind Woofy's ears.

'Phew, Woofy stinks,' she says, smelling her hand and laughing. 'Let's give him a bath.'

'You don't bath dogs like Woofy,' Jamie says.

'Why not?'

'Because he's a working dog.'

'I bet he'd like to have a bath.'

'I guess.'

Washing Woofy does sound like fun. They fetch a bucket from the laundry and a bottle of Mum's shampoo from the bathroom, then lure the old dog onto the middle of the dried out front lawn. Willis fills the bucket from the garden hose, switches off the tap and dumps the water over Woofy's back while Jamie holds his collar to stop him from running off. Together, they begin to lather him until he is more bubble than dog.

Woofy is not happy. His legs tremble. His tail is tucked under. Every now and then, he tries to shake the water off until both Jamie and Willis are covered in water and bubbles and Willis is laughing.

Despite himself, Jamie is smiling. He goes to the tap, turns it on and brings the hose over to begin to wash the bubbles off.

'Maybe we should use the bucket,' Willis says, 'so we don't waste the water.'

'There's enough water. It comes from the Great Artesian Basin which is like a huge underground lake.'

'You're pretty smart, hey?'

Jamie likes that she's worried about wasting water but even more, he likes that she thinks he's smart. Woofy shakes himself again, showering them in doggy spray and they both fall down laughing. Two wagtails flitter about their heads and Woofy takes the opportunity to slink away and hide under the oleander bush.

Later, they sit together on the lounge room floor with a plate of sandwiches between them. Willis's hair is still wet from the shower she had after they washed Woofy and she's tied it away from her face.

'Ask me something,' she says. 'Anything.'

'Um, um.'

'Anything you like.'

'Why're you called Willis?'

She smiles. 'Do you like my name? I only got it today when I arrived on Moonbroch.'

He frowns.

'I decided I needed a new name.'

'But ...' Jamie's mouth is open as he considers the strange idea that a person can simply change their name on a whim. He only thought you could change your last name if you were a girl who got married.

'You can't just change your name,' he says.

'I did.' She chews her sandwich.

'What was it before you changed it?'

'Willy.'

He puts his hand over his mouth and giggles.

'What?'

He looks at his feet and giggles some more.

'What's so funny?'

'Willy,' he says, his eyes becoming moist with mirth.

'What's wrong with Willy?'

'It's ... it's ...' More giggling. 'You know ... a boy's rudey parts.' He flaps his hand towards his shorts.

She tosses her head back and laughs along with him.

'Good thing I changed it then,' she says. 'Can't have me being named after a boy's rudey parts, can we? Both Willy and Willis are short for my full name, which is Wilhelmina Johnson.' She smiles her bright smile and puts on a posh voice. 'My mother told me I was named after a princess, someone called Princess Wilhelmina Helena Pauline Maria of the Netherlands.'

'What's the Netherlands?'

'A place in Europe.'

Jamie takes another bite of his sandwich. He never knew anyone who was named after a princess.

'Ask something else?' she says.

He shrugs. 'Can't think of anything.'

'Okay. Then tell me something about yourself.'

'Like what?'

'Um … let me think.' A mischievous sparkle comes into her eyes and he gets the impression she's playing a game with him. Then she says, 'Will you tell me about your super-powers?'

His eyes pop.

'I saw the notebook with *Jamie's List of Superpowers,*' she says, still smiling. 'I thought maybe you'd like to tell me about it.'

She knows about that!

That was PRIVATE!

She might just as well have thrown a hand grenade — his shock would have been the same. To make matters worse, her mouth is twitching like she's trying hard not to laugh. Like she thinks the notebook is a joke. Or she thinks Sophie is dumb for writing the list. He swallows. His eyes flicker in the direction of Sophie's closed bedroom door. Why did she go in there after she'd promised Dad not to? How could she have intruded into something so private? He feels rage radiating out from his core. His fingers curl into fists.

'You're stupid,' he says, throwing his half sandwich back onto the plate and scrambling to his feet.

Her eyes widen in astonishment.

'Why am I stupid?'

'For going where you're not meant to and for playing tricks. You're a stupid girl and I don't want you here.'

His face is flaming as he runs from the room.

————

Willis chews her bottom lip as she looks down at the sleeping form of the small boy. The way his mood had changed so rapidly has left her shaken. One minute he was giggling hysterically about her silly name and the next, he'd gotten into a temper because he thought she'd gone into his sister's bedroom.

Now he's sprawled across his parents' bed, fast asleep. His forehead is moist with perspiration but she thinks he'll be okay, so she retreats quietly and heads back along the breezeway towards the kitchen. As she passes the station's phone, situated just outside the kitchen door, it tingles, and she snatches up the handpiece before it has a chance to ring properly and wake Jamie. She expects it is Moira checking in.

'Hello?'

'Hello.' The woman's voice is soft. A wispy, broken sound.

'This is Moonbroch. Willis speaking.'

'Um ... Sue McKenzie, Willis. How's everything going?'

The mother!

'Hi, Mrs ... um ... McKenzie. Everything is going fine, thank you.'

'I'd like to ... can you put Jamie on, please?'

'Jamie?'

'Yes. Jamie. I'd like to speak to him.'

'Hold one moment, please.' She puts down the handpiece and walks back along the breezeway to the room where Jamie is still sleeping soundly in the middle of his parent's bed. Then, with long, graceful strides, she returns to the phone. 'Um ... Mrs McKenzie? It's Willis, again.'

'Is he coming?'

'He's sleeping.'

'In the middle of the afternoon?'

'Should I wake him? Do you want me to wake him?'

'I ... no, best to let him sleep, I guess. But you'll need to see he keeps regular hours while you're there. He does best if he has a good routine.'

'I'll try and keep him to a good routine, Mrs McKenzie. I promise. It's just ...'

'He probably needs a good sleep now that John and I are both out of the house.'

Willis can't think of anything else to say. She can hear the sound of the woman breathing over the crackles on the line and thinks she might be crying.

'Okay, then,' Mrs McKenzie says eventually, 'I'll call back another time.'

Once Willis has hung up the phone, she slides her back down the wall until she's sitting on the floor with her knees drawn up to her chin. Shit! Crap! She'd just sounded like a useless person to Jamie's mother. Like an incompetent, dumb person. What if Mrs McKenzie doesn't like her? What if next time Mrs McKenzie calls to talk to Jamie, he says he doesn't like her either? What if he tells his mother that Willis is a horrible, mean person who went into Sophie's room after promising not to? What if Mrs McKenzie doesn't want her here anymore and she has to return to Sydney and go back to being Willy before she's even had the chance to prove herself as Willis? She likes it here in the outback. She doesn't want to go back to being Willy.

When he wakes, it takes a few moments for Jamie to figure out where he is, but the sea creatures on the bedcover and Mum's familiar scent reminds him. He thinks of Granny Linley who always sleeps in the afternoon and wonders how she's doing in the hospital with the stroke. Then he remembers the person who is now using the spare room. Willis. Willy. Wilhelmina. Princess. He remembers the way he had yelled at her, called her stupid and run out of the room like a baby. Too bad. She's just a big, old, sticky beak and he doesn't like her anyway. Does he? He's not sure. It *was* fun washing Woofy.

The golden light in his parents' bedroom tells him he needs to get going on the afternoon jobs. It's not long until dark and the fruit trees should get the hose for at least an hour; Mickey, Dozer and Hebe need a run out on the flats before they get fed; the chooks need to be fed; the eggs collected.

Hearing the click of the kitchen screen door is enough to get him off the bed and out to the kitchen where he pulls on his boots. He grabs his bushman's hat and turns to get the scrap bucket for the chooks, but the bucket is gone. She must be going to try and do the jobs on her own. As if she would know what to do. Crossing the dead lawn under the lop-sided clothesline, he sees her up ahead with the scrap bucket swinging from her hand. He's still angry with her. She's dumb. She doesn't even know the way to the chook yard and is going the long way around past the hangar.

He's about to short-cut past the meathouse and surprise her by already being there when she arrives but something stops him in his tracks. It's the way she moves. Like a world-famous dancer. Like Anna Pavlova. Watching her grace captured in the sharp light of the afternoon sun, he starts to question his idea that she could have gone into Sophie's room — maybe she didn't do it after all.

'You know, if you call me a stupid girl, it means you're a sexist pig, because you think all girls are dumb sluts,' Willis says while scattering pellets across the ground for the chooks to eat.

Jamie doesn't answer, mostly because he doesn't understand what she's talking about but also because he wants to ask her outright if she went into Sophie's room — he's just not sure he wants to know the answer.

'I'll forgive you,' she says, 'because I understand why you did it. Okay?'

Jamie watches water from the hose splatter into the chook's drinking trough. A few drops mark his dusty boots.

'Jamie? Did you hear me?'

He wants to answer but is having trouble with the words, so he shrugs and grunts.

'Jamie. Look at me.'

He looks stubbornly into her blue eyes.

'Was that Sophie's notebook? The one with the super-powers list?'

He nods.

'Did you think I took it from Sophie's room?'

Again, he nods and bites his lower lip.

'I didn't go into her room. I made a promise not to and I always keep my promises. The notebook was in my room, next to my bed, under some old magazines.'

They stare at each other for a few seconds, then she straightens and turns her attention back to feeding the chooks.

'I know you feel sad about your sister dying and every-thing,' she says after a few moments, 'but don't take it out on me. Okay?'

He turns off the tap.

'Do you think we can be friends again?' she says.

He nods. He really does want to be her friend.

'Pinkie promise?'

He frowns and looks at the ground.

'You don't know what a pinkie promise is, do you?'

He shakes his head.

'Here. Put out your little finger. Like this. Now hook your finger with mine. That's a pinkie promise. It means we have to keep our promise to each other to always be friends.'

And her dazzling smile spreads around him, soothes his ruffled feathers and makes him feel happy again.

The next day, sheltering from the heat under the air conditioner in the lounge room, Willis begins to tell him stories about her life. He's fairly sure she's making the stories up but, nevertheless, she is an excellent story-teller, giving just enough detail to leave him wondering — could that really have happened?

She tells him she is an orphan and a twin. Before her parents died, they worked for the secret service (for which country she fails to say) and were killed while trying to smuggle state secrets out of Russia. After this, Willis and her twin sister, Giselle, were raised by nuns in a little convent on a remote, rocky island called Widdershins Island, in the middle of the Black Sea. The two little girls were happy in the convent until, one day, pirates came and killed all the nuns and took the girls to the Romanian mafia to be sold as white slaves. Willis was rescued by gypsies and the head gypsy, Longyear Byen, smuggled her to Australia and paid the Johnson family to raise her as their own.

'I don't know what happened to my sister but now that I'm finished school and officially an adult, I plan to go to Europe and try to find her — dead or alive.'

Then, as if it's no big deal, she says, 'You can tell me about Sophie, if you want. I will understand. I know what it's like to lose a sister.'

Jamie goes motionless and stares at the floor. Even thinking about Sophie makes his insides hurt. He doesn't want to — can't — *talk* about it. It's too hard.

'It's your turn to tell a story and I want to hear about Sophie.'

He shakes his head and gets to his feet. 'We have to go let the dogs out for a run.'

She unravels her long legs and stands too. 'Okay. You can tell me later.'

They follow the dry creek bed all the way to the crossing while Mickey, Dozer, Hebe, and Woofy scamper through the scrub nearby with their noses to the ground. Unlike Granny Linley, Willis doesn't seem to notice the heat or dust or flies, but she's very observant about everything else, always drawing his attention to tiny creatures or unique colours or unexpected scents. She says she's never been on a station before, especially one as fantastic as Moonbroch, and she asks him a lot of questions about it, which makes him feel clever and important. He tells her how the sheep eat mulga trees in a drought and how a gecko can drop off a piece of its tail if you try to catch it.

They're in the kitchen when the phone rings. Glancing at the clock, Jamie sees it's already eight-oh-seven.

'Can you get it?' Willis says. She's in the middle of icing a cake to look like a rainbow and has a spatula in one hand and a bowl of yellow icing in the other, so he puts down the teaspoon he's been using to scrape icing from the inside of the bowl and goes to answer the phone. It might be one of his parents.

'Hello.'

'Hi Jamie. How's everything?' It's only Mrs Tanning from the bank. Unlike his parents, she calls every night.

'Good.'

'Been having fun?'

'Yes.'

'What have you been doing?'

'Nothing.'

'You been swimming?'

'No.'

'Driving the ute?'

'No.'

'Seen any snakes?'

'No.'

'Can you put Willy on?'

Resisting the urge to giggle at the use of Willis's old name, he leaves the handpiece hanging on the end of its springy cord and goes back into the kitchen.

'She wants to speak to Willy,' he says, giving her a cheeky grin.

She rolls her eyes at him, puts down her icing tools and goes to the phone.

'Moira. I told you. I changed my name to Willis.'

...

'Everything's good. You don't have to call every day, you know. We're fine.'

...

'I can handle it.'

She's leaning against the wall with her back to him, but Jamie can tell she's getting agitated.

'Uh-huh.'

...

'What kind of things?'

...

'You didn't have a problem dumping me out here *alone* three days ago and now you think I can't handle it?'

...

'WHAT? NO WAY.'

...

'What'd you do that for? Shit.' Willis bangs the hand-piece back into the cradle and marches back into the kitchen.

'What?' Jamie asks, frowning.

'Moira. She doesn't freaking understand anything.'

'Why?'

Willis is pacing up and down, biting her nails and not explaining what has upset her so he starts banging his foot against the leg of the table. Not loudly, just enough to add to the general disharmony in the room.

'Cut it out,' she snaps at him.

'What?'

'The banging.'

'Why're you angry?'

She flops onto her chair in front of the half-iced cake.

'Because Moira's a stupid, shitty person.'

'What'd she do?'

'She says she doesn't think we should be out here alone because I'm too young and inexperienced to take care of you. She reckons if something unpredictable happens, I won't be able to handle it.' She points her long, graceful finger at her chest. 'I'm eighteen. I'm meant to be an adult and I *can* handle it. Your dad knows I can, or he would never have left me here with you.'

'Mrs Tanning changed her mind.'

'What do you mean?'

'She was okay with you coming here and now she's not, so she changed her mind.' His face pinches into a frown. 'Is she coming to take you back to town?'

Willis rolls her eyes and smiles. 'No, silly. I'm not going anywhere. But she's arranged for her busy-body mother, Aggie, to come and stay with us. How long does it take to drive from Sydney, do you know? One day? Two days?'

Jamie shrugs. 'You're from Sydney?'

'Yeah, but I caught a bus to Brisbane and another bus from there, so it took me longer. If Aggie drives straight here, it won't take so long. Oh God!' She presses her hand dramatically against her forehead. 'She might be here as soon as tomorrow.'

'Can we have cake soon?' Jamie asks, not overly worried about the impending arrival of Mrs Tanning's mother, Aggie. What harm can come of it? It's always fun when Granny Linley is here.

But Willis isn't done with her outrage and rakes him over with indignant eyes. 'You'd better be careful around Aggie, Jamie. She's a witch. For real. I'm not lying.'

Jamie doesn't believe in witches but as with everything Willis says, he's left with a sense of doubt. What if there really are witches? What can a witch do to him?

'You'll probably like her at first, but you'll soon figure out what she's really like. She's the kind of person who sucks all the happiness out of the world until nothing good is left.'

A small shudder rattles his bones and, with as much hostility as he can muster, he sticks out his chest and says, 'People can't turn up at our place whenever they want, you know. I'll tell Mum and Dad we don't want her here.'

'Moira already spoke to your Dad and he agreed for her to come.'

While Jamie is still processing the idea of Aggie being a witch, Willis gets out of her chair, fetches the butcher's knife and begins carving into her unfinished rainbow cake.

'Cake?'

Her smile is back as she passes him a plate covered in sticky, half-iced cake.

'Let's forget all about Aggie and enjoy ourselves while we can,' she says, shovelling an enormous spoonful into her mouth.

CHAPTER 9

Cass assesses her situation. She's about three metres from the top of the cliff where a small, robust tree is growing horizontally out from the rock. The tree has broken her fall, but her hands are bleeding from where she grabbed its rough branches, one of her nails is torn, her left knee has smashed against the rock and is throbbing like crazy, and the sight of the treetops far below is making her head spin.

'Cass?'

She looks up. Despite his fear of heights, her father has projected his entire torso over the edge.

'Cass,' he calls again, 'are you okay?'

'Dad.' Her voice comes out like a tiny squeak and she tries again. 'I'm okay.'

'Can you hold on? Are you secure?'

'I think so.'

'Good. Just keep holding on. Okay?'

With a quick heave, he pushes his body back onto the relative safety of the ledge.

'Dad? *Dad*.'

He hangs his head over the top once more.

'I'm here, love. It's just ... I don't see any way to get to you. I might have to go for help.'

'No, Dad. Don't leave me. Please don't leave me. I can't hold on. What if the snake comes back?'

'The snake will be long gone, love. Just hold on and don't worry about the snake. Okay? Give me a minute and I'll try the phone.'

He backs away from the edge, out of sight. After a minute or two, she hears him start to yell. 'Help. Heeeellllp. Coooeee. Anyone?' Then he flattens himself out at the edge once more and calls, 'You still okay?'

'Yes. No. I feel like I'm slipping.'

'Shit. Okay. Let's figure this out. I'm not sure that little tree will take my weight even if I could make it down to you.'

From her precarious position in the tree, Cass can see that his breath is shallow, like he's panting, and his face is red and wet with sweat.

'Do you think you can describe what the cliff face looks like from where you are? Tell me why there's a tree growing out of the rock?'

Small birds fly about as she begins to examine the vertical surface above her head. There is variation in shape and texture and colour. The cliff is weathered and cracked in places and anywhere there's a smattering of soil, a small clump of vegetation is growing. A near vertical crevice, stained darker where water sometimes flows, begins where the tree is and stretches almost all the way to the top.

After she has relayed this to her father, he asks, 'Is there any way you can wriggle along the tree to where it comes out of the crevice? The trunk will be stronger at the source and if you can get your leg over and straddle it, you'll be more stable and not have to worry so much about your hands slipping.'

'I can't.'

'Just take it slow. Can you move your right hand a tiny bit closer to the cliff? Just a few inches?'

More than an hour passes while her father painstakingly talks Cass through the manoeuvre. Eventually, she reports that she is straddling the tree trunk, facing the cliff and narrow crevice.

'That's fantastic, Cass. You deserve a rest. Are you able to get your backpack from your shoulders? Carefully?'

'Got it.'

'Okay, unzip the top and get out your spare water bottle. Have a few slow sips and hold the water in your mouth for as long as you can.'

'Dad?'

'I'm here.'

They're no longer within sight of each other but their voices are clear in the perfectly still afternoon.

'I'm sorry for breaking my promise about the phone. And I'm sorry for getting us lost and … for not being good at anything. I'm sorry for being …'

'You've got nothing to be sorry for, love. It's me who should be saying sorry. It's me who …' It sounds as if his words are causing him pain.

'Dad?'

'Yeah?'

'Why did you stay away so long? Did I do something wrong?' Two tears drop onto her flushed cheeks.

'No, love. Of course not.'

'Then why?'

Except for the twittering of a few birds, silence. Then he says, 'It's complicated.'

'Were you working away? Like on a secret mission? Or sick or something like that?'

Another long pause, then, 'No. That's not what happened.'

'What then? I have a right to know.'

'I'm sorry, love. I can't talk to you about why I stayed away. Not without talking to your mum first.'

'Why not?'

'Because I told her I wouldn't talk to you about it. I promised her.'

Cass frowns. She's not sure what he means. What does his absence have to do with her mother? Did her mother make him stay away?

'Was it Mum's fault? Did she stop you from coming to see me?'

He doesn't answer.

'Dad?'

'Let's wait until we get you home safe and sound and we can all talk about it together. Okay?'

'Do you hate her?'

'Of course not.'

'Then why don't you ever come inside and say hello to her when you pick me up? Why do you never see her?'

He sighs. 'As I said, it's complicated and I promised her I wouldn't talk about it.'

She picks some bark from the branch of the little tree.

'Do you think it'll hurt when I hit the bottom?' she says.

'Cass. You're not going to fall.'

'If I try and climb back up, I'll fall. If I stay here on the tree, I'll eventually go to sleep and fall, or I'll die from thirst and fall.'

'How much water do you have in your bottle?'

'About half.'

'Okay, I want you to screw the lid back on carefully and put the water bottle inside your shirt. Is your shirt tucked into your shorts so it can't fall out the bottom?'

'Yes.'

'Good. Now I want you to describe the crevice to me in more detail. How wide is it? How deep? Is it big enough for you to wriggle into?'

Cass is silent for a few minutes while she finds a secure branch to hook her backpack onto. Then she assesses the size of the crevice, trying hard not to think about the creepy crawlies inside.

'Near the bottom where the tree comes out, it's narrow, about the thickness of my arm, but further up it widens a bit,' she calls out.

'Is there any chance you could fit inside?'

'I ... I ... maybe if I stand on the tree trunk and turn sideways.' Her sudden panic is like a giant set of beaters stirring up the fluid inside her stomach.

'I'm going to be sick,' she calls.

'It's normal to feel like that, Cass. Take a big breath, as deep as you can; hold the air in your lungs, then let it go slowly.'

Her father talks to her like this until her panic subsides, then tells her to drink more water from her bottle.

'For this next part, I want you to leave your pack behind. Okay? It'll only get in the way.'

He talks her through the task of using the rough surface of the cliff to pull herself up until she's standing balanced on the narrow tree trunk. Twice, her hand slides loose from the rock, sending a shower of pebbles towards the treetops below, but she doesn't fall. It's as if his voice is a rope keeping her safe. Once she's standing, he gets her to turn sideways to the cliff and push her right leg into the crevice, then steadily, inch by inch, to wriggle up until most of her body is wedged inside the wider section. It's wider than she'd thought and there's even a tiny ledge she can sit back against.

'Well done, Cass,' her father says after she describes her new, slightly safer position inside the crevice. 'I'm so proud of you. What you have just achieved is incredible.'

'Thanks, Dad.'

'Do you think you'll be okay to stay there while I go for help?'

So focused has she been getting into the crevice, she hasn't noticed until now that the day is already ending. Outside, there's nothing to see but a shadowy grey haze. Inside is pitch black.

'Dad? No. You can't leave.'

'I don't think anyone is coming to look for us, love.'

'No-one knows where we are, do they?'

'No.'

'What about Winter? She'll come find us. I'm sure she will.'

'I don't think she … She won't know where we are.'

Cass remembers Winter's obsession with Nancy Drew books and her words from yesterday — *Da de da dum, Winter to the rescue* — and she feels a bit light headed and slightly hysterical. She resists the urge to burst into laughter.

'You don't know Winter, Dad. I think she'll be able to save us, for sure.'

Her father's silence lets her know that he doesn't think Winter is a valid rescue option. Why would she be? How can she possibly know where they are? Most likely, she'll have knocked a few times, assumed Cass has forgotten she was visiting and gone back to Brisbane with her Poppy.

'Dad?'

'Cass?'

'You can go for help.'

'You sure?'

'Yes. But promise me you'll come back. Promise you won't leave me here.' Her voice is wispy and high pitched.

'Cass ... of course I'll come back. I'll always come back for you.'

A few birds are still fussing around outside getting ready for bed. Her stomach rumbles and she needs to pee. Her hand hurts.

'Cass?'

'You didn't come back last time.'

'Cass ... I ...'

Tears wet her face.

'I thought you were going to get help?'

'We'll have to wait until morning. My torch battery's flat and it's stupid for me to go crashing around out here in the dark. So, here's what I'm going to do. As soon as it's completely dark, I'll light the Trangia. Hopefully, you'll be able to see the glow of the flame. Or I'll light a fire. Then I'll cut my rain jacket into long strips, tie them together and lower you down some food. How does that sound? I've even got some pancake mix left over from this morning. Okay?'

'Sounds good, Dad. I ... I'm glad you're here.'

'Dad?'

'I'm here, Cass. I'm not going anywhere.'

'Thanks for the pancakes.'

'It was my pleasure.'

After several attempts, he'd managed to position the plastic bag containing the food close enough for Cass to reach — pancakes, muesli bar and apple — and she'd been able to distract herself with the food for a while.

'Dad? I need to pee.'

'Just do it.'

'In my pants?'

'Sure. Why not?'

'Yuck.'

'Better out than in, love.'

She allows the warm urine to flow from her body, forming a stain on her shorts and wetting her legs. It's good to let it go.

CHAPTER 10

The day is still early when Willis bursts, smiling, into Jamie's bedroom.

'Come on Jamie. Let's go out before it gets too hot.'

She no longer seems concerned about the woman, Aggie, coming to Moonbroch, so he doesn't bring it up. He uses the bathroom, then dresses in shorts and a t-shirt, takes a few gulps of orange juice, shoves the vegemite toast she gives him into his mouth, pulls on his boots and hat, and goes outside.

Willis empties the chook bucket and throws some pellets to the chooks while Jamie turns the hose onto the fruit trees and lets the dogs out for their morning run.

This morning, they don't follow the tracks to the crossing or the shearing shed. Instead, Willis marches straight out across the flats and Jamie has to periodically trot to keep up with her easy, graceful stride. In a good season, all kinds of grasses grow on the flats and sometimes the whole area is a sea of yellow and purple wildflowers, but because of the drought, it is now mostly neverfail grass or bare ground.

The golden light of early morning sits heavy in the air. Out to the left, the land slopes away towards the claypan, with patches of yellow cane grass nearer to the creek. The course of the creek is marked by taller gum trees and ahead and to the right is the red sand and mulga country. On the airstrip, an early whirly wind is spiralling dust into the air.

'It's going to be a scorcher,' he tells her.

'This is sooo amazing,' she says, twirling around with her arms spread wide. 'Sooo, sooo amazing.'

Jamie nods. Stifles a yawn. Pushes his hands into the pockets of his shorts.

She looks at him. 'Isn't this amazing?'

He shrugs. 'Sure.'

'Hello, universe!' she yells, going back to twirling. 'My name is Princess Wilhelmina of the Wide Brown Land and I am glad to be alive.' She stops and grins at him again. 'You do it.'

'What?'

'Yell out to the universe. Say anything you like.'

'No way,' he says, pushing his hands deeper into his pockets and grinning nervously.

'Why not?'

'Because it's dumb.'

'No, it isn't. Are you scared to try?'

'No.'

'Then do it. It feels so good.'

He shakes his head.

'Stretch out your arms, like this,' — she stretches her arms wide — 'and yell. Whatever you want. *Hello, world. I am Willis and I am free. I am a giant, fat bumblebee.*'

She runs in circles, laughing and yelling and flapping her arms up and down like wings. Mickey and Dozer run in crazy, wild circles around her while Hebe barks at the spectacle. Jamie doesn't move, but he's smiling. It does look funny.

'Come on Jamie. It's fun.'

He raises his arms half-heartedly with his elbows curved. 'My name is Jamie McKenzie. I ... I ...'

'Louder,' she yells. 'Be free.'

He isn't able to let go and be mad like her.

'Tell you what,' she says. 'I'll go lock up the dogs and turn off the hose and wait for you in the shearing shed. You might find it easier if I'm not here.'

Calling Mickey, Dozer, and Hebe to come for their breakfast, she strides away, her long hair swinging. And, once again, he's captivated by the floaty, graceful way she moves. When she and the dogs are out of sight, Jamie sits on the ground and gouges a hole with a stick. He coaxes an ant onto the end of the stick and moves it through the air like the ant is flying. It's not that he's scared to yell and scream and run about. He isn't. He and Sophie did crazy stuff like that lots of times. It's just … Sophie isn't here anymore.

He gets to his feet.

Spreads his arms wide.

'I am Jamie McKenzie,' he says.

And again. Louder. 'I am Jamie McKenzie. I'm glad to be alive.'

And again. Louder. 'I am Jamie McKenzie and I am alive.'

With arms stretched wide, he begins to run in circles, shouting, '*I am alive, I am alive, I am alive!*'

Willis is waiting for him inside the shearing shed.

'Did you do it?'

'Yes.'

'Really?'

'Yes.'

She laughs and claps her hands. 'Well done, Jamie.'

She passes him a bulging, wet hessian waterbag. He screws off the lid and tips the cool water into his mouth and a good deal more down the front of his shirt. Then he screws the lid back on, drops the waterbag onto the shed floor and heaves himself up onto the wool classing table.

'What'll we do now?'

In her effortless way, Willis swings onto the table next to him. She is smiling.

'What do you want to do?'

He shrugs. 'I don't know. We could have a race.'

'But that wouldn't be fair. I would beat you in a race.'

'Not if I get a head start.'

'Okay. We'll play a game where —'

One of the dogs barks. A few short yaps, then silence.

Her voice fades away. She drops gracefully from the table and goes to lean against the thick beam that supports the door frame. When he squints his eyes, the blinding light from outside makes her look fuzzy around the edges. Her body is rigid and tense. It looks like she's listening for something. He listens too and can just make out the distant hum of an approaching vehicle — still a long way off, but sound carries in the sharp desert air.

'How the hell did Aggie get here so quickly?' she mutters, glancing at her funny, child's watch.

Jamie goes to stand by her side and peers out. 'It might be someone else,' he says.

'No. It's her.'

'How do you know?'

'I just do.'

A spire of dust shows where the approaching vehicle is passing through the stony hills.

She looks down at him. 'Are you ready to play that game?'

'Yes.'

The dogs bark again.

'There's a shirt hanging over the back of the chair in your parent's bedroom. Your mission is to get that shirt and put it on before Aggie, the witch, can get you. Remember, she's evil and will cause you great harm if you fail your mission but if you succeed, you'll be safe. She won't be able to hurt you while you are wearing that shirt.'

Her words are spoken with such urgency that it feels like they're doing more than just playing a game. This feels real and the anticipation of participating in a daring adventure excites him.

The sound of the car and the position of the dust spire suggests it is already at the crossing.

'You need to go now,' she says. Her eyes are wide as she reaches out and gives him a gentle push. 'You'll have to run faster than you've ever run in your life and stay out of sight in the trees. Come through the back door of the house. I'll distract her for as long as I can. But you've got to hurry.'

Jamie sprints down the stairs.

'Good luck,' she calls.

He runs hunched over behind the outer fence of the sheepyards until he reaches the gidgee, then sprints through the trees, past the old gravestone under which someone called Mary Withers is buried, past the disused windmill and down to the creek. He follows an erosion gully towards the back of the homestead, then makes a bolt across open ground and, with an audible grunt, commando rolls behind some corrugated iron sheets his father has stacked against the house yard fence.

He inches towards a thicket of mostly-dead bougainvillea near the back gate, listening for the car, but it must have already arrived. The dogs have stopped barking. Even with all the running practise he did when he was trying to fly, he has a stitch and his chest is heaving. He sucks in a lungful of air in preparation for the final sprint to recover the shirt before he has to face the witch. He visualises his objective — one of Mum's old t-shirts draped carelessly across the back of the chair in the corner of the bedroom next to the floaty, cob-webby curtain. He can't remember noticing it and wonders how Willis knew it was there. When had she been in Mum's bedroom?

A wet nose pushes into his armpit from behind and he gives the old dog a quick pat, then checks that the way is clear and dashes across the brown lawn, through Mum's dead rose garden, up the stairs and into the laundry. While kicking off his boots, he listens for voices, expecting Willis and Aggie must now be in the kitchen, but hears only the car starting up again. And the dogs barking again. He sneaks over the dusty wooden floorboards in the breezeway in his socks. Success is close.

Once safely inside Mum's room, his eyes go straight to the chair over which, as Willis has said, a shirt is draped. The material is soft-looking. A smoky grey colour. Even without being able to see the owl picture on the front, he recognises it. It was Sophie's favourite. So striking are the owl's eyes that when Sophie wore it, he often felt as if the owl was watching him.

A crushing sadness roots his feet to the middle of the floor. His eyes are hot and he doesn't think he's going to be able to take the final few steps to retrieve the shirt. He can't wear Sophie's shirt. He can't. Just like he failed at getting a superpower, he's going to fail at this too.

'Here you are, then.'

He jumps with surprise and spins towards the source of the husky voice, his heart accelerating. The witch is here! In each hand, she holds a suitcase — one is brown vinyl and the other is green canvas —which she heaves onto Mum's tropical bedspread, then she slides her oversized handbag from her shoulder and plops it down as well. It looks like she's planning on staying a while *and* it looks like she's planning to sleep in Mum's bed. His nose crinkles as he detects the pong of cigarette smoke.

'Hi,' she says, tilting her forehead towards him so that several new chins appear at her throat. Her voice is lilting and slow, like she thinks he might be deaf or dumb or a baby. 'I'm Moira's mum, Aggie, and you must be young Jamie McKenzie. Moira's told me about the tough time you've been having, poor, wee love, and I only hope I can help in some small way.'

When it becomes obvious Jamie isn't intending to respond, Aggie continues. 'So, what game have you and Willy been playing?' She chuckles. 'You're red in the face and all out of breath like you've been running from the devil. Has Willy been making up stories to scare you? She does that you know. Always making stuff up.' She shakes her head. 'Always trying to create a drama.'

Jamie's head snaps towards the doorway where Willis is standing. Something is wrong with her. She's as tense as a trapped fox and her eyes are sharp and manic. Her mouth is thin and flat and Jamie can't figure out how she can have changed so profoundly in such a short amount of time. The girl before him is an utterly different creature to the one he'd left at the shearing shed only minutes earlier. When she speaks, her voice is clipped and hollow.

'My name is Willis now,' she says to the woman, then to Jamie, 'Did you get the thing you came here for?'

'I ... I ...'

'What thing?' asks Aggie, raising her eyebrows and looking suspiciously around the room.

'Just this old shirt,' he says, stepping over to the chair by the window. He pats the wet stain on the front of his own t-shirt. 'I spilled water on this one. By accident.'

He whips off his own and pulls the owl shirt over his head. Strange. He'd always assumed Sophie was bigger than him because she was older, but while the shirt had been floppy and loose on her, it fits him perfectly. The fabric is wonderfully soft. Bluer than he remembers. When she'd worn it, he'd thought it had been grey. He smooths it over his chest and looks down to see the picture he already knows is there. The wide-eyed owl.

He looks at Willis and notices a tiny twist of approval in the corner of her stiff mouth. Her nod is almost imperceptible, enough to let him know that he's succeeded in the mission and will be safe from the witch, except ... the game no longer seems important. Because of the change in Willis, he suspects there's been an unexpected alteration to their circumstances that he's yet to find out about. A gnawing sense of foreboding takes hold in his belly.

Aggie declares that she's in need of a cup of coffee and musters Jamie ahead of her out of Mum's bedroom with Willis following behind. As they pass Sophie's closed bedroom door, he stops and glares bravely up at the new arrival.

'No-one's allowed in there,' he says to Aggie.

'I understand, little man. You can trust me not to step a foot inside your poor, dear sister's bedroom.'

She tries to ruffle his hair but he dodges out of reach and carries on down the breezeway and into the kitchen ...

Then stops in surprise.

Because sitting in Dad's place at the kitchen table is a man he's never seen before. Willis only said it would be Mrs Tanning's mother, Aggie, coming to stay. Nothing about anyone else. He spins around, looks into her pale, troubled face and realises that she's as shocked as he is. And maybe a little frightened, as well.

He turns back and studies the man — stocky, middle-aged, wearing a buttoned-up chambray shirt, shorts, and elastic-sided boots which he hasn't bothered to take off before coming inside. The man lights up a roll-your-own cigarette and draws smoke deep into his lungs, then blows it back out, making a big cloud in the middle of the room.

CHAPTER 11

While still recovering from the shock of finding a strange man in the kitchen, Jamie realises that Aggie is talking to him. She's explaining how she and the man, who is called Onfro, drove *all* the way from Sydney yesterday in Onfro's car; and how Mrs Tanning has driven them out to the station early this morning before she starts work at the bank because Onfro's little car wouldn't have handled the rough, station roads.

'Moira said sorry she didn't stop and say hello, but she had to get back to the bank for an important meeting.'

'Why'd he come?' Willis nods towards the man.

Aggie puts her hand on her hip. 'Onfro is here as a favour to me so you be nice to him. Without him, I wouldn't have been able to come and take care of poor, wee Jamie while his parents are away.'

'We didn't need your help,' Willis says.

Aggie's laugh sounds like a whip crack. 'Oh, dearie me, Willy. Do you really think you'd have coped on your own?'

'I was coping just fine.'

'Well,' she shrugs and looks around with a chuffed smirk, 'your work here is now done. Thank you, but it's time to let me and Onfro take over. You know how good I've always been with littlies and Onfro will love doing the outside chores, won't you, sweetie? He's always fancied living out on a station. Always dreamt of owning your own place, haven't you?'

With growing alarm, Jamie studies the three people before him. Onfro sits hunched forward holding his smoke between yellow-stained fingers while Aggie stands behind him, rubbing his broad shoulders in a surprisingly intimate gesture. Willis leans in the breezeway door, her eyes bright with frustration and unshed tears. Her arms are folded over her chest.

'How about getting us a cup of coffee?' Aggie says to Willis.

'Get your own coffee,' she says.

''Ang on, girl.' Until now, Onfro has been silent, allowing Aggie to do the talking, and the speed with which his demeanour changes is alarming. He drops his smoke into an empty teacup and leaps to his feet. 'You'll stop being so rude and do as you're told.'

'Why should I? Apparently you're here to help out, so do it yourself.'

He reaches forward, snatches hold of one of her thin wrists in his enormous hand and twists her arm. 'I said, you'll do as you are told.'

'Get your filthy mitts off me.' She uses her voice like a weapon, low and cold as steel, and he drops his white-knuckled hands to his sides. His jaw is clenched, hard as rock, as if it takes all his willpower not to slam his fist straight into her face.

'You'll get yours,' he mutters, then stomps through the screen door, allowing it to bang behind him.

Jamie stares at the floor. His knees feel wobbly and he presses his hands against the table to stop himself from toppling over.

'I can't believe you brought him here!' Willis says to Aggie.

'I know you're mad at him for reporting you to the police that time,' she says, her hands twisting around each other. 'But he was only trying to do what he thought was right. He's a good man, Willy. If only you would give him a chance, you'll see that.'

'Except, he isn't a good man. He's a sleazebag.'

Aggie looks at Jamie, smiles nervously and says, 'You'll never get far in life if you go around lying about people all the time. You need to grow up, Willy.'

'I already told you. My name is Willis. And I don't lie.' Words softly spoken. Not yelled. Then, she walks off as well, in the opposite direction from the man.

Jamie stands frozen in the maelstrom of emotions left behind, unsure what to do next.

'Well, that went well,' Aggie mutters to herself, then to him, she says, 'Sit up at the table, wee man, and let's have a cuppa. How does that sound? And we can have a nice chat and get to know each other.' She nudges him towards the table and gently presses down on his shoulders until he sits. Then she fills the kettle and fusses about opening cupboards and humming to herself.

Then, unexpectedly, Willis returns. She gives Jamie's shoulder a small squeeze as she passes behind him, marches into the pantry, gets down a large cane basket from the top shelf and bangs it with her flat palm to knock off some of the dust. Next, she starts putting items into the basket — a bottle of fruitcup cordial from the fridge, two plastic tumblers, a block of long-life cheese, two apples, three carrots, a tomato, the remainder of a leg of cooked mutton, a butcher's knife, bread, butter, a jar of peanut butter, two teaspoons, a packet of Arnott's Iced VoVos and a bottle of Rid insect repellent. Jamie wonders if she's planning to go on a picnic.

While Willis fills her basket, Aggie puts on the kettle, spoons instant coffee into two mugs she's collected from the drying rack, then examines the contents of the fridge, sniffing at the bottle of milk. Both the girl and the woman hum while they work, each pointedly ignoring the other.

Once she is finished packing goods into the basket, Willis looks at Jamie and says, 'Get your boots and hat, Jamie. We're outta here.'

Aggie's jaw drops. 'Outta here where?' she says, but Willis doesn't even look at her.

Jamie retrieves his boots and hat from the laundry floor, then joins Willis outside. They walk together towards the shearing shed, the heavy basket swinging between them. Once inside the cavernous, darkened space, they place the basket in the middle of the wool-rolling table where Woofy won't be able to reach the food. Then they walk over to the

dusty, unkempt shearers' quarters and fetch two foam mattresses, four cotton mattress covers, two pillows, and two
pillow slips.

'We'll be comfortable as,' Willis says, as she uses an old
straw broom to sweep the floorboards in the shed. Under
the dust, the boards are a rich, golden colour; greasy from
years of contact with the lanoline-rich wool. Next, she gets
Jamie to help her put slips on the pillows and covers on the
mattresses. They spread the spare mattress covers over the
top.

'It's better here, don't you think? Cooler than in the
shearers' quarters. More atmospheric. It'll be like we're
camping out. Doesn't that sound like a fun thing to do?'

Jamie agrees that camping out in the shearing shed with
Willis does sound like fun, but he's still too upset about the
unexpected arrival of the man to lend much enthusiasm to
her plan. His thoughts are still back in the kitchen of the
homestead, remembering the way the man had sat at the
kitchen table with his boots still on, smoking and flicking
ash into a teacup, and the way he'd suddenly gotten mad
because Willis said she wouldn't make him a coffee and how
he'd jumped up and grabbed her by the arm and yelled at
her. Jamie had thought he was going to hit her. What if he
gets angry like that again? What if he comes after them in
the night?

As if reading his thoughts, Willis says, 'Don't worry
about Onfro, Jamie. If we stay down here in the shearing
shed and keep out of his way, he'll not bother us. He's not
going to come after us or anything like that.'

'But ...'

'He's a dickhead with a bad temper, not an axe murderer.
We'll be alright. I promise.'

Jamie decides the best thing to do, as soon as he gets the
chance, is to radio Dad and let him know about the bad man
who has come to Moonbroch. Meanwhile, he intends to lay
low, and where better to do that than in the shearing shed?

They sit cross-legged on mattresses facing each other, eating mutton and Iced VoVos, and drinking room-temperature cordial. Woofy sits opposite the food, alert and ready to accept any food offered while a pool of drool coalesces on the greasy floor between his black and white paws.

Willis produces a pack of playing cards from her pocket and begins to shuffle them.

'I found these in the quarters. Know any good card games?'

Jamie likes it in the shearing shed with Willis. He loves the way she's constantly telling him intriguing stories or coming up with crazy ideas for games to play. It's nice being the focus of someone's attention and two days pass without incident. They see Aggie twice, once when they go up to the house to let the dogs out for their run and once when they go to replenish their food supply and get some more clothes, soap, toothbrushes, books and board games. Jamie considers slipping away to the office to radio Dad, but it feels impossible with Willis always by his side.

When they go to the house, Willis is friendly towards Aggie, assuring her that they are having fun camping out and for her not to worry. But underneath the friendliness, Jamie senses the strain.

'Are you enjoying yourself?' she asks the older woman conversationally while packing the still-warm muffins Aggie has baked for them into a Tupperware container.

Aggie sighs. 'It'd be better if I could get some more time with young Jamie. After all, that *is* why I came. Maybe it's time he moved back to the house.'

Willis looks up sharply.

'With us out of the way, you get to spend more time with *him*.' She jerks her head towards the breezeway. 'You should be pleased.'

The woman blushes. There's a smudge of mascara below her right eye. 'I guess so. It's just … Onfro's been kind of preoccupied since he got here.'

'What do you mean?'

Aggie's mouth twists into a tight smile and she waves her hand dismissively. 'Just some business stuff he's trying to get sorted. He spends all his time in the office and on the phone.'

Jamie's eyes widen. He doesn't like to think about the man being in Dad's office. Something about his presence feels wrong, but he has no way of discussing his concerns with Mum or Dad without someone listening in.

'If he's that busy, maybe he'd be better off back in Sydney,' Willis says.

'No. He needs to be here —' Aggie suddenly looks flustered and clears her throat. 'He *wants* to be on Moonbroch, is what I mean. He *wants* to be here.'

Willis picks up the basket and rests it on her hip. 'Well, as long as he's here, we'll not come back to the house. Come on, Jamie. Let's go.'

The next day, Jamie and Willis are sitting cross-legged on the mattresses playing snakes and ladders when Onfro turns up at the shearing shed. Jamie nearly passes out with fright when he sees the man standing in the doorway watching them, his body silhouetted by glaring sunlight.

'This 'as gone on long enough, Willy,' he says, once he realises that his presence has been noticed. 'You're upsettin' Aggie by keepin' the boy down here and it's got to stop, you hear. He's to come back to the house with me right now.'

Jamie drops the dice back onto the snakes and ladders board and looks anxiously at Willis for instruction. His heart is thumping like crazy, but she seems completely calm, frozen like a statue in her cross-legged position opposite him. A tiny smile turns up one corner of her mouth. He notices a glint of feline stubbornness in her eyes and realises she has no intention of doing what the man wants.

She shakes her head and says in a soft clear voice, 'Jamie is staying here with me.'

The man steps towards them. Now that he's away from the glare of the door, Jamie can see that his face is red and shiny with sweat. 'You'll not speak to me that way, Willy, and you'll fuckin' do as you're told, you hear. Or there'll be consequences.'

She lifts her head slowly, languidly, so that she's staring straight into his enraged face. The little smile is still flickering in the corner of her mouth.

'Such as?' she says.

The man clambers forward, his attention so focused so completely on Willis that he doesn't even look in Jamie's direction. He moves fast and in an instant, he has his sausage fingers around Willis's thin arm. He pulls her to her feet.

'You're out of control, girly,' Onfro says. 'You need to learn some respect.'

'You don't scare me,' she says.

'You should be scared. You should be very scared.'

Jamie has never been so scared in his life. The man is undoing the buckle of his belt with one hand and pulling free the leather strap. His other hand is still holding Willis's arm.

'Let go of me, you stupid moron,' she screams, trying to twist her arm free from his grasp. 'Leave me alone.'

Jamie is on his feet, backing away towards the holding pens, eyes wide and hyperventilating with fear. He remembers a time when he'd gotten so mad with Sophie that he'd hit her and his father had sat him down at the kitchen table and explained that it was wrong to hit girls. Hitting girls was even worse than lying and stealing and you should never do it, no matter what.

But the man has the end of the belt wrapped around in his hand and it makes a whistling sound as it arcs through the air, then a loud slapping sound as it strikes Willis's bare thigh.

'Learn some respect,' he grunts, and swings the belt back for another strike.

Without further thought, Jamie charges forward and slams his shoulder into the man's side. He starts pounding him with his fists.

'Stop it,' Jamie screams, tears wetting his face. 'Stop it.'

The man pivots sideways in an effort to avoid his punches, which causes his elbow to smash so hard into the side of Jamie's head that the world around him fills with spangles of light. He thinks his eardrum might have burst, or he might have gotten brain damage, and he's wondering what to do about it. Should he give up trying to save Willis and maybe start crying, or should he keep fighting? Nothing in his previous experience has ever involved a muscly, middle-aged man strapping a teenage girl or knocking him in the head. Before he can decide how to react, Woofy joins the battle. He rushes in, yapping and showing his teeth like he would if he was asked to push sheep up the drafting race.

'Ah. No way,' the man says, letting go of Willis and turning his attention to the old dog.

'Run,' Willis screams at him. 'I'll meet you at the gecko tree.'

She ducks behind the wool classing table.

Jamie wants to run, but the man is now sinking his boot into the old dog's ribs for a second time and Woofy is yelping with pain.

'Woofy!' he screams.

Before the big man can strike again, Woofy responds to Jamie's voice and scurries away from the falling boot.

And, barefooted, Jamie runs. Along the dusty road, back past the homestead and out towards the crossing.

Woofy runs by his side.

CHAPTER 12

The sound of the ute starting up reaches Jamie's ears and he stops running. It can't be Willis. She hasn't driven the ute once since she's been here and Jamie is fairly sure she doesn't know how. No. It won't be her. It'll be the man. Coming after him. He needs to get off the road. Willis said to go to the gecko tree. She must have meant the box tree that grows out from the edge of the creek. They'd sat under that tree the day he'd told her about how geckos drop off their tails when an enemy tries to grab them.

He veers away from the road and into the scanty scrub until he reaches the creek, then follows the sandy waterway until he comes upon Willis who is perched on an exposed root under the big old tree. He's impressed to see that she has his bushman's hat, his boots, his socks, and the hessian waterbag, which he accepts gratefully.

'Thanks,' he says, catching sight of the red welt on her thigh. He looks to her face which is in deep shade, cast by her broad-brimmed hat, and guesses she's been crying. He doesn't know what to say to a crying girl, so instead, he sets about pouring some water into his hat for Woofy and takes a few gulps himself. He carefully screws the lid back into place, then sits on the shaded sand and deburrs his bare feet. When he can't feel any more prickles, he pulls on his socks. His boots. His hat. The speed with which everything went wrong has left him shaken and in shock; and now he moves through each task robotically, with a determined focus.

She smiles. 'You okay?'

He doesn't know how to answer, so he studies the owl on the front of his t-shirt. Its wide eyes look up at him.

'What do you think we should do now?' she asks.

He looks into her troubled face, then his eyes are drawn once more to the mark on her thigh. They can't go back to the shearing shed. It wouldn't be safe.

'Do you have a driving licence?'

She shakes her head.

'I know how to drive,' he says. 'But you might need to help with changing the gears.'

She shakes her head again. 'I don't think Onfro will leave the keys to the ute where we can find them. He'll have taken all the keys. Do you know how to hot-wire a car?'

'Huh?'

'Doesn't matter,' she says, snapping a twig between her fingers.

Jamie lets his breath go with an audible sigh. 'We can walk out to the highway and hitch a ride to town.'

'How far is it to the highway?'

'Twelve k.'

He watches Willis thinking over his suggestion, then she shrugs. 'Sounds like a plan.' She pulls a tube of sunscreen from the back pocket of her shorts. 'Put this on first so you don't get burnt.'

She falls into an easy stride by his side and no more words are spoken as they make their way along the sandy creek bed towards the crossing. The crossing is the only way into and out of the homestead. Once there, they will need to follow the road up through the stony hills until they come to the highway where they can hopefully flag down a passing car. Or truck. If one comes along.

As they approach the crossing, Jamie swallows down his rising anxiety and begins to peer cautiously ahead, trying to see if the man is there waiting for them.

'No-one's there,' Willis says, passing Jamie the waterbag. She puts her hands on her hips and stretches her back.

'How do you know?'

'I'm paying attention to the little creatures.'

He immediately starts to notice the sound of the birds.

'If he was hiding, the birds would be quiet,' he says, 'and if he was moving around setting a trap, the birds would be noisy.'

'That's what I reckon.'

They come out onto the crossing which is made from ironstone pressed into compacted clay. Every time the creek floods, the ironstone loosens and Dad has to go up into the stony hills to get more rock. It's a good thing it hasn't rained for so long because Jamie doesn't think Dad has the heart for collecting ironstone any more.

Jamie looks one final time across the flats to where his home is perched low on the horizon in the far distance, then he and Willis turn away towards the highway. For a while, they stay in the scrub in case the man comes looking for them, but after a while, they begin to relax and trudge along the road.

Hours pass in silence. Despite the sunscreen, the scorching sun burns the exposed skin on Jamie's arms and legs. Blisters begin to form on his hot feet. Once again, as she has been doing regularly since they left the crossing, Willis passes him the waterbag and tells him to drink. He splashes a few precious glugs into his hat for Woofy and pours some down his own parched throat.

Then she reaches out, takes the waterbag from him, fetches the lid from his other hand and screws it carefully back in place.

'Jamie?'

He hears her voice as though from a great distance.

'Jamie, look at me.'

He lifts his face in the direction of her voice and squints to avoid the pain caused by the bright sun shining into his eyes.

'Crap,' she says.

She pushes him down onto the ground, under the sparse shade of a mulga tree. Pulls off his hat. Carefully pours a splash of water on the top of his head and starts rubbing the moisture down over his burning face with the palm of her hand.

Woofy barks a warning.

A vehicle is approaching.

It's travelling in from the highway and not coming from the direction of the house. And it's moving unusually slowly, cautiously negotiating the rough terrain and carrying a pillow of dust along with it, like a passenger.

'Thank God,' Willis says, her voice husky with dryness. She leaves him under the tree and positions herself in the middle of the road, ready to stop the car and make all their problems go away.

Jamie is hot — or maybe cold — he's not sure. His head hurts. He closes his eyes. Lowers his face until it is resting against the wet hessian of the waterbag, which is almost empty and drying out around the edges.

Stones crunch under the car's tyres as it comes to a stop. The ignition is turned off. And there's silence. As if the whole world has stopped to listen to the dust settle.

Then he hears Willis's voice. Spoken very softly. Like a whisper.

'What the hell?' she says.

What the hell.

The words are so soft, they might not even be real. They might be just a trick. Except he knows what he heard. And he knows they're not a trick.

What the hell.

He also knows it's not her actual words, but rather, the tone of her voice, that has caused his body to fill with dread.

He opens his eyes.

Walking through the stony hills with the awful sun beating down on their heads, Willis was terrified that Jamie might die. She promised Mr McKenzie she would take good care of him and she had failed. In her mind, she kept thinking about those two young boys who had died on a station in Western Australia a few years ago. She still remembers their names — James Annetts and Simon Amos.

But that won't happen to us, she'd kept thinking. We must be nearly at the highway. We've got water. We'll be okay.

But when she'd passed Jamie the waterbag that last time, she'd noticed his flushed face. And the way he'd stood on the road with the bag in his hands, staring into space like he'd lost his mind. That's when the stark reality of the truth had slapped her in the face and she'd realised they were in deep shit. She'd taken the waterbag from his hands, screwed the lid carefully back into place, then pushed him down into the shade under that spindly tree and begun to wet his face.

Please God, help us, she'd prayed silently, even though she wasn't sure there was such a thing as God. I'll do anything you want but please, help us. Please don't let Jamie die.

Then Woofy had barked. And a car was approaching from the highway.

Now she's standing in the middle of the road on unstable legs waiting for the car to come to her. *Thank you, God. Thank you.*

The car is a four-wheel drive. Beneath the dust, she can see the gloss of new, white paint. Inside, a sole occupant is perched forward on his seat gripping the steering wheel — like he's not used to driving in the outback. He stops the car three metres from where she is standing and something about his face is familiar …

'What the hell?' she mutters.

Jamie gets to his feet but stays back under the shade of the mulga tree while Willis remains motionless in the middle of the road with her arms wrapped tightly across her chest.

The new arrival is more like a boy than a fully-grown man. His clothes are a black t-shirt, stubby shorts that emphasise his skinny legs, and rubber thongs. He wears sunglasses and his dark hair is unbrushed and kind of knotty at the back; and the beginnings of a wispy beard is evident on his chin. His unkempt, scrappy appearance reminds Jamie of a character in one of Sophie's books — Cluny the Scourge, an evil one-eyed rat.

'Willy,' ratboy says loudly, walking towards her. 'How the hell are you?'

'Ray.'

Ratboy stops. 'What sort of welcome is that?'

'Sorry. It's just …' Her tone is conciliatory.

Ratboy's mouth turns upwards like he's trying to smile.

'Don't give me your bullshit, Willy,' he says. 'When my girl suddenly goes missing without telling me where she's going, what am I to think? That she doesn't want me around?'

'Ray. There's something more important.' She steps forward and touches his forearm.

'What's more —'

'I'm worried about Jamie. I think he has heat stroke.' She nods to where Jamie and Woofy are partly concealed by the tree's shade. 'Can you help get him back to the homestead? We need to cool him down and get some more water into him.'

Ratboy starts to laugh.

'Classic Willy,' he says. 'Classic fucking Willy. Everything is always such a big drama with you.'

'Ray. I'm serious.'

'What's in it for me?'

She freezes for a second, then squares her shoulders, tilts her hips slightly and looks into his face. 'Whatever you want, Ray. Just … please help me get Jamie safely back to the house.'

'Whatever I want?' He's grinning. And bouncing up and down on the balls of his thonged feet. And rubbing his palms together. 'Whatever I want? *Whatever I want?* Ha. Ha. Can't wait for that.' He licks his lips. 'How about a little taste of what's to come?'

'No.' She beckons to Jamie. 'Quick. Get in the car.'

Jamie's aching head is filled with half-formed questions that he can't quite articulate — Who is ratboy? Why is he here? Why does Willis think he has a stroke? Is it the same as the thing that put Granny Linley in the hospital? Will he have to go to hospital too? Will he die? Why did Willis say they needed to go back to the house? What will Onfro do to them if they go back there? Shouldn't they go to town?

She presses her hand gently against his shoulder. Pushes him forward. 'It'll be okay. Ray is a friend of mine.'

His feet feel heavy and robotic as he walks towards the white four-wheel drive and climbs onto the back seat. It is very clean inside. There is a new-car smell.

'Move over,' Willis says. 'I'll sit in the back with you.'

He shuffles across to the middle of the seat, feels around behind him for the seat belt and clicks it into place. She climbs in beside him while ratboy gets into the driver's seat, turns the ignition and revs the engine.

'This car has great air-conditioning,' he yells back to Willis. 'Feels like a fucking European winter.'

He pulls the automatic gear selector to Drive, presses down on the accelerator and the car jerks forward.

Jamie bolts upright and shouts. 'Wait.'

'Fuck!' Ratboy hits the breaks. 'What?'

'We forgot Woofy.'

'God. I can't believe we almost forgot Jamie's dog,' Willis says.

'Aw, fuck,' says ratboy. He clicks the selector back to Park, leaps out and starts calling, 'Here boy. Here boy.'

But Jamie knows the old dog won't come to a stranger and he's trying to unfasten his seatbelt so he can get out and call Woofy himself. But before he can even get his seatbelt clasp to unfasten, ratboy is back in the driver's seat, slamming the door.

'Fuck 'im,' ratboy says, and revs the motor. 'Let's go.'

'No.'

'Ray.'

'He can fucking stay here if he's that stupid. I don't want him stinking up my nice clean car, anyway.'

Jamie has finally undone his seatbelt and is scrambling for the door. Ratboy accelerates down the road.

'Wait,' yells Jamie and Willis wraps herself around his small body to stop him from opening the door and jumping out. He begins screaming and kicking his boots against the back of ratboy's seat until ratboy starts punching his fist through the gap between the seats.

'Make him settle down,' he yells at Willis and she holds on tighter.

'Shhh,' she whispers into his ear. 'Shhh. It'll be okay. We'll get you home and then I'll come back and get Woofy in the ute. I promise. Shhh.'

Jamie shoves her away and twists around so he can see out the back window where he gets one final glimpse of his old friend, standing alone, panting, under the straggly mulga tree on the side of the road.

CHAPTER 13

Winter waves goodbye to her grandfather, Poppy, from the front verandah of the cottage. He'd wanted to come in and meet Cass and her father but Winter had said no. She didn't want him grilling Cass's father or making Cass think she is overprotected or immature. It's bad enough that her parents won't let her have her own phone.

'You can come and meet them when you get back,' she'd said, flashing him her signature smile and getting out of the car. 'See you at six.'

Once he's disappeared down the street, she takes a deep breath to calm herself and knocks on Cass's father's front door. She's finally about to make a new friend. Maybe even a best friend. At least, she hopes so. She'd found it hard moving schools a year ago and trying to make new friends, particularly when most of the girls in her class seemed to be so totally self-obsessed. Cass is part of a big group of girls who hung out in the quadrangle at lunchtime, but Winter had spoken to her a few times in class and she seems really nice. Which is why Winter took the risk and wrote the friendship note. Of course, she'd regretted it immediately, and then, when Cass hadn't called, she felt humiliated.

But then … Cass *did* call. Yesterday. And here she is.

Winter knocks again. Harder. She cups her hands and peers through the glass in the front door at the dim interior. Shiny floorboards. A large bookshelf with framed photos. Lounge chairs and a television. She walks to the end of the verandah where there's an empty carport and beyond that, a cobwebby shed with a broken door, which she investigates — a few old pieces of furniture, two boogie boards. Half a motorbike.

No car.

Her heart sinks. Maybe Cass and her father are running late getting back from wherever they've been. That's a better scenario than the alternative — which is that Cass has forgotten about her coming over.

She calls out a few times around the back, then returns to the front verandah, sits down on the top step and jiggles her large spiral notebook free from the confines of her backpack. Folded inside the notebook are four A4 pages printed from Poppy's computer, each page containing a copy of an old newspaper article about a small boy from western Queensland called Jamie McKenzie. The articles are from 1990. Back then, Poppy had worked as a journalist for a newspaper group called the Daily and Sunday Sun; and when she'd told him that Cass's father's name was Jamie McKenzie, he'd said he once worked on a story about someone with that name and looked it up.

Winter doesn't know if the small boy in the newspaper stories is the *same* Jamie McKenzie as Cass's father. It could be a coincidence. But a ten-year-old boy in 1990 would be in his mid-thirties now — which *is* realistic. And Cass did say he was a bushie.

She opens the pages on her lap and begins to reread the articles. There's something about two people who drowned in a flooded creek but mostly, the stories are about this amazing child who lifted a car and saved a teenage girl's life.

… boy in outback Queensland who lifted a car

… no way he should have been able to lift that car

… not physically possible

… adrenaline

… a miracle.

One article describes him as Australia's littlest superhero.

Looking up from her reading, she snaps off a sprig of lavender from the bushes that grow along the edge of the verandah, crushes it between her fingers and holds it under her nose. Does Cass know her father was once famous? Does she know that people once called him a superhero? Cass doesn't seem to know much about him at all. Will she be impressed that Winter has these old stories? Or will she be annoyed? Or upset with her?

She wonders about the girl who Jamie McKenzie saved. The stories said she had horrific injuries. Did she recover? Did she go on to have a good life?

She folds the pages back into her notebook, sets the notebook down on the verandah and does some yoga poses — the mountain, the tree, the dancer, and warrior III. She drops her right hand onto the ground, lifts her left leg and breathes through the half-moon pose. But she's bored. The chirp of crickets makes her sleepy. She checks her watch. Where is Cass?

Leaving her notebook and backpack on the front verandah, she goes around to the back and calls again. Then she tries the back door.

The unlocked back door opens straight into a kitchen where she helps herself to a glass of water. Then she decides to use the bathroom. After this, she goes past the study nook into the lounge room and checks out the photos on the bookshelf. Just a quick peep and she'll get out of there. One is of a girl who *looks* like Cass. But there are no photos of Cass. Strange. What if this isn't Cass's father's house?

She checks out the bedrooms. In the second bedroom, she notes the unmade double bed, the items of clothing on the wicker chair, the toothbrush and the pot of strawberry-flavoured lip balm — all good evidence that Cass has been staying in this room. Then, under a glass vase on the dressing table, she finds definite proof that this is the right house — it's the friendship note she gave Cass at the end of the school year. Embarrassing!

So where is Cass now? Why isn't she here?

What if something bad has happened to her?

Back at the study nook, she sits down at the computer.

'Let's see what's in your browser history, Mr McKenzie,' she mutters. 'Let's find out what dastardly deeds you've been planning. A few jiggles of the mouse and … yes, here we go. The beast awakens, ready to reveal all your secrets.

You don't have a password, Mr McKenzie? That's dumb. Good for me but dumb for you. Everyone should have a password. Don't you know that? Especially if you've got secrets, which I suspect you do.'

While participating in her imaginary conversation with Mr McKenzie, she clicks her way confidently into Chrome and opens up the browser history. Some of the girls at school think she's a luddite, or they would if they knew the meaning of the word, but she actually spends a lot of time on a computer at Poppy's house. She spends a lot of time at Poppy's house. Period. Because her parents are so often away overseas.

'So, what do we have here?' she says, leaning forward. 'Main Range National Park — Goomburra Section. I'm onto you, Mr McKenzie. I'm on to you.'

'Cass has gone missing,' she tells her grandfather when he returns to pick her up at six. 'There's evidence she's been here but no sign of the actual person.'

'Poor old you,' he says sympathetically. 'Being stood up by your friend is not nice.'

She puts her hands on her hips. 'That's just it. I don't think I've been stood up. At least, not deliberately. I think something bad may have happened to them.'

'And why is that, Ms Drew?' The skin around his eyes crinkles with amusement.

She pulls a sheet of paper from the pages of her notebook and holds it up for him to see. 'Because of this. It's a map.'

'I can see that.'

'I printed it off their computer.'

'You went into the house?' He frowns and rubs the side of his head.

'The door was unlocked and I thought it would be okay if I had a quick look around for clues on account of me being an invited guest and not a stranger.'

'Winter! You should never go snooping in someone's house when they're not home.'

'But if I hadn't gone 'snooping,' — she holds her hands up by her ears like inverted commas — 'I wouldn't have found this.' She waves the map under his nose.

'How is the map relevant?'

'They downloaded it last night so it must be where they've gone. What if they didn't come back because something bad happened to them?'

'Or because they forgot you were coming.'

'I really don't think that's why they're not here, Poppy. I've got a bad feeling about this. A really bad feeling.'

He smiles and shakes his head. 'You get a bad feeling about lots of things, Winter. It's because you have such a vivid imagination and I love that about you. But right now, we probably should be heading home.'

'This is different, Poppy.'

By the way he keeps rubbing the side of his head, she knows she's won. He now has a bad feeling about the welfare of Cass and her father as well, and he's not going to want to leave Toowoomba until he knows that they're okay.

She and her grandfather — they're alike when it comes to solving mysteries.

As the day darkens, Winter and Poppy sit side-by-side in Poppy's van, watching the cottage and silently chewing their food. Both are deep in thought. Spread across the wide console between them are several containers of food including bean salad, fresh tabbouleh, home grown avocado, falafel balls, quinoa salad. All delicious.

Winter loves it when her parents go away and she gets to stay with Poppy. He owns a market garden out in Moggill where he grows all kinds of organic fruit, herbs and vegetables. Some of the produce is sold direct to the markets but most gets turned into a wonderful array of salads that are sold to local delicatessens and cafes. She always feels happy and proud to sit beside him in his *Poppy's Real Food* van and she knows he loves having her with him.

'How'd your visits go today?' she says. 'Anyone interested in buying your yummy food?'

'I came to see one place in particular, and they've already placed an order, and a couple of other places said they'd taste the samples and get back to me.'

She gives him a high five. 'Well done.' After a pause, she says, 'Do you think we're being silly sitting out here waiting for Cass to come home? Maybe she doesn't even want to see me.'

He turns towards her. 'It's not costing us anything to sit here and eat our dinner. It's a nice street. The jacaranda trees are pretty and we've got nowhere else we particularly need to be ... and I get to enjoy dinner with my favourite granddaughter.'

She laughs. 'Your only granddaughter.'

'Most people these days wouldn't stop and say — is my friend safe? They would simply ignore their gut instinct and hurry on with their busy lives. I think it takes courage to recognise a gut instinct for what it is and act upon it, which is exactly what you are doing. If Cass and her dad turn up safe and sound, then great. No harm done. But if they really are in trouble, us sticking our necks out might mean they get the help they need.'

'But we're not sticking our necks out. We're sitting here eating our dinner.'

'We will.' He shuffles about in the semi-darkness of the van and produces his mobile phone. 'We'll start by making some phone calls. You don't happen to have Cass or her father's mobile phone numbers written down in that giant notebook of yours, do you?'

Around midnight, after they've finally managed to talk to the police, Winter and Poppy return to Cass's father's house and park under the jacaranda trees out front. Winter wanted to go straight out to the National Park, but Poppy has insisted they sleep first.

'There's nothing we can do until daylight and we'll be no use to anyone if we charge out there in the middle of the night and get ourselves into trouble. Meanwhile, we can wait outside their house in case they come home.'

After checking that the house is still empty, Winter lays back her seat and sleeps soundly. Then, something wakes her. A deep rumble — half sound and half vibration. Raising her seat to an upright position, she checks the time on the van's clock — 3:34 a.m. — then peers out at the quiet street which is lit in places by the soft glow of street lamps. She quickly identifies the source of the disturbance. A motor bike is coming up the street, moving slowly despite her sense that it is a powerful machine. It looks as if the rider is trying to read the house numbers on the letterboxes. He (or she) stops the bike about twenty metres further up the street and dismounts. Takes off his helmet. It's definitely a man. Dressed in leather. He saunters down the street, back towards them, and enters the picket fence at the front of Cass's father's house.

'Poppy,' she says quietly. 'Are you awake?'

From where he's stretched out in the back of the van between the eskies of food, he responds immediately to her voice.

'Are they home?'

'Shhh. Look.'

He wriggles through the space between the seats and climbs into the driver's seat.

'What is it?'

She nods towards where the man in leather is cupping his hands over the windows and peering into the house.

'Who do you think that is?'

'I'll go see.'

Before she can stop him, Poppy is out of the van and approaching the stranger. She winds down her window so she might have a better chance of hearing what is being said.

'Hello there,' Poppy says as he goes up the front path.

The man spins towards the sound. 'Jesus, mate, you scared the shit out of me.'

Winter is tense as she watches the man's body language — at first, borderline aggressive, but quickly settling in response to her grandfather's passivity. The two men shake hands.

Then Poppy leads the man back to the van.

'This is Ray,' he says.

CHAPTER 14

In the backseat of Ray's four-wheel drive, Willis closes her eyes. If Ray thinks she's asleep or unconscious, he might stop showing off and drive a bit more carefully. She'd seen how cautiously and slowly he'd been driving when he was on his own but now that she's in the car with him, he's driving like a maniac and fishtailing all over the road. And he's not concentrating on the driving because he's too busy talking at her, loudly, about how clever he's been to track her down and good thing too or she might be fuckin' dead meat and isn't this just classic Willy, her getting lost in the outback. She wants to tell him that she's not technically lost, and not to swear in front of Jamie, but she's worried that anything she says might antagonise him and cause him to drive faster. Her first priority is to keep Jamie safe.

She's fifty-fifty about whether she should have gotten Ray to take them into town or back to the station. The station is closer but if Jamie really does have heat stroke, then maybe he should go to town where there will be a doctor. Except, it's probably quicker to get the flying doctor to come to the station than drive all that way to town. She just hopes she's made the right decision.

Having to go back and face Onfro is something she'd rather not have to do, because, despite her bravado around him, he terrifies her. However, she must do what's best for Jamie. She made a promise to Mr McKenzie to take care of him and she intends to keep it no matter what.

On top of everything else, she'll now have to deal with Ray. Shit! Crap! What the hell is he doing here and where did he get this brand-new four-wheel drive from? She's grateful he came along when he did, of course, but she doesn't want him here. He'll expect everything to be the same as it was in Sydney and she's not the same person she

was back then. She knows it's only been a week. But …
she's changed.

As soon as they arrive at the homestead, Ray leaps out
of the car and starts calling out.

'Help. Help. We need help.'

Out in the stony hills, he'd thought her situation was a
joke and now he's trying to act like the hero … saving lives.
She clenches her jaw with frustration.

Shit, he annoys her!

Twenty minutes later, Willis leaves Jamie at the house with
Aggie and ratboy and prepares to go back to the stony hills
to collect Woofy, like she'd promised she would. Onfro is
going to drive her in the ute.

'We won't be long,' she says, disappearing through the
screen door.

'Wait.' He follows her outside and glances worriedly to
where Onfro is waiting.

'Don't worry about him,' she says. 'He's just a harmless
old man. Unless I stir him up, of course. Which I'm not
going to do.'

Jamie is worried about her going off with the man who,
a short while ago, had beaten her with his belt. But what can
he do? Someone has got to get Woofy.

Once she's gone, he returns inside where Aggie fusses
over him with wet towels and cold drinks. She keeps putting
her hot pudgy hands against his forehead and muttering,
'You're okay, little man. No need to worry. You're okay.'

He's drunk three glasses of cordial and thinks he might
vomit over the kitchen table at any moment. Is there any
need to worry about that, he wonders?

In the middle of the table, Aggie places an enormous
plate filled with ham, cheese, salad, nuts, and crackers, and
while ratboy is busy shovelling the food into his mouth, he's
also busy talking.

'Life in the outback suits you, Aggie,' he says, spraying cracker crumbs over the table. 'You're looking real good. Thanks for the food, by the way. Delicious. And thanks for arranging for me to come and for your daughter hiring the car and everything. She seems nice, your daughter. What's her name? Moya?'

'Moira.'

'Moira, the bank manager. She must have lots of money, hey?' He chuckles.

'Just make sure you do what you're here to do, Ray,' Aggie says. 'Willy needs to be gone. By tomorrow.'

Jamie sits up straight and looks from Aggie to ratboy. That's why ratboy is here? To take Willis away? Willis is leaving? Leaving him alone with these people? With one hand either side of his thighs, Jamie grips onto his seat. The chair suddenly feels like a brumby, wild and unpredictable. Ready to buck him off.

'Don't worry. I can handle Willy,' ratboy says. 'It'll not be a problem.' He shakes his head. 'But isn't that just classic Willy. Imagine her going off and getting lost like that. One road in and one road out and still, she gets lost.'

He pushes a slice of ham wrapped in a lettuce leaf into his mouth with his fingers. It's too much for Jamie. He jumps to his feet and glares at ratboy.

'Her name isn't Willy. It's Willis. And ... and we weren't lost,' he yells. 'You ... you idiot.'

Ratboy's eyes widen with surprise.

'Whoa, sport,' he says. 'Settle down.'

'There, there,' says Aggie as she moves behind him and attempts to manoeuvre him back onto his chair.

'He's just a bit out of sorts, is all,' she says to ratboy.

'I. Am. Not. Out. Of. Sorts,' he screams, pushing her away. 'I am not ...'

He's burning up with anger and wants to hit out at these stupid people who are so mean and dumb and don't even know that Willy is the wrong name. But he's also at grave risk of crying and he doesn't want to do that in front of ratboy. So he runs. Down the breezeway. Into his bedroom. Bangs the door. Flops onto his belly on the bed. Arms over his head.

After a few minutes, the door opens.

'Mind if I come in,' says Aggie.

He doesn't answer. The floorboards creak under her feet and he feels the movement of the mattress as she sits down.

'Onfro is so sorry about what happened, Jamie,' she says. 'Truly he is. He feels just terrible. He never meant any of it to happen.'

She pauses.

'It was my fault, you know.'

She sniffs. Is she crying? He rolls onto his side so he can see her face.

'I just wanted to feel useful and help take care of you, is all. To think, because of me, you might have come to harm.'

'He hit her,' Jamie says, his voice scratchy and stretched with emotion.

'Oh, I'm sure he didn't hurt her. Young Willy can be just so challenging, sometimes. It'll do her some good to get the strap occasionally.'

His father's words echo inside his mind. There's never any excuse for hitting a girl.

'You've got to understand it from Onfro's side, Jamie. He was in the Army as a young man and he had to go to war in a terrible place called Vietnam; and ever since, he's suffered from something they call PTSD which gets worse when he's under pressure … and young Willy pushes his buttons. You know that. You've seen it. It's like she wants him to snap and hit her.'

'Why'd he come if he hates her that much?'

'He's here to help out while your parents are away. That's what good people do. They help out when others are having a tough time.'

'We didn't need help.'

She laughs and flutters her hands. 'This is a job for grownups, Jamie. Willy is way too young to handle it. And from the moment we arrived, she's made absolutely no effort to get along, so I really can't say I feel sorry for her at all. She got what she deserved.'

Aggie stands and dusts her hands down the front of her dress.

'I'm only sorry you got caught up in our troubles, especially when you've got your own sorrows to be dealing with, so let's hope things settle down once she's gone.'

He still hasn't had a chance to process that Willis is leaving and is still thinking over the significance of this when Aggie says, 'Your mother called. A few times.'

Willis sits as far from Onfro as the seats in the ute will allow and keeps her eyes directed towards the scrub, searching every shadow for the possible outline of a dog. At the place where they'd met Ray, both she and Onfro get out of the car.

'Woofy,' she calls. 'Here, Woofy.'

Onfro whistles.

But Woofy is not there.

'Probably a good thing if he doesn't come back,' says Onfro.

'What do you mean?'

'Dogs like that ought to be put down before they end up biting someone.'

Willis recalls that, when Jamie had become involved in her struggle with Onfro in the shearing shed, Woofy had shown a few teeth and maybe growled a little. But she'd never felt the old dog capable of biting anyone. However, she doesn't want to get into an argument with Onfro again, especially when they're on their own out in the scrub, so she ignores his idiotic statement and remains silent.

In fact, neither speaks another word until they're nearly back at the homestead.

Then, Onfro breaks the silence. 'Jamie needs to sleep back at the house. In his own bed.'

Not wanting further conflict with the man, Willis nods her consent. 'I'll put the mattresses back in the quarters and move our stuff back to the house this afternoon.'

'Not you.'

'Why not me?'

'You can stay in the shed with your boyfriend tonight.'

Jamie will be frightened at the house without her and upset about Woofy missing. Also, as soon as Ray and she are alone, he's going to expect payback — for her leaving Sydney without telling him — and reward — for saving her life.

Her head is spinning. She doesn't want to stay in the shed with Ray, but if she insists on staying in the house, what might happen? Onfro could lose his temper again and next time, the beating could be much worse. And Ray will still want to sleep with her, wherever she is, and he won't care who hears them having sex. If they're in the house, she won't have any chance of resisting his advances. She'll just have to lie still and take it in silence.

A tiny shudder of fear and loathing causes her to tremble.

'What about after tonight?' she asks. 'Do I get to move back to the house tomorrow?'

He pats the steering wheel with his blocky hand. 'You won't be here after tonight. Your boyfriend has come to take you back to Sydney.'

'Are you serious?'

'Aggie had such high hopes coming out here. She's disappointed at how it's all turned out.'

Willis's mouth is dry and her words come out as a whisper. 'She has no right.'

He pats the steering wheel once more. 'What's done, is done.'

'But ... but what if I try really hard ... what if ...' Tears are clouding her eyes.

'Bit late for that.'

'No. I can do it. I promise. Just let me stay with Jamie. Please.'

He drives the ute past the house and along the dusty track to the shearing shed, then turns and looks dispassionately at her tear stained face. A leery smile turns his plump lips upwards.

'Get a good night's sleep.'

Ray is already at the shed. She can hear his music playing inside. Loud, discordant music that smashes mindlessly against the subtleties of the natural landscape around her.

Inside, she sees him first, sucking on a joint and spinning around in a kind of slow-motion dance.

'Willy,' he yells over the music when he notices her standing anxiously in the doorway. 'How fuckin' great is this?'

'Turn it down,' she yells back and attempts a smile. He's in a good mood. Maybe it won't be so bad.

'What?'

'I said, turn it down, you idiot.'

He switches the music off and comes over to her. She can smell the sickly scent of marijuana in the air.

'Babe. You've been crying.'

She nods.

'Didn't find the doggy, hey?'

She shakes her head.

'Never mind.' He looks at the joint between his fingers. 'Here. This'll make you feel better.'

She takes the joint carefully between her fingers, holds it to her mouth, draws the smoke deeply into her lungs and holds her breath for a few seconds, the way Ray has taught her. It's strong shit. She can feel the effects immediately — like tiny trains chugging through her veins.

'Go again,' Ray says.

And she does.

'Mum?'

'Jamie-love. It's so good to hear your voice.'

'Mum, I —'

He looks to where Aggie is standing, leaning against the wall in the breezeway, listening.

'Is everything going okay? Have you been managing to get the chores done every day?'

'Yes. I —'

'Aggie told me you and Willy have been having a great time camping in the shearing shed and playing all sorts of games.'

'Yes.'

'And Aggie sounds like such a nice lady. I've spoken to her every day since she arrived. She's been keeping me up to date.'

'Mum?'

'Yes, love?'

He looks sideways at Aggie. 'How is Granny?'

'As well as can be expected. I've been telling her about all the fun you've been having.'

The call to his mother leaves Jamie with an overwhelming sense of impotence. He wants so much to tell her about Onfro, the man who hits girls, and about getting heat stroke in the stony hills, and about how the horrible ratboy left Woofy behind. He wants to cry and plead with her to come home. But it will take more than a supervised talk over a crackly phone line for such words to be able to come out of his mouth. Also, with Aggie standing against the wall, smiling and nodding, he starts to wonder if, maybe, things aren't so bad after all.

After hanging up the phone, he takes a bath, then returns to the kitchen to see if Willis is back with news about Woofy.

'You'll want a clean shirt,' Aggie says, her mouth twisting with disapproval at the sight of Sophie's old t-shirt with its ever-watchful owl on the front.

He shakes his head.

'You sure? That one's filthy.'

When he doesn't respond, she continues. 'You're a funny one, aren't you? Well, never mind. We need to get this food down to the shearing shed. I think it's cool enough to walk. What do you reckon? Feel like a bit of exercise?'

She seems to have already forgotten that he and Willis have been out walking most of the day and that he has heat stroke. Or that he's got blisters on his feet.

He decides to go barefoot. When they arrive at the shed, ratboy comes out to greet them, takes the bags of food and sets them down on the top step. He's very charming and immediately starts flirting with Aggie until she's giggly and blushing.

'Ray. You're such a scream,' she laughs.

Jamie wants to go into the shed and ask Willis about Woofy, but ratboy is blocking his way, so, while he waits for them to finish talking, he gouges a hole in the ground with his toe.

'See you later, then,' Aggie says eventually, still smiling at ratboy. 'Come on Jamie. We'll leave the love birds alone to have some fun.'

'But …'

'You thought you were staying here?' Aggie rolls her eyes at ratboy and stifles a chuckle by putting her hand over her mouth. 'Oh, dearie me, no. That's not going to happen. Willy's not going to want you around while she's got Ray to keep her company.'

Ray is nodding. 'Off you go,' he says and flicks his fingers towards Jamie in a dismissive gesture.

'Hey. There you are.' Willis appears at the doorway of the shed.

'We're just leaving,' Aggie says.

'Jamie stays with me.' Her words are slurred and her eyes look glassy. She points at her chest and stomps her foot, knocking over one of the bags of food. Two red apples roll down the stairs. Plonk. Plonk. Plonk. 'I'm the looker afterer of Jamie McKenzie,' she says.

'You're in no fit state to look after anyone,' Aggie says sourly. 'Come on Jamie.'

Little puffs of dust rise around her thonged feet as she begins to march back down the dirt track towards the homestead.

'Piss off, you old witch,' Willis says in a stage whisper at her retreating back. Then to Jamie, she says, 'Stay with me, Jamie. I need you.'

He looks at Aggie's retreating back and then at Willis. Is he meant to decide what to do? There doesn't appear to be any safe option.

Then ratboy comes down the steps and starts flicking his hand in front of Jamie's face like he's shooing a fly. 'Piss off home, little boy. We don't want you here.'

Willis makes a sound. Maybe a laugh. Maybe something else. He stares at her. Unsure. She seems like a stranger. Like someone he's never met before.

'Aw, fuck Willy. Just tell him to piss off,' says ratboy.

'Jamie stays …' She stomps her foot again. Another shiny red apple rolls out of a bag and plonks down the steps.

Then Jamie decides. He turns away. Follows Aggie down the road towards the house.

'Jammmiiieee … Don't leave me.'

He keeps walking.

'Jammmiiieee. Jammmiiieee.'

He doesn't look back.

In the growing gloom of twilight, he and Aggie feed the dogs and chooks, top up their water and run the hose on the fruit trees. While they work, she explains that Woofy is still missing.

'Onfro and Willy didn't find him,' she says, 'but we can leave some food out for him in case he comes back later.'

'Can't. Ants,' Jamie mutters. He's so knotty inside that he finds it difficult to do more than grunt.

When they enter the kitchen, Onfro is sitting at the kitchen table rolling a cigarette.

'Hello, love,' Aggie says, rubbing her hand across his broad shoulders. 'Feeling any better?'

'I'm going to bed,' Jamie says, not daring to look in the man's direction. 'Good night.'

'But … what about dinner?' Aggie says.

Jamie rubs his tummy. 'I'm still full from before, which was very nice thank you very much.'

'Don't forget to brush your teeth.'

'I won't.'

'Okay. See you in the morning. Sleep tight.'

'Night,' the man says, his own eyes locked downwards at the cigarette in his yellowed fingers.

Willis flattens her palm against her mouth and allows the tiny blue tablets Ray has given her slide between her lips and come to rest on her tongue. Saliva pools around them.

'This is so cool,' chortles Ray, loading more CDs into his portable stereo.

Willis moves to the open door, gazes out at the bruised evening sky and wonders how Jamie is getting on up at the house and if he has managed to do the dogs and chooks and fruit trees without her. She regrets the way she acted earlier. It'd killed her to see the anguish on Jamie's face when he'd been made to decide whether to stay with her or go with Aggie, and even more when she'd had to watch him walk away up that lonely road towards the house.

Thump. Thump. Thump. Ray's choice of CD sounds more like mass murder than music and she rubs at the goosebumps that have appeared on her bare arms. Maybe he'll get so smashed he'll forget about wanting to have sex with her.

The tablets weigh heavily on her tongue. Why doesn't she simply swallow them? It'd be easy to let them slide down her throat. Some of the drug has probably already entered her bloodstream, so why not? It's what everyone would expect her to do.

Everyone, except Jamie.

He expects better of her. She's sure of it.

She brushes her fingers across her mouth in one smooth movement that puts the tablets back into the palm of her hand, then she pushes her hand deep into the pockets of her denim shorts and wipes the sticky tablets onto the cotton lining.

Next morning, Woofy still isn't home. After they've done the chores and eaten breakfast, Aggie suggests she take Jamie in the ute to look for him. He forces the window of the ute down with his hands because the window winder is broken, hangs his head out and calls until his voice is hoarse. But to no avail. The old dog seems to have vanished.

When they arrive back at the house, Onfro is outside raking up dead leaves into a large heap in the corner of the yard. A sprinkler is spraying a circle of water over the lifeless lawn.

'Any luck?' he says.

Aggie shakes her head. 'We can go and have another look this afternoon.'

Jamie glances at Onfro's big boot, remembering how he'd used it to kick Woofy.

'Any sign of the kids this morning?' Aggie asks.

'All quiet on the Western Front.'

'I heard the thumping of their music most of the night so they're probably sleeping it off.'

Onfro leans on the rake. 'Rain is coming. Big storms north of Charleville, heading south, so they'll need to be leaving soon. We don't want them getting stuck here.'

Rain is coming?

Jamie feels as if a hush has suddenly fallen over the land. As if all the plants and all the creatures are leaning inwards. Listening. Not quite believing.

He feels strangely giddy. Could it be true? There's not a cloud in the sky. But he can feel it. Like a darkness pressing down on the blue from above. Invisible. Oppressive.

CHAPTER 15

It's nearly midday when Ray nudges Willis awake. The shearing shed is steamy hot and even though she's only wearing a t-shirt and pair of knickers, her body is clammy with sweat. She has a nasty headache that can't be a hangover because she'd had hardly any alcohol to drink. And other than the few puffs on the joint, she'd not taken any drugs. More likely, her headache is the result of the hours she'd spent walking in the boiling sun the previous day.

His breath is hot in her ear and she realises he's on the mattress next to her, his pelvis hard against her lower back. His hand is inside her knickers, between her legs.

'You're as wet as a wild sow, Willy.'

'No.' She tries to pull his hand from her crotch.

'You want it. I know you do.'

'Ray. No. I can't. Not here. Not in the middle of the day.'

The more she tries to free herself, the rougher and more insistent he becomes.

'My head hurts,' she moans. 'I need water.'

'Fucking typical.' He lifts his body over hers. There's a mean glint in his eye and his breath is sour.

'Stop it. I said no.'

'You always fucking say no, Willy.'

He's tugging her knickers down with one hand while holding her arms over her head with his other and she can't believe how strong he is.

'What if someone comes? What if Jamie comes? Do you want that little kid to see you with your dick out?'

Ray is thrusting himself at her, trying to penetrate, but he's gotten too soft to get it up and she realises he's already ejaculated. She lies perfectly still with her eyes closed for a moment, hoping he'll be fooled into thinking she liked what he just did.

'Fuck,' he moans, flopping down next to her. 'You stupid cunt.'

As soon as his weight is off her, she wriggles free, stands, pulls up her knickers and looks around for her shorts.

'You had to go and talk about that idiot kid in the middle of us doing it, didn't you?'

He's on his feet too, fists clenched.

'It's like you're so obsessed with that useless fucking kid, you can't stop talking about him.'

She quickly pulls on her shorts and checks the pocket for the tablets he'd given her the previous night. They're still there. With her unlaced Doc Martens on her feet, she grabs her towel and toiletry bag.

'I'm going to the bathroom … to wash off the stink of you.'

But he doesn't hear because he's already turned on the stereo — the same loud, thumping, jarring, screaming music he'd played all night while he got smashed and she watched on, smiling, agreeable, approving. Vigilant. Subtly deterring his advances.

But all her efforts were for nothing because he got her in the end, didn't he? Or did he? She isn't sure how to classify what just happened. Did that count as sex?

The ablutions block is set amongst some straggly trees about half way between the shearing shed and the quarters. A plant called a bindi-eye grows like a mesh across the ground outside.

Once inside the corrugated walls, she bends forward and holds her towel and toiletry bag like a cradle over her stomach, which feels sick and crampy, like she might be getting her period even though she's not due. She's still trying to steady herself when she hears the ute driving by. It stops at the shed.

She wedges her towel and toiletry bag between some corrugated iron sheeting and a water pipe, then quickly crosses the distance back to the shed and conceals herself behind a water tank that's bolted onto the back of a trailer — for fighting bush fires, according to Jamie. Peeping out from her hiding place, she sees Onfro banging on the side of the shed with a stick.

The music stops and Ray's head appears from inside. 'What?'

'We've brought Willy's things,' says Aggie. 'I'll put them in your car, so you won't have to stop by the house and pick them up on your way. You need to get going.'

'What's the big hurry?'

'Rain's coming,' says Onfro.

'Rain? Bullshit.' She can hear the disbelief in Ray's voice.

'We have an agreement.' Aggie's voice sounds shaky.

'And we expect you to stick to it,' says Onfro.

'Okay. Fuck. We'll go. Just give us half an hour to get our shit together. We just woke up and Willy's in the shower.'

'Not a minute more, you hear?' says Onfro.

Willis imagines Ray rolling his eyes.

'You'll need to pay me before I go,' he says.

'Moira will give you the cash when you get back to town with Willy,' says Aggie. 'That was our agreement.'

The cramped, sick feeling in Willis's gut is not going away. She should have realised that Ray was getting more out of this trip to the outback than the pleasure of seeing her. He's being paid to take her back to Sydney. But why would Aggie and Onfro go to so much trouble and expense to get rid of her? It doesn't make sense. Is she really that bad?

She hunches low as Onfro and Aggie drive away. Then Ray is yelling, loudly enough for her to hear from inside the ablutions block. 'Willy? You done? We've got to get out of this shit hole!'

When he doesn't get an answer, he springs down the steps and walks towards the ablutions block. She holds her breath and waits until he's more than half way to discovering she's not there, then she slips quietly away and vanishes into the scrub on the northern side of the shearing shed.

The mulga gives way to gidgee and a few box trees and before long, she comes upon the weathered gravestone of Mary Withers. The engraving has been carved and blackened so that it stands out from the background — name, dates of birth and death, then a short epitaph at the bottom. Willis squats on the grave and runs her fingers across the letters.

Dearly beloved.

Dearly beloved!

Suddenly, she has no breath. Her chest heaves as she struggles to draw air into her lungs. Her entire body begins to shudder. She drops to her knees in the sandy soil on top of the grave and begins to sob. And sob. And sob. As painful as it is, she seems entirely unable to stop.

'I want to be dearly beloved too,' she says eventually, wiping the back of her hand over her eyes. 'I want someone to care about me and protect me from people like Ray. And Onfro and Aggie. I want someone who will say, "No, you cannot stay in the shearing shed with that boy. You are not to have anything to do with him because he does not respect you."'

She gazes around at the sage and rust landscape and, inexplicably, in the middle of all this grief, the words of her school counsellor, Mrs Batzloff, come back to her.

You have the power to decide what kind of life you want and what kind of person you will become. Don't let others take that power away from you.

What kind of life do *I* want, she asks herself? She doesn't know. All that's clear, right now, is that she wants to stay on Moonbroch and continue to take care of Jamie, like she promised Mr McKenzie she would. She wants Ray to leave. And, of course, she wants Aggie and Onfro to disappear from her life forever.

It doesn't feel like she has the power to make any of these things happen. Ray, Onfro, and Aggie are all too strong. So what's she expected to do? Should she go to Ray and say, 'Sorry, old chap, but I don't want you here, so can you please leave? You probably won't get paid because I'm not leaving. I'm staying here — with Jamie.' It won't work. Ray doesn't cope with rejection and he'll do almost anything to get his own way. He always finds a way to win. Onfro is the same — he uses his foul temper to frighten people into giving him what he wants — and Aggie … she lives in fantasyland and doesn't listen to a word anyone else says.

She wiggles around until she's sitting cross-legged on Mary Wither's grave, facing the gravestone.

'What would you do, dearly beloved?' she says. 'If you were me, what would you do to make Ray go away?'

She thinks back to last night. About how Ray's eyes had kept drifting towards the open doorway and the open windows. He'd insisted on keeping all the lights on. And rather than go outside to pee, he had, disgustingly, used one of the holding pens.

He was scared.

Another memory floats into her mind. One from when she and Ray were about fifteen and they had decided it'd be fun to spend the night in a cemetery. All was going well until, around midnight, they'd started to get this uncanny sense that they were surrounded by ghosts. While she'd loved the otherworldly thrill of the experience, Ray had totally freaked out. He'd run off between the shadowy graves screaming and later, by the side of a road far from the cemetery, he'd curled into a ball and cried because he was afraid of ghosts.

'What's that, dearly beloved? You think I should have a séance? What a genius idea.'

She high fives the gravestone. 'Sophie McKenzie is about to become my new best friend.'

Jamie waits until Aggie and Onfro leave in the ute, supposedly to look for Woofy, then goes to Dad's office to check out what's changed in there since Onfro moved in. Lots of papers are strewn over the desk along with a dirty coffee mug and an ashtray full of roll-your-own cigarette buts. The drawers in the filing cabinet are not closed properly.

Suddenly, he freezes. In the kitchen someone is opening the cabinet doors and banging them closed again. It can't be Aggie and Onfro. He'd seen their dust as they passed over the crossing on their way to look for Woofy and if they'd changed their minds and come back, the dogs would have started barking.

What if it's ratboy?

'Jamie. Jammmiiieee,' a voice calls.

It's Willis. He sighs with relief.

Then frowns. Life since he moved back to the house with Aggie and Onfro hasn't been too bad and he's almost convinced himself that it would be better if she did stay away. If it wasn't for her, Woofy wouldn't be lost and ratboy wouldn't be here. Maybe Aggie is right and she did deserve to get the strap.

'Jamie, didn't you hear me? I said, have you got any candles?'

Her long, lean body appears in the office doorway. Unbrushed hair. Bloodshot eyes. She looks terrible.

'Are you leaving?' he says, trying to make his voice sound indifferent because he can't stand her knowing how much he cares. 'Aggie said you were leaving.'

'Aggie is a liar.'

'Then you're staying?' He feels happier.

She sits down on the office chair in front of him. 'Do you want me to stay?'

'Yes. But no-one else. Just you.'

'Well, that's what I'm working on, Jamie. First, I have to get rid of Ray. Then I'll see if I can figure out how to get rid of Aggie and Onfro.'

'He has to go *now*. Once the rain gets here, he won't be able to get over the crossing.'

She rolls her eyes skywards. 'It's not going to rain.'

'Yes, it is. By tomorrow.'

'Really? Then I'll need to get rid of Ray tonight. That's why I need the candles.'

'What are you going to do with them?'

'I'm going to have a séance.'

'What's a séance?'

She hesitates, and he guesses she's trying to decide whether to tell the truth or make something up.

'It's this thing where you pretend to talk to ghosts,' she says.

'How's that going to make him leave?'

She gives him a mischievous smile. 'Ray is terrified of ghosts. If he thinks there's ghosts on Moonbroch, he'll take off for sure.'

'But ghosts aren't real.'

'To Ray, they are. Can you help out with some candles?'

He bends down and pulls a tatty cardboard box from the bottom of the bookshelf, inside which are bundles of long tapered candles, narrow jars half filled with rice to stand the candles in, and boxes of Redhead matches.

'Yay.' Willis claps her hands. 'This is perfect. Thank you, Jamie. You're the best.'

'They're in case of a black out,' he says. 'How many do you need for a séance?'

'All of them.'

She scoops up the box. 'When I see you tomorrow, he'll be gone,' she says.

'Wait.'

She turns back. 'What?'

Sitting on the wide ledge above Dad's desk is a framed photo of Sophie. Jamie lifts it down, brushes off dust and cobwebs, and studies the black-and-white picture. The photographer has artfully captured her movement as she's rotated towards the camera and a lock of blonde hair covers one eye. She's laughing. Dad always said the photo was his favourite.

Jamie holds it up. 'Use this.'

Her jaw drops. 'You sure?'

'Yes. Sophie won't mind pretending to be a ghost for one night.'

Jamie can't sleep. It's too hot. The clammy heat presses down on him like a blanket and it feels as though a thousand tiny bugs are buzzing around his ears. But it isn't just the bugs. It's the questions that whir unrelentingly inside his head.

Why does Onfro spend so much time in Dad's office? Why are there papers spread across the desk and filing cabinet drawers left ajar? And why does Aggie want to get rid of Willis so badly? Both Onfro and Aggie were furious when they found out that ratboy was staying one more night, and Jamie had had to hide in the schoolroom all afternoon pretending to do schoolwork on the holidays. Will Onfro hit Willis again when he discovers ratboy has taken off without her?

And what about Woofy? Why hasn't he come home? Is it Jamie's fault for taking him in the first place? Or because he was too weak to stand up to ratboy? Too afraid. A scaredy cat. Always too afraid to act. He'd not known how to help Sophie when she got sick or Willis when she got hit, and he doesn't know what to do about Woofy. He wants to be able to make a difference in his own place and the limit of his power is completely devastating.

Sound drifts through his bedroom window, tinny and distant. He thinks it might be music coming from the shearing shed but when he tries to hear it again, he can't separate it from the orchestra of bush creatures preparing for the rain. He wonders how the séance is going. Imagines Willis and ratboy's faces aglow in the flickering light of the candles and ratboy's eyes. Wide with fear. Because he's scared of ghosts.

They'll need to be careful not to knock the candles over. But what if they do and the shearing shed catches on fire? He remembers last summer, the shed at Walluma had burned to the ground. And one in New South Wales as well. Dad has already lost his heart for most things on Moonbroch and a burnt-down shearing shed might be the end of everything. He needs to warn Willis to be careful with the candles.

He slips out of bed. All is quiet. The house is in darkness. He goes quietly down the breezeway and through the kitchen, pulls on his boots, grabs the torch and eases himself silently out the screen door. Clouds are blocking the starlight, making the night a solid black. The air smells airier. Discordant calls from the frogs, awake after their long, drought-time slumber, send shivers along his spine and all his instincts scream for him to return to the safety of his bed. But he has to tell Willis not to knock over the candles. He doesn't want Dad to lose his heart. He wants Dad to come home.

When he gets there, the shearing shed appears to be in darkness. And silent. Willis and ratboy must have already gone to sleep. He's about to turn back to the house when he spies the tiniest flicker of yellow light coming through a propped-open window. Did they go to bed without putting out the candles?

He switches off the torch and peeps through a crack between the door frame and the corrugated iron sheeting. Inside, a sphere of soft light has been created by a circle of at least twenty candles and inside that circle of light sit Willis and ratboy, cross-legged, facing each other, holding hands; and propped up between them is the photograph of Sophie. Willis looks magnificent. Mesmerising. Her long blonde hair is swept up onto her head so that only loose tendrils are left to drop softly by her face. Her eyes are closed and her lips are moving. Jamie can't hear what she is saying over the sounds of the bush creatures outside. Even the birds are restless in their nests.

Suddenly, she lets go of ratboy and reaches her long pale hands into the air above her head, graceful, like a dancer.

With the backdrop of candle light, the scene is very dramatic. Jamie holds his breath, expecting to see the murky outline of ghosts come floating down from the rafters at any moment. Maybe, there'll even be a girl who looks like Sophie.

But nothing happens.

And ratboy starts to get twitchy, stretching his neck and scratching his nose.

'Ray,' Willis says, dropping her arms. 'It won't work if you don't take it seriously.'

'It's not going to work,' he says, yawning.

'It *is* working,' she says, her eyes luminous with reflected light. 'I can feel it.'

'This is bullshit. You're so dumb, Willy.'

She looks stricken. 'This place is full of ghosts.'

'You're so full of bullshit.' Ratboy picks up the photo of Sophie and begins to examine her face with an intensity that makes Jamie sick.

Without thought, he reaches down, picks up a rock the size of his fist and feels the weight of it in his palm. Then he walks silently down to the corner of the building and around to the back side where a small gate opens into the space below the floorboards. Every year, after shearing, his entire family gets under here and rakes out the sheep manure for Mum's garden — at least, they used to. When there was sheep and a garden. When Sophie was alive.

He can hear voices above his head.

'I thought it'd be fun,' says Willis.

'Well it isn't. Jeez, you're getting boring Willy. I came all the way from Sydney to have some fun and you decide to have a fucking séance. For real? What are you? A baby? A little girl? You think you're too high and mighty to do normal stuff anymore. In case you haven't noticed, you've been living in a fucking shed,' says ratboy.

Jamie feels around until he locates the water pipe that runs across the underside of the floorboards. Then he lifts the rock and taps it gently against the pipe.

Tap. Tap. Tap.

'Shhh. Listen,' says Willis.

As though a conductor has raised his baton, the bush creatures go silent. The unexpected absence of sound is completely unnerving and Jamie can feel the gooseflesh rising on his arms. He lifts the rock once more.

Tap. Tap. Tap.

'What was that?' says ratboy. Both the pitch and volume in his voice has lifted.

'I don't know,' Willis says.

Tap. Tap. Tap.

There's a scurry of feet as ratboy runs across to the door and down the steps.

'Get a fucking torch.'

But he won't be able to see Jamie under the shearing shed because the corrugated iron sheeting goes all the way to the ground.

Tap. Tap. Tap.

'Come and sit back down, Ray.' Willis's voice is so calm, she sounds almost like a ghost herself. 'Sophie wants to talk to us.'

'Are you fucking serious?'

'I am. Sophie is here. Just like I said she would be.'

'No fucking way.'

Tap. Tap. Tap. Tap. Tap. Tap.

Tap. Tap. Tap.

Footsteps sprint across the floorboards overhead, like someone is frantically gathering together their belongings.

Tap. Tap. Tappity. Tap.

'Ray. It's alright. Come and sit down.'

'Fuck you, Willy,' he says. 'You're such a freak.'

When he hears the white four-wheel drive starting up, Jamie drops the rock, crawls back to the little gate he'd used to get under the shed, climbs out, dusts himself off with the palms of his hands and goes back to the corner of the building to see what is happening. And by the time ratboy's vehicle is speeding towards the crossing with only the red fuzz of his taillights still visible, Jamie is sitting silently on the steps next to Willis, a tiny smile on his face.

Willis looks at her watch. 'Midnight.'

He nods.

They go inside, blow out the candles and lie down together on one of the shearer's mattresses. Willis pulls a cover over them.

'We did good,' he says in the darkness.

'Yeah! We did.'

'And Sophie.'

'Sophie did good too.'

After a while, he speaks again.

'Can't imagine why you'd want a boyfriend like him.'

CHAPTER 16

'Ray is a friend of Jamie McKenzie,' Poppy tells Winter as he drives his van away from Cass's father's house.

'If you're his friend, how come you didn't know which house was his?' says Winter from the back of the van where she's moved to make way for the man in leather.

The man jerks his head up and turns around to where she's sitting behind Poppy, as though he's surprised to be challenged by a girl. Then he smiles, so she gets a good whiff of his sour breath. 'I haven't seen him in a while.'

'And you just decided to visit him in the middle of the night?'

'I'm sure he wouldn't have minded the early wake up call. I mean, the McKenzie family and I go way back. I've known Jamie since he was a boy and I'm sure he would've been thrilled to see me at any time of the day or night.'

'Good timing,' says Poppy. 'And great that you can come out to Goomburra to help with the search.'

The man shrugs. 'Nothing else to do. I'm only in Too-woomba to catch up with Jamie so I might as well pitch in.'

Something is fishy about this man. Winter is sure of it. Her stranger danger beacon is all lit up and she's giving Poppy the full benefit of her death stare though the back of his head, but to no avail because Poppy has an insatiable curiosity about people. He can't help himself. It's what he does. He talks to people and he gets them to say all sorts of weird stuff about themselves — a leftover from when he was a journalist, she supposes. He's not about to let a potentially interesting character like Ray slip through his fingers.

Ray has a boastful way about him and, she suspects, a tendency to exaggerate. He tells Poppy he's been friends with the McKenzie family since he first went out to their station as a young man and, before long, Poppy has him talking about the time those two people drowned in the creek and Jamie McKenzie earned the title of Australia's littlest superhero.

Ray shuffles in his seat. 'I knew that old couple who drowned. Such a great pair, they were. He was a return serviceman, you know, and she was a real good cook. But as for the boy, Jamie ... well, you can't believe everything you read in the paper, you know.'

'What do you mean?'

'Well ... I wouldn't have called that kid a hero, if anyone had asked me.'

'But you were friends?'

'Err ... well, I was older. But sure. Now we are.'

'It must have been awfully traumatic for the little boy. I mean, he did witness the drownings of the two people who were meant to be looking after him, didn't he?'

A tiny snort escapes Ray's nose. 'As I said, you can't believe everything you read in the paper.'

'Meaning? The boy didn't witness —'

'Meaning, there's more to that story than everyone realised. Much more. But I'm really not at liberty to say.'

Poppy pauses a few seconds before asking, 'You knew the girl involved, didn't you?'

Winter thinks her grandfather is only guessing that Ray knew the girl who was saved by young Jamie McKenzie.

'I did.'

Yes!

'What was she like?'

Ray flinches, as if the question makes him uncomfortable. Then he shrugs. 'From what I've heard, she wasn't a very good person. Kind of lower class. After all the stuff with the drownings was over, the McKenzies banned her from ever having anything to do with their family again.' He chuckles. 'They kicked her out.'

A minute goes by in silence, then Ray continues.

'Who knows what she was capable of, back then?'

More silence.

'I mean, whatever she did, she got away with it, didn't she?'

'What do you think she did?'

'I'm not at liberty to say.'

'But you know something?'

'I might.'

Despite her interest in the way Poppy and Ray lunge and parry with their words, and her fascination with the story about Jamie McKenzie and a mysterious girl from years ago, Winter can't keep her eyes open. She fights the urge to sleep but it's too strong and eventually her head flops to the side and their words fade away.

Cass spends her long night in the crevice with two main worries — fear that unseen creatures are queueing up to bite or suck her skin and her aching tiredness. Her urge to sleep is a terrible drag but she knows if she nods off for even a second, she's likely to slip out of the narrow space and plummet to her death. On the upside, the glow of her father's fire on the rock ledge above is visible and the sound of his voice helps to keep her awake.

They talk, but not about anything big or important. Mostly, they play guessing games like 'Animal, Vegetable or Mineral' and 'I Spy', which is funny because there's nothing to see except the glow of his fire. He teaches her something called a phonetic alphabet — Alpha, Bravo, Charlie. Whenever her eyes drop closed and she's sure she'll not be able to get them open again, he encourages her to talk, laugh, shout, slap her face, take sips from her water bottle or pinch the tender skin between her thumb and index finger.

She hears a noise that's different, and after listening to it for a few minutes, asks, 'What are you doing?'

'Making a rope,' he answers. 'I got the idea after I lowered the food down to you.'

'What are you making it out of?'

'I'm shredding my backpack and plaiting the strips to-gether. It's pretty strong.'

'What are you going to do with it?'

'I thought we might use it to get you back up the cliff.'

'No way, Dad. It's too dangerous.'

'Everything about this situation is dangerous. You falling asleep is dangerous. At first light, if I go for help, it might be hours before I get back and I'm not sure you'll be able to stay awake that long. What if you fall asleep while I'm not here?'

She yawns. How she'd love to drift into the oblivion of sleep. But going to sleep means certain death. There's nothing holding her into the crevice except her pushing against the rock and she needs to be awake to do that.

'A rope sounds good, Dad.'

With the first glow of the new day, her father says, 'I'm going back from the edge for a few minutes, Cass. I need to test the rope to see if it's strong enough. I'll tie it to a tree and see if it will take my weight, and while I'm doing that, I want you to sing. Loud, so I can hear.'

'What'll I sing?'

'How about Old McDonald?'

After a few minutes spent working her way through the animals on the farm, a few zoo animals, a leech going 'suck, suck' and a snake going 'hiss, hiss', her father is back at the edge.

'It's good. Strong.'

Cass hears the faint whack of something hitting the rock above her head. She reaches up and gets her fingers onto the soft, thin rope her father has made.

'Got it,' she says.

'I've put a loop in the end. Try and get your head and arms through the loop so that it's under your arm pits.'

'I can't—' She stops herself from speaking words of defeat. She's been awake over twenty-four hours and survived losing her phone, a leech sucking her blood, a snake nearly biting her, falling over a cliff, a night wedged in a crevice, and the humiliation of having to pee in her pants. Now she just wants to get out of here and have a sleep. She removes the empty water bottle out of her shirt and pushes it deeper into the crevice, takes one long breath, fills her lungs until they hurt, and lets the air out in a long stream. She clenches her jaw. Locks her teeth together. Then she wriggles up until her head and torso are free from the crevice. She pushes herself up with her feet until she can grab the rope above the loop.

'Got it. Hang on, Dad.'

'I got you,' he says.

She manages to wriggle her body inside the loop and holds on tightly as her father takes up the slack and the rope begins to strain.

'Don't look down. Don't look down.' She chants the words softly to herself while her heart pounds and her teeth clench so tightly she nearly breaks her jaw.

She feels herself being hauled slowly upwards away from her safe hole in the rock. It soon becomes obvious to her that this could take a very long time if she continues to hang like a dead weight at the end of the rope, and the more time she hangs over the abyss, the more likely it is that the rope will break or her father will drop her. She needs to find a way to contribute. Using her natural athleticism and agility to reposition herself, she presses her feet against the irregular surface of the cliff and begins to push herself upwards. Unexpectedly, as soon as she does this, she stops thinking about the rope breaking. Or about falling. She's too busy concentrating on where she's putting her feet. The higher she goes, the bigger her smile and by the time she climbs over the top of the cliff, she's laughing.

'That was awesome fun,' she says, scrambling away from the edge. 'And easy, too. I can't believe I spent the whole night down there when it was so easy to climb up.'

Her father eyes are burning with tiredness and relief, but he's smiling too. He puts his arms around her and pulls her close. Rocks her back and forward and kisses the top of her head.

'You're one hell of a girl, Cass,' he says.

'I love you, Dad,' she says, hugging him tight.

'I love you too.' She doesn't remember him ever saying those words to her before.

'Thanks, Dad.'

'How about a cup of tea? There's enough water left.'

'Yes, please! But first, I need to pee, and this time not in my pants. I can't believe I had to pee in my pants.'

After checking for snakes, they sit on the wide, rock ledge with their mugs of sweet tea and watch the spectacle of the sunrise. They listen to the forest creatures starting their day. It feels good to be together. To be alive. Half an hour ago, Cass thought she couldn't possibly stay awake. Now she feels more awake than she's ever been.

'I always have good adventures with you,' she says.

'You think this was a *good* adventure? And here's me thinking it was a complete disaster.'

'It's only a disaster if you don't get through it. But we did get through it. So that makes it a good adventure.'

Winter jolts awake as they enter the National Park carpark at the end of Goomburra Road and the first rays of sunshine are tipping the tops of the tallest trees. The carpark is in a large clearing about a hundred metres across, sandwiched between thick rainforest to the north and dry forest to the south. Around the edges, most of the grass is shrivelled and yellowed, giving it a dusty, barren feel.

While Poppy and Ray go to shake hands with two police officers — a man and a woman — and a park ranger, Winter climbs down from the van and surveys the scene. Lined up against the rainforest side of the carpark are four vehicles — Poppy's van, police and ranger cars, and an older style 4WD that must belong to Jamie McKenzie, Cass's *bushie* dad. In the far, south-eastern corner of the carpark, a glint of reflected sunlight catches her eye and she identifies a fifth vehicle parked behind some bushes. In the early morning light, with the sun in her eyes, the small sedan is almost invisible, and she caps her eyes with her hand to see it more clearly. She imagines that she can see someone in the driver's seat.

'You must be Cass's friend, the young lass who raised the alarm.'

The lady police officer has left the men talking about plans for search and rescue and is standing next to her, hand extended. 'I'm Constable Susanne Rush.'

'Hello,' Winter says and shakes her hand, then points towards the concealed vehicle on the other side of the carpark. 'Do you know who owns that car?'

Constable Rush looks momentarily caught off guard and a little uncomfortable. 'Don't go over there, will you?'

'No. But why?'

The officer presses her hand against her lower back as though she has back pain. 'You don't know who it might be.'

'Okay.'

Strange.

Winter has a thought that the person in the faraway car might be Cass's mother. The police would surely have contacted her when they found out Cass was missing. And Cass's mother would have driven straight here. But if it is Cass's mother, why is she parked so far away? Why isn't she here talking to the police?

'Your Mum's not going to be happy when you tell her about your adventure,' her father says.

'I won't tell her.' Cass starts to comb her tangled hair with her fingers.

He moves uncomfortably. 'I'd hate you to feel you have to lie.'

'It won't be lying. I just won't say anything about it. It can be our little secret.'

He sets his mug down onto the rock. 'Secrets can get pretty heavy if you're having to carry them around by yourself.'

She stops messing with her hair and studies his precious face. The exhaustion in his eyes. His stubbly chin. 'You carry secrets, don't you, Dad?'

He's silent for a while, then nods. 'Yeah. I do.'

'Heavy secrets?'

He nods.

'Maybe if you share them with someone, they won't be so heavy.'

He smiles. 'Wise words from one so young and you're absolutely right. But right now, we need to go home and catch up on some sleep. Ready to go?'

By seven a.m., at least a dozen people have assembled in the carpark. Most are volunteers. Folding tables and chairs have been set up. Maps spread out. Plans made. Poppy has scored a job that involves sitting at a table looking official. Ray is seated by his side, painstakingly writing down people's names as they register.

Winter leaves the activity and wanders up past the toilet block to where the walking trails start. She stands in front of a National Park sign, not to read about the local flora and fauna but so she is in a better position to see the person in the blue car — who she's decided is definitely a woman, even though her hair is tucked inside a cap. The sedan is angled side-on to the open forest and from the assembly area, the woman was mostly out of sight; but from this angle, Winter can see her quite clearly. She appears to be very alert, her attention focused on the people preparing to search for Cass and her father. Strange that she doesn't walk over to see what is happening.

Winter doesn't know why she's so curious about the woman — probably because of the way the police officer had reacted when she had asked about the semi-concealed car. She's considering ignoring the officer's request to stay away and going over to say hello when the sound of laughter drifts towards her from the forest. She spins around to see a tall, blonde girl and a man coming along the track between the trees, both laughing. While there's a weariness about them, they seem otherwise unharmed and very happy to be in each other's company.

'Cass,' she calls, a huge smile breaking over her face.

'Winter? You're here?'

The two girls race together for a hasty hug, both talking at once. Cass introduces Winter to her father, who has nicely crinkled blue eyes and says to call him Jamie. He apologises for not getting Cass home in time for her visit and thanks her for coming to find them.

'I knew she would,' Cass says proudly.

Other people soon begin to realise that the lost have been found and Cass and her father are quickly surrounded.

'Talk later,' Winter says to Cass. She's never been particularly comfortable in a crowd and doesn't want to hang around Cass like a third wheel, so she retreats to the van and leaves them to deal with all the attention. Because of the way Poppy has backed into the parking space, from the passenger seat, she gets an excellent view of everything that is happening.

Cass's father shakes everyone's hand and thanks people and apologises for the trouble they've caused while Cass floats by his side with a grin on her face like she's just won the lottery. The man police officer asks them some questions while the park ranger thanks the search and rescue people and tells them they're free to pack up and go home. Poppy and Ray get busy packing up the tables and chairs. Meanwhile, the lady police officer, Constable Susanne Rush, crosses the carpark to the blue sedan and talks to the woman inside.

When she returns, she signals to her partner that she'd like a quiet chat and he joins her over by Poppy's van. Winter considers making a little cough to warn them that their conversation is not private, but her curiosity wins out over her need to warn them of her presence and she decides to stay quiet. They talk in hushed whispers about something called a DVO.

Next, the woman police officer calls Cass's father over to the van.

'Now we don't want any trouble,' she says. 'But we need you to know ... Mina Johnson is here. She wants to take Cass home.'

Mina Johnson? That must be Cass's mother. She *knew* it!

Cass's father frowns and wipes his palms against his thighs. 'Mina?'

The woman nods in the direction of the small sedan behind the bushes.

'Okay ... Thanks.' He scratches his bristly chin. 'I'll go talk to her. I'm guessing she's pretty upset about our situation.'

The woman rests her hand against his upper arm, enough to restrain him.

'You know you can't do that.'

'I can't go and talk to her? Why?' He sounds mystified.

'Just stay here. I'll send Cass over.'

'But ... Okay. Sure.'

Stranger and stranger, thinks Winter, as the policewoman speaks to Cass. Cass's parents must have had a very bad divorce, *and* someone must have forgotten to tell the dad about it.

'Mum's here.' Cass is smiling as she speaks to her father. Someone has obviously forgotten to tell her about the bad divorce too. 'She doesn't want to come over. I'll go see.'

With confusion dripping from his pores, Cass's father watches his daughter's graceful swinging gait as she crosses the carpark to speak to her mother.

Even though she hasn't had a shower, smells like pee, and needs about forty hours sleep, Cass thinks this has been the best morning ever. But why is her mother here? Acting strange? She'll most likely ruin everything. Nevertheless, Cass is feeling magnanimous and decides to give her mother some air time before explaining that she will, in fact, be returning to Toowoomba with her father and coming home at the end of her pre-arranged eleven-days. And not before.

She opens the passenger door and slides into the seat.

'Cass. You smell.'

'I peed my pants.'

Her mother looks out of place in the forest. Her eyes are bloodshot and her mascara has smudged.

'Oh, Cass.'

She gives her mother an I-don't-care-that-I-peed-my-pants look and says, 'What's up?'

'I need to get you something to sit on,' her mother says, crinkling her nose. 'Hang on. There's a towel in the boot.'

She presses the boot button with her manicured finger and gets out to fetch the towel. Cass tries to get out as well, but her door won't open. It must have the child safety lock on. She twists around to tell her mother to open the door but stops when she catches sight of her father across the carpark, staring at her mother. She's in front of the boot, staring back at him. Both seem frozen in time, as if, for them, the entire world has disappeared and only the two of them remain.

How long is it since her parents have eyeballed each other like this, she wonders? When he'd come to pick her up a few days ago, she'd had to go down to the carpark on her own to meet him. And now that she thinks about it, every time she's gone with him before, her mother has arranged for a friend or a neighbour to pass her over and welcome her home. She can't ever remember seeing her parents together.

Yet, she's never had the impression that they hate each other. On the contrary, even though they rarely speak about each other, she's always had the sense that they like each other very much.

Suddenly, without even getting the towel from the boot, her mother is sliding back into the driver's seat.

'Quick. Put your seatbelt on,' she says.

'No. I —'

As though he has read her mother's mind and knows what's about to happen, her father begins to run towards them. But her mother takes no notice of him. She reverses the car in a wide arc then scrapes the gear change into drive.

'No. Let me out,' Cass yells, frantically tugging at the useless door handle.

Dirt, gravel and dry grass sprays from the back wheels as her mother pumps the accelerator to the floor. Galloping after them, her father appears wild with panic and confusion. Behind him, the woman police officer is running too.

'Mum. Stop. Please. I knew you would ruin everything.'

She is crying. She presses the button to open her window and gets it a quarter down before her mother's hand slams over hers to stop her.

'Dad,' she screams.

He's still running but getting further and further away as they accelerate out of the carpark.

CHAPTER 17

Jamie's head is filled with the sound of fairies! Thousands and thousands of them. Cheering. Clapping. Dancing.

He knows it's not real fairies making the noise — because there's no such thing as real fairies — but nevertheless, he keeps his eyes closed and listens to them.

It's a good sound. A comfortable sound.

Perhaps, now, Woofy will come home.

Slowly, piece by piece, he begins to recall all that happened during the night — the frogs waking up after their long slumber, him going to the shearing shed, the candles, the séance, tapping the pipe under the floorboards, ratboy thinking it was Sophie's ghost … the glow of taillights disappearing into the night. Hooray! He and Willis had done it together. They'd gotten rid of ratboy.

'Morning, sleepy-head.'

He opens his eyes. Willis is sitting cross-legged on a shearer's mattress brushing out her wet hair and smiling at him. Her breath smells like toothpaste.

'Aggie came looking for you,' she says.

His heart skips a beat. Damn! He'd forgotten about Aggie and Onfro. Acting like they own the place. Touching his family's things. Looking through Dad's office. What'll they do when they find out that ratboy left without Willis? Uneasiness stirs inside him.

He sits up and matches Willis's cross-legged style.

'She was worried you'd run away again,' says Willis, pulling a knot loose. 'Said for us to come to the house for some lunch.'

He frowns and rubs his hand across his face. 'What time is it?'

'Nearly lunchtime.'

'What'd she …?'

'She didn't say much, but I think she's pretty mad that Ray left without me. But hey, what's she going to be able to do about it now that the rain's here? Thanks for your help, by the way. You did great.'

He looks around. Without the fluoros on, the inside of the shed is always gloomy, even on the brightest of days. But the light is different this morning. And the sound is still inside his head. The fairies are still celebrating.

He gets up from the mattress, goes to the open door and looks outside.

Yes! The rain *is* finally here.

It's coming down so fast it looks like streaks of water running down panes of glass. There are puddles on the ground. *The fairies are dancing on the roof.* That's what Sophie always said, whenever it rained. *The fairies are having a party. They're dancing on the roof.*

After so long and everything that's happened ...

Last time it rained like this, he and Sophie had run bare-foot into it, splashing through the puddles and waving their hands over their heads. Laughing until they were doubled over.

'Cool, hey?' says Willis, moving to share the doorway with him. 'Wanna get wet?'

He nods.

'Come on then.'

And together, they run fully clothed into the rain.

Willis isn't sure they should go to the house, but Jamie says it'll probably be alright because they've been invited for lunch. Somehow, since ratboy left and the rain came, he feels a tiny bit less frightened of Aggie and Onfro. Even Onfro hitting Willis seems less horrifying than it once had because, mostly, the strange man tends to stay out of everyone's way. And Aggie seems nice enough. At least, his mother had thought so.

Besides, he's hungry.

Aggie is at the kitchen table with a jumbo crossword puzzle spread out before her and a mug of coffee cooling by her elbow.

''Bout time you got here,' she says, taking the biro from her mouth like she thinks it's a cigarette. 'Go around to the laundry, take off your muddy shoes and get dry before you come into the house.'

People always take their shoes off at the screen door, but Jamie won't risk an argument by pointing this out. He wants food.

'Come on,' he says to Willis and steps back out into the rain.

On their way to the laundry, they pass the window to Dad's office. The lights are on and the solitary figure of Onfro is hunched over Dad's desk studying some papers, a plume of smoke coiling into the air from the ashtray. Jamie stops midstride and stares through the rain-speckled glass at the stranger sitting in Dad's place. The man's presence feels wrong — like a wild goat running with a mob of sheep.

The man looks up. He glances at Jamie for only a second, disinterested, then his gaze shifts to Willis and his face freezes over, sending a shiver of foreboding along the full length of Jamie's spine.

'Come on, Jamie,' she says, turning away. 'Just ignore him.'

Inside the laundry, she pulls off her muddy Docs and wraps a towel around her shoulders.

'You have first bath,' she says, 'and you don't need to wear this stinky old shirt anymore. You can get a clean one.'

He looks down at Sophie's soaking and stained owl shirt, then back up into her eyes. There's a sharpness behind the blue. Like she's holding back a thousand tears.

'Will you wait for me?'

'Of course I will. Don't worry. As soon as we've cleaned up and eaten, we'll go back to the shed together. Okay?'

Despite Aggie's invitation to come to the house for lunch, there doesn't seem to be any food on offer, so Willis fetches a bowl of Weet-Bix with milk and honey.

'Oh, Willy, your clothes are all wet,' says Aggie, looking up from her puzzle.

Willis shrugs. 'My clothes bag is in Ray's car.'

She sits down, puts a spoonful of Weet-Bix into her mouth and chews slowly.

Aggie watches her for a moment, then says, 'Moira called. She said Ray was waiting for her when she got to the bank this morning.'

'He must have wanted to get paid.'

'Paid?'

'I know you and Moira paid him to take me back to Sydney.'

The older woman shrugs. 'She had to call the police.'

'Really? Was he arrested?'

'No. He took off before they got there.'

Willis stops chewing and stares at Aggie. 'Why did you do it? Why'd you get him to come for me?'

Aggie crosses her arms and shuffles her feet under the table.

'It's just ...'

'What? Say it.'

'Jamie's dad had promised Moira he'd make a payment to the bank as soon as he got back from a flying job down south. He's in awful financial trouble, you know. Anyway, the night before he was due to leave, he called her to say that now he couldn't go because he had to stay home and take care of Jamie. Of course, Moira didn't want him to miss out on the work, so she sent you to Moonbroch. There wasn't time to find someone better but when she told me what had happened, Onfro and I offered to help out. You know how much I like to help those less fortunate than me and Onfro ... well, he has a good sense for business and thought he might be able to help the McKenzies sort out

their finances. Don't you see? This was a much more satis-
factory arrangement than having you here. And when you
refused to get along with Onfro ... well, you've brought all
this trouble on yourself, Willy.'

Willis's eyes are glassy. 'But I'm the one who talked to
Mr McKenzie. I'm the one he agreed could look after Jamie.
Not you.'

Her bowl of Weet-Bix is forgotten. She's sitting forward
on her chair gripping the edge of the table.

'That young boy needs responsible adults in charge of
his care,' says Aggie, 'not an out-of-control teenager.'

Willis gets to her feet. 'You think you know what he
needs. But you're wrong. I bet no-one thought to ask him
what he wanted.'

'Jamie is not old enough to know what he wants. If you
hadn't got here first and filled his head with silliness, there
would never have been a problem.'

'Is everything okay in here?' Onfro enters the kitchen
from the breezeway. He looks from Willis to Aggie.

Willis sits back down. Drops her eyes to the table. 'Fine.
Everything is fine.'

While she is crazy with frustration at Aggie's inability to
see things from her side, it's not worth getting into an argument with Onfro. Her objective is to get in, get food and
get out. Safely. With Jamie.

Onfro sits at the table, close enough so that his knee
knocks against her leg, then interlaces his chunky fingers
and leans forward as if they're about to share a secret. A
smile twitches on his mouth.

'You must think you're pretty clever?' he says, softly.
'Your boyfriend gone and you still here?'

When she doesn't answer or look up, he nudges her with
his knee and says, 'Answer me, Willy.'

'It's not my fault he took off in the middle of the night.'

'You must have done something to drive him away.'

'No ... I ...'

'Well. Never mind that now.' He shakes his head. 'I have some good news.'

She looks up.

'I know where that old dog is.'

'He's alive?'

'Yes.'

Her heart skips a beat. 'Where?'

'He's made camp over at the rubbish tip.'

That doesn't sound right. Why wouldn't Woofy just come home to Jamie?

'I need you to walk over there and fetch him home,' he says, his voice soft with menace. 'Right away.'

Willis stands and steps back, glad to put some distance between herself and Onfro.

'Okay. I'll just get Jamie.'

Onfro holds up his hand. 'Go on your own.'

'Why?'

'Because I say so.'

A warning is blasting in her mind, telling her that something is off. Like he's setting a trap. But she can't figure it out.

'Leave Jamie here to have some lunch,' Aggie says, twisting her hands together. 'He'll be okay while you're gone. It can be a nice surprise for him when you get back.'

She looks from Aggie to Onfro.

'But … I have to let Jamie know that I'm going first.'

'No,' says Onfro, shaking his head. 'Just do this one little thing to show us you're sorry, Willy. That's all we're asking. Then, maybe, we can let bygones be bygones.'

On the way to get her Docs, she hears water running down the drain in the bathroom. Jamie has finished his bath. She knots her laces with white knuckles, swallows down the bile in her throat and goes quietly out into the grey, rainy day.

'There you are,' Aggie says as he arrives at the kitchen door. 'How are you, Jamie? Starving? Hop up here at the table and let's get you fed, then, hey?'

He remains at the door. 'Where's Willis?'

Aggie shrugs and shakes her head. 'You know what Willy's like.'

'Where is she?'

'She's taken her boots and gone. Why she wants to be going out in this weather, I'll never know.'

Aggie takes a plate of cold, soggy toasties from the fridge and sets them on the table. 'Want a fruitcup cordial?'

'Yes. Please.'

Willis leaving without him feels like a terrible betrayal after she said she would wait. Should he follow her or should he wait for her to come back? In the end, his hunger makes the decision for him and he takes his place at the table.

'As of mid-morning, the phone lines are out,' Aggie announces unexpectedly as she sits back in front of her crossword. 'Onfro's been on the radio all morning keeping up with what's happening with the rain. He used to have something to do with communications in the Army, so he's a good man to have on the job.'

Jamie keeps his head down and chews his sandwich, but his body is rigid with interest in what she is saying.

'They've had over ten inches around Charleville and there's a big flood coming down the Paroo, so Ray got out just in time. Another few hours, he may not have made it.'

Jamie swallows a mouthful of food. A sip of his cordial.

'I managed to get calls out to both your Mum and Dad and I've let them know we're battening down the hatches. Told them everything was under control and not to worry.'

Mostly, Jamie avoids thinking about his parents, but, suddenly, the pain of their absence seems almost unbearable, particularly since Willis isn't here to distract him. A giant-sized lump is blocking up his throat, so big it's hard to swallow.

'Don't you love wet days?' Aggie says, peering out at the endlessly falling rain. 'After you've finished eating, I thought we could play some board games together. Would you like that?'

CHAPTER 18

Along with everyone else, Winter's attention has been fully captured by the drama that has unfolded in the carpark — Cass calling out to her father as the blue sedan sped away, him chasing after them, the police officer chasing after him. Then, once the car went out of sight down the road, he had dropped to the ground and covered his mouth with his hands, like he'd been in shock. And the police officer had squatted by his side and spoken to him for a long while.

It was all very strange and mysterious.

Winter had seen Cass's mother properly for the first time when she'd gone to fetch something from the boot of her car. Just before she took off. A tall and slender woman who moved in the same languid, graceful way that Cass did, except, possibly, she might have had a slight limp. With her hand on the boot, she'd paused for a moment to look across at all the people who had gathered to help find her daughter. Her eyes had found Cass's father. And the way they stared at each other! It wasn't how Winter thought people would look if they hated each other. The connection and emotion that passed between Cass's parents was something altogether different. Something outside her scope to explain. Something with the power to bring tears to her eyes.

But then, Cass's mother's gaze had shifted to her left and Winter had seen her stiffen; and her mouth had formed a perfect o. Twisting in the passenger seat of Poppy's van, Winter saw the man she and Poppy had brought to Goomburra with them. He was standing back in the crowd.

He's the reason Cass's mother has taken off in such dramatic fashion, she realises. Cass's mother knows the man who claims to be Jamie McKenzie's friend. The man called Ray. And she's terrified of him.

On her lap, Winter's notebook is opened to the page she has dedicated to Cass's father. At the top, she's written *Jamie*

McKenzie in large, bold letters, and the page is more than half full of notes. Her last entry is *DVO,* which is what the police officers had said when they were whispering by the side of the van. As soon as she can, she intends to find out what it means.

Directly above *DVO,* she has written *Ray, long lost friend?*

She chews the end of her pen for a moment, then underlines Ray's name. Twice.

It takes Jamie some time to convince the police that he's not about to jump in his car and chase after Cass. For some reason, they're convinced that Mina has a DVO out against him — they'd had to explain that a DVO is a domestic violence order, which means he's not allowed to go anywhere near her. Apparently, she'd told them that when she'd first arrived in Goomburra. Why would she do such a thing? The idea of him being violent towards any woman, and especially towards her, is so alien it makes him feel sick. When he asked the police if they'd checked the validity of her claim, they said they couldn't because they were out of range.

Shit! What an awful, embarrassing mess. He feels like a criminal.

In a daze, he accepts that the police also don't want him driving himself home and he agrees. He knows he's too shattered, physically and emotionally, to drive safely. One of the volunteers, a man called Ray, steps forward and offers to drive him in his car; and he climbs gratefully into the passenger seat.

Once Ray has driven slowly out of the carpark with Cass's father, and all the packing up has been done, Poppy climbs wearily into the van.

'Too much action for an old man,' he says to Winter. 'And after all that, you didn't get to spend time with your friend. What a shame. She seems like such a lovely girl.' He reaches over and gives Winter's arm a gentle pat.

'Did you notice that the man, Ray, who was supposed to be Jamie McKenzie's long-lost friend, didn't even go up and say hello to him?'

Poppy frowns. Then shrugs. 'I guess he was too busy with the volunteers. Maybe he didn't want to make a fuss with so much going on.'

'But when he offered to drive Cass's dad home, Cass's dad didn't seem to recognise him.'

'Listen to little Miss Nancy Drew.' He chuckles. 'Always looking for a mystery to solve. Jamie was probably too exhausted to recognise anyone, especially someone he hasn't seen for years.'

'I hope you're right,' Winter says. 'And I hope Cass is okay. Don't you think it strange the way her mother took off?'

'You're a good friend, Winter, my love. If everyone had a friend such as you, what a wonderful world it would be.'

A small smile flickers across her face, followed by a frown. 'They didn't really need our help though, did they? Cass and her Dad? In the end, they sorted everything out on their own.'

'Yeah. I guess they did. But it's always good to know you have someone in your corner who loves and cares about you, even if you don't fully appreciate it at the time.'

Jamie keeps his eyes closed to avoid having to talk to the man driving his car. He doesn't need conversation. He needs sleep. But his mind won't stop picking over the extraordinary events of the past few days. He has a deep sense that something is very wrong but he's too tired to figure out what it is. The only thing he's certain of is that, from now on, he wants Cass to be part of his life; and, if he has to, he will fight to make that happen.

He remembers the intense joy that had surged through his body when her dirt-streaked, smiling face had finally appeared over the top of the cliff. And the way she'd said she loved him, as if it was the most natural thing in the world. How could he have been so stupid to think that he could live his life without her? Without Cass, his life is a vacuum — has felt like a vacuum these past two years. Empty and meaningless.

He allows his mind to drift. Thirteen years ago, he agreed to become Mina Johnson's sperm donor. Even though he'd only been in his early twenties, it had seemed like a good opportunity to right a wrong and help alleviate some of the terrible guilt he'd carried ever since her accident on Moonbroch, all those years ago. But he definitely hadn't thought through the implications of that decision. The pain and the joy it would bring.

He and Mina had gone to a place called QFG in Spring Hill, received counselling from a woman called Angie, and signed consent forms. Angie had stressed that even though he was a known donor, he would have no legal rights to any children — and he'd said he was fine with that because he wasn't interested in having children right now and was doing it as a favour to Mina.

At the time, he'd expected their renewed friendship to continue, but a short while after he made his donation at QFG, he received a text message from her — *J thanks for what you have done for me means a lot but … this is difficult sorry I can no longer have you as part of my life and ask that you please not try to contact me again hope you understand. M.*

Her words had hurt him more than he cared to admit; so as soon as he graduated from university, he'd taken a job as a mining engineer and moved two thousand kilometres away, to Mt Isa. There was a mining boom. The money was fantastic. He played rugby for the Wanderers, got drunk on weekends, travelled overseas for holidays, and didn't give any further thought to whether his sperm donation had ever actually been used.

Nearly five years passed.

Then, one day, he received a text message from her, asking him to call. She said she needed a break from being a single parent and was there any chance he could mind their daughter for a few days or a week.

He had a daughter? He could scarcely frame the thought that he might be the biological father of a little girl he had never met.

Mina never begged him. In fact, she made it sound as though she had other options and this was a casual request. So he almost said no. But in the end, his curiosity won out over his doubts. He got time off work and flew to Brisbane.

'This is Cass,' she said, as he dropped his chopper bag on the floor inside her front door. She might have said more, but he couldn't hear over the sound of blood whooshing in his ears. Because … the little girl before him, *his* biological daughter, was the spitting image of his sister, Sophie. Same blonde hair. Same wide, intelligent eyes. Same gentle face. There was an aura of brightness and wisdom about her and, in that instant, Jamie's heart was changed. Forever.

Mina's place turned out to be a tiny hotbox with hundred-year old plumbing, dodgy electrics and all-night ker-thumping coming from a pub across the road. It was a ghastly place to be raising a child and he quickly grasped how tough she was doing it as a single mother. He and Cass went house hunting and he bought an attractive apartment close to the city, which he then offered to rent to Mina for the same price she was currently paying.

She was suspicious about his motives and initially refused to accept his offer of the apartment, reminding him frequently that he had no legal claim to Cass. But, in the end, she accepted the apartment because she knew it would provide a better environment in which to raise her daughter. She also agreed that he could see Cass twice a year, on condition that he never discussed her existence with anyone. Not even with his parents.

When he left to return to Mt Isa that first time, Cass had clung to his legs and cried, 'Don't go, Daddy. Don't go, Daddy.'

He had never told her to call him Daddy.

Twice a year for the next six years, Jamie had travelled to Brisbane to see Cass. Mina was cautious and made a lot of conditions, but it didn't matter, so long as he got to spend time with Cass. She was a bright little girl with lots of energy and a great sense of adventure and they never ran out of things to do together.

Strangely, in all those six years, he never once saw Mina. All their communication was via phone calls and text messages, and whenever he went to the apartment to collect or return Cass, someone else was always there to greet him. Never Mina. He'd thought it strange but had never wanted to jeopardise his access to Cass by asking her why she was avoiding him.

When Cass was ten, he had taken her to Noosa for a week and they'd had a brilliant time together. Then, the day after he'd dropped her home, Mina had called to say she was cutting off all contact between them and he was no longer welcome to see her. Just like that! She gave no explanation and refused to discuss her decision, simply reminding him that, by law, he had no parental rights.

He'd been stunned, and very angry. He'd wanted to fly back to Brisbane and demand to see *his daughter* any time he liked. He'd wanted to remind her how much he'd contributed financially to their wellbeing. He'd even considered speaking to a lawyer. But there is a reason why sperm donors have to agree to follow the rules — so they don't go causing trouble down the track, disrupting lives and demanding to see children that aren't legally theirs. And the last thing he ever wanted to do was cause trouble for Cass.

So, in the end, he did nothing.

For the past two years, he had held his grief inside and never uttered a word to another living soul, but his heartache was obvious in other ways. Sometimes after rugby, when he'd had too much to drink, he'd become so argumentative and difficult that people he once considered friends started backing away. Work was no different. He'd been cautioned several times about the slipping quality of his work and the disrespectful manner in which he spoke to his colleagues. He lost himself. He certainly wasn't the man his father had raised him to be. Such was the depth of his shame, he'd eventually quit his job in Mt Isa and moved to Toowoomba, determined to start again. Determined to be better.

Then, a week ago, he'd received another text from Mina asking him to look after Cass again. The timing couldn't have been worse because he'd been booked to fly to Melbourne later that same day to partner his ex-girlfriend to a wedding. They had gone out for about a year when they both lived in Mt Isa, but she'd broken it off. Now, just when she was prepared to give him a second chance, he was letting her down ... again ... and he was fairly certain there wouldn't be any more chances. That relationship was now definitely dead and buried.

But he'd had no choice. He was never going to give away a chance to spend time with his daughter.

Even though he didn't think he was sleeping, Jamie wakes as the car bounces over the guttering and pulls into the driveway of his house. He rubs his hand across his weary face and looks at the thin, wiry man driving his car, wondering vaguely how he knew where he lived.

'I'm most grateful for your help,' he says. 'Can I drop you off somewhere?'

'No need,' the man says. 'My wheels are out front.'

In his exhausted state, Jamie is unable to connect the dots and come up with a plausible reason why the volunteer's car would be at his house, so he doesn't try.

'Would you like a drink of water or use of the bathroom before you go?' he says, hoping the man declines because he really needs to get his phone on the charger and call Mina.

The man pulls the keys from the ignition and holds them for a second too long before dropping them into Jamie's hand. He reminds Jamie of someone teasing a dog with a bone. There's a sharp little grin on his face, as if he's waiting for Jamie to catch on to a joke. Except, Jamie doesn't know what the joke is.

Then the man hops out of the car, springy on his feet, and says, 'Some breakfast would be nice.'

CHAPTER 19

Willis hates being manipulated by Onfro and despises the way he always wants to have control over her. But finding out that old Woofy is still alive is the best news she's had in ages. Already, as she walks along the bush track in the rain, she can imagine what the reunion between the boy and the dog will be like. Jamie's arms will be around the dog's stinky wet neck and he'll be laughing. Woofy's tail will be spinning in circles of joy.

After twenty minutes, she arrives at the station's dump. It's an area in a particularly dense section of scrub, twenty metres by twenty metres, and surrounded by a bank of compacted soil. Inside the bank is all kinds of rubbish — old tyres, tangles of barbed wire, household rubbish, rusted-out shearers' stretchers, forty-four-gallon drums, an ancient truck motor.

From the top of the bank, she stands still, arms folded, and scans the area. Woofy is on the floor of the dump. Out in the rain. Wet and trembling. Miserable. And chained to a steel peg.

'Woofy.' With tears in her eyes, she slides down the sticky bank of mud and drops to her knees before him in the mud. 'You're alive.'

She begins to pet him, rubbing behind his ears and chastising him for being so smelly. He isn't in great shape, but he still makes a gallant effort to wag his soggy tail in response to her fussing.

'What's Onfro got you chained up for, hey?' she says soothingly, feeling in the thick fur around his neck for a way to remove the chain.

She feels the dog flinch. Notices the way he begins to cower in fear. And instinctively, she turns towards the source of that fear.

Onfro is only two metres away, a rifle held out in front and a mask of madness on his face. There's no time to react. Her hands are still in Woofy's fur when the gun goes off.

And the old dog slumps in her hands.

She stares at Onfro. Is he going to shoot her too?

Dropping Woofy's limp body, she gets warily to her feet, her wide eyes glued to the gun. Her instinct is to run. But she doesn't. She stands her ground. Because if she runs, he might not be able to resist putting a bullet into her retreating back.

After several long seconds, with her heart trying to catapult out of her chest, Onfro slowly turns the rifle so that it's pointing to the ground. Then he steps forward, grabs the sleeve of her t-shirt and twists it up so his knuckles are pressed against her shoulder.

With his ruddy, wet face close to hers so she can smell his coffee cigarette breath, he says, 'Consider this a lesson. For every action, there *is* a reaction. 'Bout time you knew that.'

When Willis comes back to the house for Jamie, she has mud on her knees. She's upset about something, and she drags him away from the house by his wrist. He has to do a running shuffle to keep up with her long, angry strides.

'Your father has a gun,' she says, wiping angry tears from her eyes with the back of her spare hand. 'Why does your father have a gun?'

She stops and looks at him, waiting for an answer. He's scared.

'Jamie. Why does your father have a gun?'

'Everyone in the bush has a rifle.' The sound of the rain is confusing him and he raises his voice. 'It's for when they need to shoot an injured animal or a wild dog or something like that.'

'Hell. What do you think happens when a crazy dick like Onfro gets his hands on a gun? I mean, we both know he's shot people before.'

Jamie's eyes widen. 'I don't believe you.'

'Of course he's shot people, you idiot. He was in a war, remember. A*nd* he's got PTSD. Do you know what that is?'

'A disease.'

'A disease in his head.' She taps her temple with her pointer finger while tears mix with rain on her flushed cheeks. 'Onfro is crazy, Jamie. You're not safe. We've got to find somewhere for you to hide.'

'You're making it up. YOU'RE MAKING IT UP!' he screams and tries to run back towards the house. But she's still holding his wrist.

She's full-on crying now. 'You've got to believe me. It isn't safe for you to be out here.'

He shakes his head and tries harder to get free. 'Let me go. I want to go back to Aggie. Let me go.'

'I'm serious, Jamie. You've got to trust me.'

'No.'

He starts kicking at her shins.

'Jamie. Stop it. I can prove it.'

'No.'

'Just let me show you what that sick bastard's capable of. Please. So you know. Then, if you want, you can go back to Aggie.'

Jamie stops struggling. He hasn't got the strength to continue fighting her and decides to go and look at what she wants to show him because he can't bear to see her this mad and crazy. But, that's it. Once they've finished, he'll go home, to *his* house, and feed *his* dogs and *his* chooks, and do whatever *he* wants. He'll eat *his* food and sleep in *his* bed because he's sick of everyone thinking they're the boss of him. He doesn't need any of them to look after him.

Willis and Jamie stay away from the bush tracks that radiate out from the homestead and walk through the band of scrub that grows between the creek and the house, heading north. Sheet lightning reflects off the gravestone of Mary Withers as they pass and rolling thunder competes with an orchestra of a million frogs.

They arrive at the station dump. He looks expectantly at Willis, wondering what can be so important that she's dragged him here in a storm, then follows her gaze, squinting his eyes against the rain.

It takes a while for him to find what it is she wants him to see. Then his mind refuses to acknowledge what his eyes are seeing — there's not enough light, or too much when the lightning flickers across the stormy sky. Everything in the dump has been darkened by water, but his eyes, and his mind, know that the small, fuzzy object chained to a steel peg are out of place.

'If you go closer, you'll see the bullet hole in his head.'

Horror floods Jamie's body like spiders on his skin. He wants to run. He wants to push Willis over in the mud and kick her. He wants to scream and yell. And vomit. Instead, he steps down the claggy bank using his heels to stop himself from slipping, drops to his knees and slides his hand under the dog's floppy old head. Woofy. His friend and companion. The one constant in his life since Sophie got sick.

Dead centre between the dog's glassy eyes is a deep-red hole.

Willis watches the devastated young boy from the top of the bank. She'd not wanted him to see Woofy like this, but how else can she convince him of the danger he's in?

The rain falls.

Jamie bends low over the limp bundle of wet fur and rests his cheek against the dog's head, avoiding looking at the unseeing, dead eyes. Every muscle in his body is tense as he bears the first intolerable wave of grief. Clenched jaw. Toes curled inside his boots. Burning in his chest. It hurts so bad. Woofy's death seems even more shocking than Sophie's had. Sophie died remotely in a distant hospital. He had never seen her dead. But Woofy is here. In his arms. He brushes some blobs of mud from the dog's rump and remembers how, little more than a week ago, he and Willis had washed him with Mum's shampoo, and laughed and laughed.

Was he being punished for laughing? For having fun while Sophie was dead? Breathing deeply, he draws all the doggy pong he can get in through his nostrils, grateful that the rain has amplified the smell.

Her voice intrudes. 'Onfro chained him up and shot him. I saw him do it.'

From his lowly position on the floor of the rubbish dump, she looks like a giantess against the wild grey sky. He watches as she steps gracefully down the bank and squats beside him in the mud.

After some time, she says, 'Do you know why Onfro's here? At Moonbroch?'

He clears his throat. 'To look after me …?'

She raises her eyebrows. 'What room has he been spending all his time in?'

'Dad's office.'

'And what's he been doing in there, do you think?'

He pictures Onfro's round shoulders hunched over Dad's desk, the plume of smoke coiling into the air, the open filing cabinet and the scattered papers.

'Using the radio to find out about the rain.'

'I think he's been looking into your parents' business, going through old bills and stuff like that. Talking to people on the phone. You know what else I think?'

'What?'

'He wants to take over Moonbroch.'

Her words are so unexpected, they arrive like a slap to his face.

'... he wants to own it. Especially now it's raining, and the drought is breaking. Think about it. Moira Tanning is your parents' bank manager. She knows that since Sophie died, they've done a crap job of running the place and they're nearly bankrupt, so she blabs to Aggie who blabs to Onfro. He always wanted his own place out west. Aggie's always saying it. So, when he heard your parents were away and you were home alone with just me, he got here pronto. He wants Moonbroch, Jamie. I'm sure of it.'

But, if Onfro is here ... where will his family go? Moonbroch has been in the McKenzie family for three generations. Moonbroch is home. Jamie can't imagine ever living anywhere else.

'Mum and Dad wouldn't sell it, no matter what.'

'I know that,' Willis says, balancing her squat by leaning her hand on his shoulder. 'But Onfro and Aggie don't. They think it'll be a walk in the park to take this place over because Moira has told them how badly your parents are doing since ... since Sophie died.'

'Mum and Dad love Moonbroch.' His chin quivers as he says the words, because he's not sure they do anymore.

'Yeah. I'm sure they do. But whenever they're here, they're reminded of Sophie every minute of every day and it hurts. It hurts real bad. Which is why Onfro must have thought they'd be happy to sell and move away.' She gazes around at the bleak landscape. 'Onfro must have thought the death of Sophie would be enough, but he underestimated your parent's attachment to their land. Your parents aren't prepared to sell, and it's making him crazy. Crazy enough to kill Woofy.'

Jamie hasn't a clue how to handle Willis's theory about Onfro wanting to take over Moonbroch so he sinks his hands into Woofy's fur and waits for her to continue.

'Onfro is the kind of man who likes to get his own way,' she says. 'If one dead child isn't enough to make them sell, what about two? That's probably what he's thinking. What if their other child has a terrible accident and dies too? Surely that will be enough.'

Jamie starts to shiver. He's been in wet clothes for much of the day, but this is more a response to his fear than anything physical. He scans the scrub around the perimeter of the dump. Might they be planning to kill him?

'I'll protect you,' she says. 'I promise.'

'How will you?'

She stands, pushes her hands against her lower back and stretches her spine like a cat, then offers him her long, pale hand and pulls him to his feet. Woofy's lifeless head flops back into the mud.

'I've been thinking about it. The meathouse might be the safest place for you to hide. It's out of the rain and close to the house so I can keep an eye on you, and I don't think they'll look in there. They're more likely to concentrate their search around the sheds and quarters, don't you think?'

The meathouse is a tiny, screened outbuilding for hanging sheep carcasses overnight. Whenever meat is needed, Dad cuts a sheep's throat, strips off its wool, empties out its guts and hangs it from a giant, steel hook in the meathouse. Next morning, he cuts the carcass into legs, shoulders and chops for Mum to bag up, label and put in the freezer. At least, that's what used to happen before Sophie got sick. Now, the blood stains have darkened to black, and dust and spider webs have gotten caught up in the greasy fat that coats the walls and floor.

'I don't want to …'

'Trust me,' she says, 'it'll be the safest place.'

CHAPTER 20

Huddled in darkness on the concrete floor of the meathouse, Jamie is too frightened to lean against the spidery, corrugated iron walls that fill the lower half of the tiny shack, so he presses his back against the meat block in the middle of the room, draws his knees against his chest and clutches an old meat cleaver firmly between both hands, ready to battle whatever strikes first — Onfro or a snake.

His eyes strain to see in the dark and his ears are alert to every noise coming from the house, which is difficult over the patter of rain on the roof and the chattering of his teeth. The skin on his bare legs and across the back of his neck crawls with imaginary redback spiders.

After a very long time, he hears the screen door of the kitchen open and close.

'Jamie,' Onfro calls. 'You need to come home. Now.'

'Come on Jamie. Where are you?' calls Aggie.

Their voices are thick with concern and he's tempted to come out of hiding and go inside for a hot bath and some dinner. Even the smell of old blood and rancid fat can't overpower the hot, meaty aroma wafting out the kitchen and suddenly, sitting here in the dark in his damp clothes seems stupid and babyish. He stands and peeps out the fly screen that encloses the top half of the structure. Kitted out with boots, rain jackets and torches, Onfro, Aggie and Willis stand in the house yard — Onfro is holding Dad's rifle — and they're squinting into the blackness of the stormy night as if trying to figure out how one goes about finding a missing ten-year-old in the rain and the dark. His hand reaches for the door.

'Jammmiiieee. Jammmiiieee.' There's a manic wildness to Willis's voice when she calls his name. Like a warning.

Heart pounding, he drops back to the floor, aware that Aggie is chastising Willis for not treating the situation seriously enough and Willis is telling her to lighten up.

'I really don't see what all the fuss is about,' she says. 'He'll turn up when he gets hungry. He always does.'

Jamie drops his head forward onto his knees and tries — and fails — to muffle the sound of their voices by pressing his hands over his ears.

'I'll let the dogs out,' Onfro says. 'I'm sure they'll be able to find him.'

If Jamie had hidden at the shed or quarters, like he'd wanted to, the dogs would have found him for sure. But they're not allowed in the house yard where the meathouse is. It would take a lot of coaxing to make them break the rules and he doesn't think either Onfro or Aggie know much about dogs.

'Don't forget your gun, soldier man,' Willis taunts. 'Bang. Bang. Shoot all the poor little doggies.'

'Shut the fuck up,' growls Aggie. 'If it wasn't for you, none of us would be in this mess.'

Jamie rocks slowly to and fro. He starts to count in his head. One, two, three. Four, five, six. He remembers one time he had gone all the way to five hundred without losing count. They had been in the Landcruiser, going to Toowoomba — him, Mum, and Sophie — to see the specialist about Sophie's nosebleeds and bruises. She was in the front, he was in the back, and Mum kept yelling at him for kicking the back of her seat, which he hadn't been doing on purpose. Mum had said if he didn't sit still, she'd stop the car and put him out and he had yelled back that it was too boring and there was nothing to do.

Then Sophie had twisted around, smiled and asked, 'What number can you count to?'

'I dunno,' he'd said.

'Think you can count to forty?'

'More than that.' His School of the Air teacher, Mrs Hendy, always said he was good with numbers.

'Go on then. Let's see how far you can go.'

Before he knew it, they had been in Dalby with only an hour to go.

Clang. Clang. Clang. Clang. Someone outside the meathouse is running a stick across the corrugations in the iron sheeting.

'Jammmiiieee,' Willis calls from right outside. 'Jammmiiieee. Where are you?'

He's not sure if she means for him to come out or stay hidden. Is he really in danger? Or is this just another of her crazy games? Like the day when Aggie and Onfro had arrived, and she'd had him run through the scrub to the house to fetch Sophie's shirt? He's still trying to decide if it's a game or serious when her voice trails off.

He stands and takes another peep. Willis has gone into the hangar, pretending to look for him, while further away, walking towards the shearing shed, he can see the glow of two torches. Onfro must already have let the dogs out. What if he shoots them?

Jamie pushes the meathouse door open and bolts across the yard and into the kitchen without bothering to take off his boots. Just past the kitchen is the phone and Granny Linley's number is written on the wall. Holding his breath, he lifts the hand piece to his ear. No dial tone. Just a whole bunch of scratchy noises. And he remembers Aggie saying how the phone lines were out due to the rain.

He dials anyway.

'Mum. Mum.' There's no response.

The radio! He runs to Dad's office, but the radio doesn't seem to be working either. Onfro must have done something to it.

No-one is coming to help him.

There's no-one to stop Onfro from shooting the dogs or whoever else he wants. And no-one is coming to save them. Because of the rain, the road will be out. And a plane can't land in the dark without flares. There's no-one to set the flares.

His only chance, he realises, is to walk out to the highway, like he'd tried to do the day Onfro hit Willis. He's got to try again. If he goes in the dark, he doesn't have to worry about sun stroke like last time.

But first, he's got to get the dogs.

Back in the kitchen, he opens the fridge, gulps down four mouthfuls of milk straight from the bottle, wipes his mouth and burps. A pot of casserole is cooling on the sink, so he shovels a couple of spoonsful into his mouth and upends the rest into the chook bucket. Dogs have the power to smell a thousand or a million times better than a human so maybe they'll come to the smell of a bucket of stew. He'd like to change his clothes but there isn't time, so he grabs the bucket and slips back through the screen door into darkness.

Behind him, the homestead lights soon become fuzzy blobs in the distance, as remote as the moon, and above, the stars have been vanquished behind a thick blanket of cloud. He's thankful he once spent so much time practising the bat's superpower of seeing in the dark. Without the use of his eyes, his other senses begin to spread across the landscape like tiny tendrils, seeking a path through the darkness.

His nose takes strange comfort in the smell of veggie scraps and stew rising from the bucket swinging by his side and his ears are vigilant for the excited pant of the dogs. Or the sound of Onfro coming after him with the rifle. At least he won't be able to come after him in the ute without getting bogged on the flats. The only way is on foot and the old man is slow and will never be able to catch him. For some inexplicable reason, Jamie wants to laugh out loud, but he holds back the hysteria. Running for his life is a serious business.

The rain stops. Suddenly. One minute, he feels the wetness of it on his face, and the next, nothing. He stops walking and listens.

Puffing and pleased with themselves, the dogs arrive by his side and are welcomed with pats, muttered praises and a good sniff of the treat inside the bucket. However, the reunion can't distract him for long because another sound, a horrifying rumbling noise, is now demanding his attention.

The creek is up.

A big flood, by the sound of it.

'Jesus Christ,' he says to the dogs. 'What're we going to do now?'

Dozer nudges the bucket.

'At a time like this, all you can think about is your stomach?'

Hebe barks. One quick yap.

'Shhh. You've got to be quiet or they'll come find us.'

Another bark.

'Here.'

He quickly reaches his hand into the bucket and scoops a handful of the slop onto the ground, makes another pile a bit further away and then a third. The dogs immediately plop their behinds on the ground and wait for the command to eat.

'Okay,' he says, his own stomach rumbling. 'Good dogs.'

The dogs rush forward and gobble the food, while Jamie tosses the bucket away and wipes his hand down the front of his shirt.

He feels his way off the road and finds a tree that is large enough to sit against and face the direction of the homestead. He wriggles his bottom until he's comfortable then draws his knees to his chest. Once the dogs have ensured themselves that all three piles of food and the bucket have been licked clean, they join him. Hebe curls against his left leg, Mickey against his right, and Dozer settles next to his feet.

'We'll wait 'til daylight,' he says, 'then we'll see about getting over the crossing. Don't worry. I won't let the bad man shoot you. It'll be alright. You'll see.'

He doesn't sleep. Occasionally he nods off, but the lolling movement of his head against the tree trunk always pulls him back to consciousness. There's comfort to be had from the dogs' body heat and the pong of their wet fur; and from his belief that they'll warn him if anyone approaches.

He thinks about the dark-red hole in Woofy's head and about what Willis had said about Onfro wanting him dead so he could take over Moonbroch. He wonders what it would feel like to be shot between the eyes. And he wonders if he'll get in trouble for staying out all night and making everyone worry about him.

The clouds begin to glow with early morning streaks of sunlight — pinks and purples and yellows. Jamie pushes the dogs away, stands, rubs his fists against his eyes and has a pee. His hair sticks out in every direction. His clothes are filthy. He's cold and ready for sleep, but he can't go home. Home is no longer the safe place it once was. Home has been taken over by aliens. And one of them has a gun.

He walks down to check the crossing and it's the biggest flood he's ever seen. A churning mass of brown water and branches. There's no way he can make it across. The rocks Dad collected from the stony hills to pave the way will have been washed away and it'll be ages before anyone is able to drive across. The only way in and out will be by air.

Hebe's warning bark causes him to jump. Distracted by the flood and deafened by its roar, he's forgotten to keep an eye out for people approaching from the house.

Willis is not more than twenty metres away, her face milky pale with fatigue. Dark smudges, like bruises, have formed under her eyes, smears of mud are streaked across her bare legs and like him, her clothes are dank and dirty.

The growl of the ute in low gear grabs his attention and he gawks open-mouthed at the ancient vehicle slipping and sliding across the flats towards them. Onfro and Aggie are visible through the mud-speckled windscreen and he doesn't understand why they're not bogged to the axle.

'Why didn't you stay hidden like I told you?' Willis says.

'I didn't want to.'

'But why?'

'… he was going to shoot the dogs.'

The ute is getting closer.

'I had it under control.'

'No, you didn't.'

Willis talks to him in a low soothing mumble, trying to calm him, but his terrified brain is refusing to pay attention. And she keeps stepping closer and closer, trying to get near enough to catch hold of his arm, but he keeps stepping back. He's scanning from her to the ute which has stopped about fifty metres away. He sees Aggie and Onfro throwing open the doors. Then, suddenly, he feels the ground beneath his feet give slightly and his eyes pop wide when he realises that he's tottering precariously on the edge of the sodden creek bank, high above the churning water.

'Jamie. Be careful,' Willis warns, her exhausted eyes filled with fear and tears.

'Leave me alone,' he says, unable to fully understand the torrent of hysteria that is thrashing about inside his body.

'Jamie. I was wrong. They're not going to hurt you. Just come away from the edge.'

Then Aggie is screaming. Screaming and running towards them with her hands flapping wildly in the air like an injured bird, and Onfro is following behind with the rifle in his arms. Aggie's cheeks are streaked with mascara smudges. Her witch's hair is fanned out about her head.

Jamie and Willis both stare, open-mouthed, at the madness charging towards them.

Aggie's arms are outstretched. Reaching for him.

But what neither she, nor anyone else, has been paying attention to is the dogs. Ever since Willis arrived at the creek, the dogs have been standing to attention, ears upright and alert, as though waiting to be informed about their role in the unfolding drama. With the excitement of Aggie's charge, the younger dog, Hebe, loses her self-control and bounds forward, right into the path of Aggie's feet. Aggie stumbles. She staggers. She slides forward on the slippery ground and before Jamie can move out of her way, she slams straight into him.

He goes backwards. Over the edge. Down towards the swirling, brown water. And Aggie comes down on top of him. Pushes him under. It's like being in a washing machine, spun round and round, knocked by debris in the water, and by Aggie's flailing body, then bumping hard against the bottom of the creek. His lungs are going to explode. He doesn't know how to get to the surface so he can breathe.

Then he feels a hand pressing against his back, pushing him up, and he's above the water coughing and gasping. Aggie is behind him holding his head in the crook of her elbow. A branch whacks him in the back and tangles around him but she uses her free hand to push it off.

'I've got you, Jamie,' she yells in his ear. 'I've got you. You're going to be okay.'

After the initial fall and struggle to get their heads above the water, they've ended up near the middle of the swollen creek, but Aggie manages to get them back towards the bank, further downstream, and Jamie is using his legs to help. A red-faced Onfro has climbed down to the water's edge and is holding out Dad's rifle as though he wants them to grab hold of the end of the barrel. He's ankle deep in mud.

'Get the end,' he calls.

'He's got the rifle,' screams Jamie and begins to thrash around in Aggie's arms.

'For snakes,' Aggie says. 'It's only for snakes. Grab the end so he can pull you out.'

She thrusts him forward.

Then he looks up into Onfro's face. And Willis's words are still in his head — *If one dead child isn't enough to make them sell, what about two? What if their other child has a terrible accident and dies too? Surely that would be enough* — and suddenly the soldier man's eyes are the eyes of a killer. He imagines those giant hands squeezing the trigger and a round, blood-red hole appearing in the middle of his own forehead.

Planting his feet firmly in the squishy mud, he grabs the end of the rifle and levers himself sharply to the left, up the slick earth bank and as far away from the man as he can get. Onfro tries to counteract this unexpected movement, but his balance, which was already precarious, has been lost and he stumbles forward. In an effort to regain his balance, he drops the rifle and falls to his hands and knees. His movement is clumsy as he attempts to get his feet underneath himself in the sticky mud.

The squelch of Onfro struggling to get out of the mud, the rumble and boom of the creek — it all fades and Jamie has the sense that's he's become trapped inside a giant, silent bubble. He's suddenly aware of his hollow stomach and a vision comes to mind of Mum in the kitchen making lunch, the snick of the knife against the cutting board as she slices up the salad, the salty taste of a piece of mutton he's swiped from the plate next to her, the smell of nearly-baked bread wafting from the bread-maker in the corner, the cricket commentators on the radio talking about short mid-wickets and silly mid-ons, a fly beating itself against the fly-screen, Dad whistling as he approaches the house for lunch. This is what he wants. He wants it so badly he aches for it. Mum and Dad have had enough sadness. He's had enough sadness. Things have to go back to normal.

The bubble around him bursts with an almost audible ping and he knows what he must do. He's going to have to be very, very brave and not at all scared because if he isn't, his family could lose everything.

He pulls the rifle from the mud and studies it for several moments. The last time he'd held this rifle was the day Dad had killed the kangaroo. The same day Mum had called to say Sophie was dead.

'Don't want to break the rifle. Don't want to waste a bullet,' he mutters and leans it carefully against the steep bank that rises above his head. A few steps further upstream, he finds a solid lump of old wood, about half a metre long, sticking out of the mud. He pulls it free and notes its weight in his hands. Then, like a cricket bat, he swings it through the air a few times. It feels comfortable in his hands. Carefully, he shuffles forward again until he's directly behind Onfro, who's still struggling to free himself from the mud.

And he swings.

CHAPTER 21

The wood collides with the back of the man's head and the force of the blow reverberates through Jamie's hands. Then, to his amazement, he hears an odd, high-pitched sound rising above the froth and toil of the flood. Onfro is laughing. Hysterical laughter. Not only has the man's physical balance gone weirdly off-centre, his brain seems to have become unhinged as well. He almost gets himself upright, but he can't seem to lift his feet out of the mud, and he staggers forward until he's knee-deep in the water. He laughs again, as if his bizarre predicament is the funniest thing that's ever happened to him.

Jamie feels as if everything is moving slow-motion. He turns to see if Aggie has noticed the man's strange behaviour, but Aggie is having troubles of her own. She's ten metres further downstream on her hands and knees trying to crawl her way to safety but her dress is tangled around her knees, limiting her movement.

He turns back to Onfro who now seems to have given up his struggle. Both his arms are held out wide, like he's part of a crucifixion with an invisible cross; then he simply falls, forward, and belly flops into the turbulent water where the current picks him up and carries him away.

An expression of horror flashes across Aggie's face when she sees Onfro go into the water. She twists sideways and allows herself to slip back into the current as well. Jamie sees her pushing strongly out towards the place where Onfro has vanished below the churning water and brown foam.

Onfro's head reappears just as Aggie reaches him and she wraps her arms around his shoulders. By now, they've been washed across towards the other side of the creek and further downstream so that all Jamie can see is their two heads bobbing up and down in the mad brown water.

He thinks they're going to make it to safety on the other side. But then, an unearthed tree that had been mostly submerged suddenly lifts out of the water like a sea monster and crashes down over the top of them. There's a tiny flash of colour. Maybe the wave of an arm.

And then they are gone.

Jamie can't stop his chin shivering and his teeth jangling together. He stares dumbly at the place where Aggie and Onfro have disappeared.

'Jamie. Jammmiiieee.'

The sound of someone calling his name is persistent but coming from a long way off.

He looks around.

'Up here.'

Willis is above him, standing on top of the bank, her anxious face shrouded by a mess of blonde hair. By her side are the three dogs.

He drops the lump of wood next to the rifle. She drops onto her tummy and reaches towards him.

'Give me your hand. I'll pull you up.'

Once he's safely back on top of the bank, she says, 'We've got to save them.'

Hebe gives a sharp bark as if in agreement, but Jamie only shakes his head and stares at the waterlogged ground.

'The current took them to the other side of the creek,' she says. 'We've got to go and help them.'

Her voice is shrill with panic.

He knows he should say something, but he doesn't know how to talk anymore. Like the vacuum of space, his whole mind is empty of everything — ideas, thoughts, emotions.

'Jamie. We have to go after them.'

He lifts his head slowly and locks eyes with her. 'Why?'

'Because … because they might be hurt.'

'I don't care.'

'But … what if they die?'

'I don't care.'

'But … if they die, people will say you killed them. That you're a murderer. They'll take you away.'

Murderer? He's a murderer? He doesn't want to be called a murderer and be sent away. He wants to stay here. With Mum and Dad. Slowly, the awful irony of his situation dawns on him. He'd hit Onfro on the head so that he could continue to live on Moonbroch with his parents. But because of his actions, he's now at risk of losing everything. It's all back-to-front. Not fair. His stomach is suddenly sick with fear.

'No-one will believe you,' he says quietly.

'What?'

'I'll tell everyone it was your fault and it was you who pushed them in. Because you wanted them dead.'

Willis's face is as pale as a corpse — at least as pale as he thinks a corpse's face would be. It's horrible seeing the effect his words have on her. But he can't help it. Blaming her is his only chance to save himself.

'Everyone will think it was you. Because you were always fighting with them.'

Tears flood her eyes as the full extent of his treachery dawns on her. A sob catches in her throat and she turns away from him. Then she's running. Through the sticky mud and turkey bush back towards the crossing.

Jamie lets out his breath and drops into a squat, careful not to put his hands or knees into the burr. It doesn't feel good to be so mean. His stomach hurts. He hasn't slept. He's barely eaten. His clothes are wet and filthy. He doesn't know what has happened to his hat. Perhaps it's back at the house or it got washed away. He doesn't remember.

He hears a mechanical sound. A loud revving. And his head jolts up.

Someone has started the ute.

Willis! It has to be Willis.

But she's not allowed to drive the ute. She doesn't know how to drive. Does she?

Is she going to drive back to the house without him?

Or … is she planning to try and cross the creek to save Aggie and Onfro?

He runs slow-motion because of the wet clay sticking to the soles of his boots and by the time the crossing is in sight, the ute is already plunging into the water. The water over the crossing isn't deep, not more than a metre, but it's the current that makes it dangerous. A city girl like Willis wouldn't know about how you shouldn't drive into flood water. He watches as the ute gets about halfway across, then the back of the vehicle lifts and the whole car spins so that it's facing downstream. It halts for one sickening moment, then is washed off the crossing and into the creek. The front driver's side slams against an old gum tree a few metres downstream and gets hooked up for a few seconds.

'Get out of the ute,' Jamie screams. He can see Willis's head inside the car. 'Get out.'

She reaches her hand through the open window and grips the top of the door frame and he thinks she's going to get out the window, but before she can, the powerful current against the side of the car causes it to flip. It slams upside down with an enormous splash so the entire cabin with Willis inside is now below the water. The upside-down car continues to spin further downstream and, after about ten more metres, becomes pinned against the earth bank.

Jamie slides down the sticky mud wall, lowers his head and arm into the tiny space between the bank and the car, and begins to feel around inside the inverted cabin for the feel of human flesh. Yes. He touches her. He's sure of it. But she's trapped. There's not enough room for her to get out.

Slithering back to the surface, he twists his body around so that his back is pressed against the muddy bank and his boots are firm against the bottom of the driver's door frame. He clenches his teeth and pushes his boots outwards, his singular purpose being to use the power in his legs to push the car away from the bank and make a large enough space for Willis to get out.

His awareness of the physical world fades and suddenly he can hear Sophie's voice inside his head — *It'll be really cool for you to have a superpower, we should write a list of all the super-powers we can think of, then we can pick the best one for you to start working on, you should concentrate on one at a time so you can focus your attention on it.*

Then, even the inside of his head becomes silent and still. The entire universe exists here and now and nothing matters except the power in his legs.

Ever so slowly, the car begins to lift away from the earth bank. One of Willis's arms appears, breaking through the surface and reaching hungrily towards the air above. But she can't breathe with her hand. She needs to get her head above water. Every muscle in his small body contracts as he pushes against the car. He pushes so hard that black blobs begin to appear before his eyes. But it's working. The space between the ute and the bank is growing and at last, her head is visible. She's gasping and gulping. Which means she's alive.

With relief, he relaxes.

And she screams.

The sound reminds him of the sound of a weaner lamb when it's first taken from its mother — a haunting, strangled sound filled with pain and horror. He realises that the car has swung around and slammed her against the bank, crushing her.

Again, he pushes outwards with his legs. His muscles twitch and tremble and he thinks he might pass out, but he just keeps pushing his feet against the car.

He's unaware that people have arrived on the bank above. He doesn't realise that they're sliding down the mud wall to assist him. His eyes close and his brain stops working. But every muscle in his strong little body is locked tight as he holds himself like a stiff iron rod, holding the space Willis needs to survive.

Only after Willis has been pulled free and dragged over the top of the bank does he let his body go limp. He's barely aware of the sounds of her screams, or of being lifted back up onto the bank and wrapped in a blanket and held in someone's arms. He's too exhausted to even open his eyes.

CHAPTER 22

Asleep, Cass looks like a little angel — an angel by the name of Sophie McKenzie, perhaps — and it takes effort for Mina to turn her eyes back to the road. Only minutes earlier, her daughter had been the she-devil, screaming threats and *I hate you*s as she twisted around in her seat to watch Jamie disappearing into the distance. Mina had been terrified she would do something stupid like grab the steering wheel, or jump out the window, and in an effort to deflect her fury, she had tossed her her iPhone.

'I found it by the side of the road. The glass is cracked but otherwise, I think it'll be okay,' she had said, biting back the urge to ask why the phone had been on the side of the road in the first place and to give her a lecture on how much the damn thing had cost.

Cass's startled blue eyes had widened and she stopped screaming long enough to switch it on.

'How did you find it?'

'I used the "Find my Friends" app.' Thank goodness, Mina thought. If it wasn't for the app, she would never have known where to find her.

But Cass wasn't thankful.

'You have no right spying on me,' she had screamed. Then she had tried and tried to call her father, her friends, then triple zero, not seeming able to understand that her efforts were fruitless because there was no reception this deep in the valley.

Mina was hurt by Cass's behaviour. She had wanted a chance to explain her actions to her daughter, but Cass was too exhausted and out of control to reason with, so she had remained quiet.

Now, thankfully, she is asleep. Looking just like a perfect, grubby little angel who makes Mina want to sob uncontrollably.

Mina checks her rear-view mirror. No-one seems to be following them. She exhales slowly in an effort to calm herself. Shit! What a mess!

Lying to the police about Jamie and the DVO had been a terrible thing to do, but what choice did she have? She couldn't have risked being seen talking to him. Her stomach twists as she recalls the sight of him across the carpark — lost and confused — not unlike the way he'd looked all those years ago, as a ten-year-old boy. But then ... her eyes had drifted from him ... to the other faces in the crowd. Jamie must have seen her stiffen. He'd known she was about to run even before the notion had fully formed inside her own head and he'd started to sprint towards her, desperate to stop her taking his daughter from him once again.

Her mind drifts back to when she'd first known him — such a funny, sad, wilful little kid. She'd been only a girl herself. A girl called Willy. Willis. When she'd first arrived on Moonbroch Station, she'd been so filled with hope that it would be the start of a different kind of life for her that she'd changed her name. From the moment she'd stepped down from Moira Tanning's car, she'd fallen in love with the place. And, of course, there was Jamie. She'd adored him right away. His intensity. His humour. The way he took everything she said so literally. His kindness towards her.

But she'd been naïve back then, thinking she could escape her place in the world. She shudders as she recalls the events that led to her accident in the flooded creek. How she had nearly drowned. The terrible shock of the ute slamming her against the bank. And the pain as they lifted her free. She remembers lying on the stretcher waiting to be taken away by the flying doctor and Jamie being so upset because he thought she was going to die. It hadn't seemed fair. He didn't deserve to have to deal with more death. So she had promised him she would live. It was the only promise she made back then that she had managed to keep.

She spent the months following the accident in the PA hospital in Brisbane and, even though the staff were wonderful, she remembers it as a time of great loneliness.

She smiles as she recalls one particular wardsman called Warren. The first day he came to take her to rehab, he had studied her name at the top of her chart — Wilhelmina — for several moments before saying, 'Where'd you get a name like that?' And when she told him her mother had named her after a Princess, he had said he couldn't pronounce such a big word and was just going to have to call her Princess Mina, if that was alright with her. After that, whenever he came with his wheelchair, he said, 'Morning, Princess Mina. How's the bravest girl in the world today?' and before she knew it, all the staff had started calling her Mina as well.

She had few visitors. The police came twice to ask her questions about how Aggie and Onfro had ended up in the creek and she told them she had no memory of anything that happened prior to her accident.

Her mother came up from Sydney, her crazy eyes flicking suspiciously at every long curtain and passing stranger. One month after that visit, her mother finally got her hands on enough medication to take her own life and set herself free from her demons. So, while Mina was struggling to recover from the accident, she was also grieving the loss of her only family member. Or, perhaps, she'd been grieving for something she'd never had in the first place.

One day, a woman she had never met turned up on her ward asking to speak to her. Even before they were introduced, she knew it was Jamie's mother, Sue McKenzie. Mina was giddy with hope that the woman had come to say thank you for minding Jamie, or sorry about the accident, or to tell her how Jamie was doing — he hadn't answered any of her letters. In fact, she hadn't heard a thing since leaving the station.

But the visit didn't turn out as she hoped. Mina's mouth twists at the painful memory.

'You've been sending letters to my son,' the woman said in an accusatory tone.

'Yes.'

Mina had promised Jamie she would write and had already posted him four letters. But with Mrs McKenzie standing sternly by her hospital bed she felt as if, by writing those letters, she had committed a crime.

'You need to understand,' Sue McKenzie had said, scrunching a tissue nervously in her right palm, 'Jamie is deeply traumatised. So much so that he has suppressed all memory of what happened while you were there. His father and I have talked about it and we think it best if you to stay out of his life. We want you to stop sending the letters.'

'Has Jamie received my letters?'

'We've not shown them to him. As I've said, we don't think it's for the best.'

'But I promised him I would write.'

'I'm asking you. Begging you. Please just leave him be. We've been through enough.'

Mina had wanted to scream. What about me? What about what I've been through? What about what's best for me?

Instead, she'd said, 'I won't write any more letters.'

What was the point in doing anything else? What was the point in trying to keep promises? It was unlikely she'd ever see Jamie McKenzie again, so what did it matter?

Her only other visitor was Ray. He moved to Brisbane and visited her nearly every day, lolling about on the end of her bed until one of the nurses told him it was time to leave or when Warren came to wheel her to rehab. They agreed they were no longer girlfriend and boyfriend — after all, her pelvis was so badly broken, she wasn't available for sex and she was in no fit state to go out on the town with him, either.

Occasionally, he offered her drugs, saying his stuff was better than the piss-weak junk the doctors prescribed, but mostly, he cheered her up with his funny jokes and thought-ful gifts and ridiculous attempts to flirt with the nurses. On reflection, even then, she knew he wasn't a good person. But how could she have let him go? She *had* no-one else.

So, she did whatever she thought necessary to get him to stick around — she soothed his complaints with flattery and always tried to win his approval by being upbeat and amus-ing. One day, thinking he would find the story hilarious, she told him that the ghostly sounds of Sophie McKenzie in the shearing shed that night had, in fact, been made by Jamie below the floorboards tapping on a waterpipe. She laughed as she told him, her eyes glistening with amusement. But Ray hadn't thought it funny. He stormed out and stayed away for a week.

When he eventually did come back to the hospital, he insisted on knowing what had happened after he left, in-cluding how Onfro and Aggie had ended up in the creek, and after making him promise never to tell anyone, she told him, only changing the detail about Jamie clubbing Onfro with the chunk of wood. In the version she gave Ray, it was her, not Jamie, who had swung that wood against the back of Onfro's head. She needed Ray in her life. Telling him she hit Onfro with the wood was an act of contrition — a way of saying sorry for laughing at him. Why did she lie about who had swung the wood? She wasn't sure. She might have been trying to protect Jamie or, more likely, she might have been trying to win Ray's approval by making herself out to be a tough girl who fights back against men like Onfro.

There had been two consequences of her loose lips. The first was that she had given Ray the knowledge he needed to control her. She had wrapped that knowledge in pretty paper and put a bow on top, meaning that, never again could she safely go against him, disagree with him or dis-please him; because if she did, he would go to the police and tell them what she had done. Which, according to Ray, was to commit murder. Whenever there was a story on the news about a person who had been arrested years, or even decades, after committing murder, he'd call her up to check she'd seen it.

'You'll never be free from what you did, Willy,' he once told her. 'Because you were eighteen at the time, you'll go to jail for sure if you're ever found out. But don't worry. I won't tell anyone.'

He was clever. He knew exactly how to create chaos with her peace of mind. At one time, before she had Cass, she decided that jail might actually be preferable to having him in her life. But once Cass came along, going to jail and being separated from her precious daughter was never going to be an option.

The second consequence of her loose lips had been that she had turned Ray's mild dislike of a ten-year-old boy into an obsessive hatred that had not lessened with time.

'What's it *feel* like to kill another person?' he'd asked her one day, while he was slouched in the beige vinyl chair next to her hospital bed with his hairy feet up on her mattress. Thankfully, the woman from the neighbouring bed was in rehab at the time and no-one was around to hear him.

When she didn't answer right away, he continued. 'I've been thinking I might try it myself. See what it's like.'

'Kill someone?' Despite her pain, she'd grabbed the hand grip that swung on a chain above her bed and pulled herself into a sitting position. 'Ray, you can't be serious.'

He had grinned at her and shrugged. 'Why not?'

'Because …' Surely, he was only joking. Feeling foolish, she'd attempted to laugh it off. 'Don't say stuff like that, you idiot.'

'I'm serious.'

'All right, then. Who?'

'Does it matter?'

'Ray, it's not funny. You're talking about killing someone you've never met just for the hell of it? You're talking about taking another person's life. A real person.'

He would have been aware of the tightness around her mouth and the shininess in her eyes, but that was exactly why he was saying such horrid things. He wanted her to feel upset. He had rolled his eyes towards the ceiling for at least five seconds, as if deep in thought, before looking unblinkingly into her eyes. 'I'm not talking about some random off the street, Willy. I'm talking about that kid. Jamie McKenzie.'

And her brain had exploded. Cold steel had run like blades through her veins and she had battled to hold his stare. Keep a neutral face. She even smiled.

'I don't care what happens to him,' she'd said, 'but I reckon you're better off picking someone you *don't* know. Otherwise, they might figure out it was you.'

'I'll be careful. No-one'll know it was me.'

'How can you be sure?'

'Because, I'll be patient. I'll wait until everyone else has forgotten all about Moon-fucking-broch and that little shit who is responsible for smashing up my girlfriend's body. I'll wait until everyone else has forgotten I ever met him.'

He'd clapped his hands sharply together an inch from her face. 'And then that little bastard'll get what he deserves.'

'Why not kill the bank manager lady,' she'd said, her voice unavoidably whiney. 'You're always going on about how that bitch owes you money, so why not her?'

She'd hated herself for throwing Moira Tanning under the bus, but she'd have done anything to distract him from Jamie.

'Shit you're dumb, Willy. People would suspect me more if I bumped her off and anyway, I'm not goin' to kill someone who still owes me money, am I?'

He'd bounced onto his feet then, making like he was about to leave, but at the door, he turned back.

'You like that fucking kid more than you like me, don't you?'

'No. I —'

'Yeah. You do.'

'Ray. Stop being a dick. You know I'll never see Jamie again for as long as I live so what difference does it make whether I like him or not.'

He'd returned to the beige vinyl chair and sat forward with his elbows on his knees and his chin resting on cupped hands.

'Promise me,' he'd said, quietly.

'Promise you what?'

'That you'll never see him again.'

She remembers she stuck out her chin as if in defiance and said, 'Okay. I will.'

'I want to hear you say it properly. I want to hear you say you won't ever see or speak to him again for as long as you both shall live.'

'I promise I'll not see or speak to Jamie McKenzie ever again for as long as we both shall live,' she'd said, then she'd closed her eyes as though she was asleep and willed him to leave.

Mina glances across at her sleeping daughter and remembers the day she had explained to Cass that she and Jamie were never actually a couple and that Cass was an IVF baby.

'If you had a choice of fathers,' Cass had asked, 'why'd you pick him?'

'I wanted to know that the person who fathered my child was someone with a good heart,' she'd said. 'Someone who is kind and intelligent.'

She takes a steadying breath and allows herself to remember the first time she saw Jamie as an adult. A Sunday. She had been walking along the river in St Lucia, near the university, where some students were playing rugby, when suddenly, this ball had come flying out of nowhere. Instinctively, she caught it and was about to throw it back when this young man had run right up to her, apologising.

Mina swallows, remembering the crashing turmoil she'd felt upon coming face-to-face with Jamie McKenzie after more than a decade. At first, she'd not been able to see past the child he'd once been — the difficult, funny, wild, grieving little boy who had once called her Willis when everyone else was calling her Willy. The little boy who had saved her life.

Jamie had abandoned his rugby game and walked with her along the river's edge until they came to a park bench, where they sat down and talked. He told her he was in the final year of an engineering degree and that his parents still lived on Moonbroch. She told him about her work at the National Bank and about her marriage and divorce. Then he brought up the topic of the accident, saying how sorry he was that she'd been so badly injured and how responsible he'd always felt. He asked if she had fully recovered from her injuries. No-one had ever shown so much interest or concern about what, to her, had been a momentous time in her life. When she became too emotionally strangled to answer his big questions, he broke them into smaller, more specific questions … about her shattered pelvis, her rehab, and learning to walk again. That's how he found out about her deep longing to have a child and her inability to conceive naturally. He took the time to ask the right questions and to listen to her — and by doing so, she was able to slowly replace the boy she'd once known with the man he had become.

After that first meeting by the river, they had met twice more. She never asked him outright to be her sperm donor and he never directly offered. The decision had simply evolved organically during their conversations, as if it was the most natural thing in the world.

Despite the ease with which she and Jamie had reconnected, she didn't reveal all of herself to him. She didn't share the desolation she felt when his mother had struck her from his life, for example. And, of course, she didn't mention Ray's dark presence in her life.

With his usual uncanny timing, Ray had arrived in Brisbane for a visit just days after she and Jamie had been to the fertility clinic in Spring Hill, bouncing energetically on the balls of his feet, attempting to disguise his cruel nastiness as fun and friendship, and fooling no-one but himself.

What if Jamie had tried to contact her while Ray was in town? If Ray ever found out that she'd been in contact with Jamie McKenzie, or worse, that Jamie had donated sperm so that she could try for a child, he'd go bat-shit crazy. If he even suspected she had a single thought in her head about Jamie McKenzie, her life could have become extremely complicated, really fast. It wasn't worth the risk; so she had sent Jamie that awful text asking him to stay out of her life. She'd been surprised at how much it had hurt to send that text. It had hurt like hell. Because she had wanted to keep him around.

Mina glances over her shoulder before merging with the traffic on the Ipswich Motorway. Not much further.

She'll definitely need to call Jamie and try to explain everything once she gets Cass to safety. Despite the threats Ray once made against him when she had been in the hospital, she's confident that Jamie is not in immediate danger. Ray's not stupid. He's not going to do anything after people have seen him in Goomburra. He never acts rashly, or in anger. His abuse is always strategic and considered. Besides, Ray's the kind of guy who gets his thrills from intimidating women and children. When he had talked about killing Jamie all those years ago, Jamie had been a child. Now he is an adult and Ray is far too cowardly to take on a grown man.

Frustrated, she bangs her palm against the steering wheel. It isn't Jamie that Ray is after. It's Cass.

She glances across at Cass whose head is lolling against the window glass. She'll be damned if she lets that creep anywhere near her daughter.

'Over my dead body, Ray,' she mutters.

Cass is woken by the sound of her mother arguing with someone on the phone. Most likely her father. She sits upright, pushes her hair off her face and gazes around. They're parked in the outside carpark next to the apartments.

'What's going on?' she asks.

'We've got to get you cleaned up, grab some things, and get out of here,' her mother says, climbing out of the car. 'I'll explain later.'

Cass freezes. Her mother's behaviour is both irrational and frightening.

'Cass. Come on. There's no time.'

Still half asleep, she follows her mother inside.

'Take a shower,' her mother says, 'while I pack some things.'

In a daze, Cass strips off her filthy clothes, drops them onto the bathroom floor and climbs under the shower. She leans her head back and closes her eyes so that the water cascades over her face. It feels so good. She could stay here forever.

'Hurry,' her mother says, poking her head through the door. 'I need you to pack enough clothes for a few days.'

Cass wraps a towel around herself, goes into her bedroom, dries off and pulls on some shorts and a t-shirt. The outfit is horrible but all the stuff she likes is back in the spare room at her father's place. Which is where *she* should be right now. If she was there, they'd probably be at the kitchen table eating a late breakfast — pancakes most likely, and orange juice — and laughing about what happened on their bushwalk, and she'd be feeling totally happy. Instead, she's being yelled at by the scary person pretending to be her mother. She sits down on the edge of the bed and begins to clean the dirt out from underneath her finger nails.

'Cass. What are you doing? I need you to —'

She glares at her mother. 'You can't make me go with you.'

'I'll explain everything in the car. Just hurry. Please.'

'I'm not going.'

Her mother's sense of urgency is terrifying, and she has no idea why she's acting so weird. Does she want them to leave the apartment so her father can't find them? Does she want to punish him for what happened in the forest?

What if he comes looking for her, and she's not here?

Her mother looks at her watch. 'We don't have time for this, Cass. Please. You're just going to have to trust me.'

'I said, I'm not going.'

She folds her arms, ready for battle.

'Cass. Please.'

'I want to see my father. You can't stop me from seeing him. I have rights.'

'This is nothing to do with your father.'

It *is* about her father. She's sure of it. Just like last time when she was allowed to go to the coast with him but then she wasn't allowed to see him again for *two* years. It's not fair. Who does her mother think she is? Always trying to control everything. Always saying when she can and can't see him.

She jumps to her feet and begins to shovel the contents of her wardrobe into a bag. Tears are backed up behind her eyes and she has to bite down on the inside of her bottom lip to stop them from falling.

'There is a man who wants to hurt you. He was in Goomburra, which is why we had to take off the way we did.'

Cass spins angrily towards her mother and screams into her face. 'You are making things up. You are a liar. I hate you.'

'Please. Cass.'

'No. I'm not going with you. I want to go back to *my father.*'

She doesn't see her mother's hand, but she feels its sting as it slaps her face. Warmth radiates from the place of impact and spreads down her throat. No-one has ever hit her before. She stands, slips her feet into her old Havaianas, picks up the bag of clothes and walks out of the bedroom.

'I'll be staying at a friend's place until Dad can pick me up,' she says with ice-cold restraint.

'Wait.'

Cass turns back and studies her mother's pale face. Her bright, teary eyes. Her shaky lips. Her mother has been the only constant in her life. The only person who has always been there for her. But she could have had a father, too, if her mother had allowed it. He wouldn't have stayed away all these years on purpose. He loves her too much to do that.

'Cass. I didn't mean to hit you. I'm so sorry.'

Cass stays silent, unable to decide what to feel — sympathy or contempt.

'I did it because I care so much about you. Everything I do is because I love you so much. You must know that.' Tears dampen her cheeks and her usually sleek blonde hair has slipped from its clasp.

Cass hitches the bag higher onto her shoulder.

'Then you shouldn't have stopped me from seeing my father,' she says, and she walks out the door.

CHAPTER 23

The volunteer makes Jamie uncomfortable. He's grateful to the guy for driving him home, but now, he wishes he would leave. He wants to get his phone on the charger and call Mina to find out what the hell is going on and why she had snatched Cass from Goomburra in such spectacular fashion. The last thing he needs to be doing is cooking breakfast for a stranger.

They enter the house via the unlocked back door. Jamie drops his keys on top of the fridge, opens the fridge door and is pouring two glasses of orange juice when the man's phone begins to vibrate. Smiling, the man holds the phone up for Jamie to see, then ducks away towards the lounge room. Even though the man keeps his voice low, Jamie is disturbed to hear the half-joking, half threatening way the man speaks to his caller.

The man doesn't return to the kitchen as Jamie expected him too after the call is finished. Is he snooping about the house? Irritated, he sets the glasses of juice on the table and goes to find him, stopping by the study nook to put his phone on the charger. The man is in the lounge room, standing by the bookshelf, leaning forward with his hands behind his back studying the photo of Sophie.

'Here you are,' Jamie says, trying not to sound too sharp.

'Pretty girl,' the visitor says, nodding at the picture.

'My sister.'

The man nods. 'Sophie.'

'You … um?'

The man turns. 'You don't remember me, do you?'

Jamie has no clue who he is, and his only cognitive thought is that he doesn't give a rat's arse who the guy is. He wants him to leave.

'Mate. If you don't mind, I really need to —' Jamie begins to say, but he's interrupted.

'They really do look a lot alike, don't they?' the man says, picking up the framed photo and continuing to study Sophie's face, seemingly oblivious to Jamie's irritation.

'Who?'

'Your sister and Cass.'

'Cass?'

'The girl you were just with in the forest. Remember her?' He uses a slow drawl, as if he's speaking to a dim-witted person. 'Blonde hair? Long legs? Saucy little number that one, just like her mother was at that age.' He licks his lips.

Who speaks about a twelve-year-old child like that? Or any woman, for that matter? Jamie is so annoyed by the man he clenches his fists.

'Look, mate. I really don't think …' Jamie stutters, stepping forward, intending to take back the picture frame with Sophie's photo.

'Ha,' the man says, tossing the picture onto the couch, leaping back and bringing up own fists as if expecting a fight. He jabs at the air a few times while springing from foot to foot like a boxer. Dumbfounded by the man's comical performance, Jamie stares.

'Nah. Fuck. I ain't gonna fight ya,' the man says, dropping his fists and grinning so that Jamie can't help but notice his bad teeth. 'It's Willy I'm mostly mad at. She's the one who's done the wrong thing here.'

Willy? WILLY? Without warning, Jamie's world suddenly becomes a whirring vortex, spinning and spinning, out of control, back and back through time. Back to … He staggers sideways and lowers himself onto the recliner.

'I might have forgotten to tell you my name,' the man says, stepping forward and offering Jamie his hand. 'Name's Ray.'

Memories, long suppressed, unfurl inside Jamie's mind. Memories of a mean, dark-haired boy who once came to Moonbroch. A boy who looked like a character from one of Sophie's books.

Ratboy!

'Here. Drink this.'

While Jamie has been sitting forward with his head in his hands for the past five minutes waiting for his world to stop spinning and hoping that the tumble of his thoughts will soon coalesce into something that makes sense to him, Ray has been busy in the kitchen. He now stands over Jamie offering a mug of thick, black coffee. Jamie accepts the beverage with shaky hands.

'Your big night might have caught up with you, mate,' he says. 'I recommend you drink some coffee and go have a lie down.' He holds up his own mug. 'I'll drink this and get on my way. Got things to be doing down in Brisbane today. People to see.'

Jamie stares at the scrawny character. 'Why are you here, Ray? What has any of this got to do with you?'

Ray sits and blows onto the surface of his coffee.

'I don't get what you mean?' he says. 'This has everything to do with me. Me and Willy have been friends since the day dot and if her kid goes missing, obviously I'm going to pitch in and help to find her. That's all I'm doing. Just tryin' to help. Can you imagine my surprise when I hear the brat's gone off with some bloke who's calling himself her father? Well, you know, I have to wonder ...'

Jamie looks up sharply.

'I am her father,' he says.

Ray shakes his head and smiles. 'Yeah, well that's not what I heard. You see, the story Willy gave me was that you were just a sperm donor and apart from that, you never had nothin' to do with her or the brat. But you'd let me know if that wasn't the case and the bitch is lying to me, wouldn't you?'

The last thing Jamie wants is to create trouble for Mina and Cass. There is something deeply disturbing and dangerous about this man, so he shakes his head and says, 'No. She's telling the truth. I haven't seen her ... well only the once really, since I was a boy.'

And he realises that that is almost the truth of it. Since she left Moonbroch, and even though they are parents of a beautiful daughter together, he's seen her face-to-face a total of only five times — not counting today.

Ray slaps the palms of his hands against his thighs.

'That's what I thought. What I don't understand is why the brat's been staying with you? What's *that* all about?'

Jamie clears his throat. 'I actually have no idea. Mina might have been having a tough time lately and needed a break … so she called me up out of the blue and asked me to take her.'

He hates speaking to Ray about Mina and Cass. The last thing in the world he wants is for Cass to be mixed up with someone like him and he can't believe that Mina is still friends with the man after all these years — or that she would let him anywhere near their daughter. The muscles in his jaw begin to ache.

'You don't reckon I'm good enough for her, do you?' Ray says.

Jamie brushes his hand over his hair. 'I don't even know you.'

'You're dead right,' Ray says, his voice edged with belligerence. 'There's a lot you don't know. I mean, where were you when Willy was lying in that hospital bed for all those months? Or when she was struggling to learn to walk again? And where were you when she was dealing with the fact that her own mother had topped herself? Or when she got married? And divorced? Your stuck-up family walked away from her and pretended you never even knew her.' He puts his coffee down on a slightly wobbly side table so that a little sloshes over the side. Then he stands. 'You know what your mother did, don't you?'

Jamie swallows and stares mutely at Ray who has begun to pace. 'She went to Willy's hospital bed and told Willy to stay away from the McKenzies. Said none of you wanted anything further to do with her. After all she done for your family, your lot turned their backs on her when she needed you most.'

Tiny droplets of spit are spraying from Ray's mouth as he speaks.

'I was the one who stuck by that girl through thick and thin. I was the only person who showed up, day after day, and held her hand through all those surgeries and all that rehab. I was the one who went to her mother's pauper's funeral in Sydney because Willy was too broken to get out of bed. I'm the one who's always been there for her.'

Ray sits back down opposite Jamie and takes a slurp of his coffee. 'But nothing I ever did was good enough for her. Once she'd met you, I was dead to her. She was always going on about it, saying Jamie did this or Jamie said that. Isn't Jamie cute? It nearly did my head in.'

Jamie's arms fold across his chest.

'I thought she'd gotten over it and moved on,' Ray continues. 'Like, she got married to some loser for a while, poor bastard, but it only lasted long enough for her to get her hands on a real nice apartment. That's the thing with Willy, you know. She's selfish. Always looking out for number one.' He sits forward. 'You seen her place? Nice. Wouldn't mind a place like that myself, one day.'

Mina had not moved into that apartment until Cass was four years old — long after she had divorced her husband. And the apartment belonged to Jamie, not Mina nor her ex-husband. Jamie had bought it so that Cass would have somewhere decent to live. But he's not about to tell Ray any of that or point out the flaws in his timeline. As Ray talks, it becomes increasingly obvious to him that Ray is not the constant, supportive friend to Mina he likes to think he is. What Jamie can't understand is why Mina even puts up with him.

'Anyway, the marriage was over,' Ray continues, fidgeting with Sophie's photo. 'Willy's living the good life in this flash apartment and next thing I know, she's preggo. Can you believe it? The slut gets pregnant.'

Jamie squirms in his seat and scuffs his hiking boots against the carpet. It's excruciating for him to have to listen to this egotistical bastard talk about Mina in this way — he'd rather smash his face to a pulp — but he needs to try and figure out what Ray is up to. What's his end game? And, what's his interest in Cass? So, he forces himself to stay calm and pretend to be interested in Ray's version of Mina's life — a version, he suspects, has little resemblance to reality.

Ray laughs. 'I'm like … huh? How the hell can you get pregnant if you can't even get laid? A nurse at the hospital explained it to me once, you know, about how she couldn't do it any more … because of her injuries.' He waves his hand casually over his crotch. 'I mightn't have been an A-grade student, but I do know *quite a lot* about the birds and the bees. 'Specially about the birds, if you know what I mean. Anyway, turns out the silly bitch had gone and gotten IVF which is where some doctor sticks this needle thing up there and injects her full of a man's —'

Jamie can't listen to any more. He springs to his feet, mutters something about needing to use the bathroom, and walks out of the room. Shit! What the hell? Ray is not the kind of person he wants hanging around his daughter. And why does he keep pawing Sophie's photo the way he does? What's Sophie got to do with any of it?

'So, I asked her who the father was, you know. No big deal. I was just taking an interest and all. And she said she didn't know.'

Jamie's pants are down, he's sitting on the toilet needing to take a shit and Ray is right outside the door, still talking. Shit!

'You don't get to meet the fathers, she told me. And I was fine with that, you know. Jeez. I didn't give a flying fuck who the guy was so long as she was happy. But the bitch is a pathological liar. Can't help herself. All along, she knew who it was. For years, she's been laughing behind my back, thinking I'm the world's biggest loser for not knowing who the ankle-biter's father is. Treating me like a piece of shit.'

Jamie hears the man's fist bang against the wall outside the bathroom and decides he needs to put his own needs on hold, go out there and force this creep from his house. He flushes the toilet as a way of warning, hoping Ray will back away, then opens the door.

'So, what I need to find out is —' Ray says, blocking his path to the kitchen, '— did you know you were the father? Right from the start, did you know?'

'You need to back away,' Jamie says in his sternest voice, holding a palm in front of Ray's face. 'Back away and leave my house, or I'll have to call the police.'

And he's shocked by the sound that explodes from Ray's toothy mouth.

'Now there's a good idea,' Ray says, staggering back into the kitchen, holding his sides laughing. 'I'm all for calling the police and telling them about our dear little Willy's evil past. I'd be curious to see what happens to that sweet kid of hers once Willy's been given a life sentence and dragged off to jail. What do you reckon would happen to the kid? Do you reckon they'd give custody to a sperm donor who she barely knows? More likely little Cass would be sent to live with me, don't you think? Me being an old friend of the family who's been around since the day dot.'

By the time Jamie has picked his jaw up off the kitchen floor, Ray is gone.

CHAPTER 24

Cass hears the door of the fire escape click closed and knows that her mother is looking for her. She can't bear to have anything to do with her mother right now — she's way too upset — so, despite the stink, she slides her back down the bricks behind the industrial bins at the back of the apartment block, pulls her knees to her chin and wipes away her tears with the back of her hand.

Growing up, her mother was always the centre of her universe — the two of them against the world. At night, instead of watching television, she would often snuggle against her mother and beg for a story; and her mother would make up vivid tales about evil antagonists seeking to harm beautiful young heroines. The characters changed — princesses, orphans, gypsies, pirates, government spies, ghosts — but the theme was always the same. There was always a bad guy chasing after a little girl and the girl always won in the end. When her mother had said they needed to leave the apartment because a man was coming to hurt her, Cass's heart had sunk. Does her mother think Cass is the heroine in one of her made-up stories? Is her mother starting to get stories mixed up with real life the same way her grandmother had once done? Cass has never met her mother's mother — she killed herself before Cass was born — but she knows that she suffered from a mental illness. Maybe her mother has a mental illness too. Maybe she'll end up killing herself as well.

Or is she just pretending so she can keep Cass away from her father?

Cass thumps her forehead a few times, trying to clear her thoughts. What is she going to do? She visualises her pale canvas backpack swaying gently from the branches of the strong little tree that sticks out from the cliff in Goomburra. Inside that backpack is her wallet, so she has no money.

But she does have her iPhone.

She pats her empty pocket. Damn. She must have left it in the car. She pushes herself upright and wanders around the side of the building to the outside carpark where her mother parked. All the doors of their car are locked. Cupping her hands, she peers through the tinted glass and can see the phone, half concealed between the passenger seat and the centre console. The thought of breaking the window with a rock crosses her mind but she's interrupted by the ping of the apartment elevator.

Quickly, she drops into a crouch behind another car where she can see the weirdly dishevelled woman who emerges. Cass barely recognises her own mother, who looks cautiously left and right before walking quickly across to the car, using the automatic unlock on her keys as she approaches. She opens the driver's door, reaches inside and retrieves Cass's iPhone. Then she walks back inside the building.

Part of Cass wants to run after her mother, wrap her arms around her and beg her not to go mad. Not to kill herself. But ... what if her mother takes her away and she never gets to see her father again. She had realised out in the forest that she loves her father, and he loves her. No-one is going to stop her from having him in her life. Ever again.

After three steadying breaths, she emerges from behind the car. With her unique, leggy grace, she slings her bag over her shoulder and slips into the back laneway that leads to Coro Drive, crosses at the lights and takes the bike path to the river.

A honeyeater fusses about in the shrubs along the river bank and out on the chocolate-milk coloured water, a City-Cat glides silently by. She crinkles her nose at the musty mud smell and squints her eyes against the glare. It's hot by the river. Her sunglasses are with her wallet. Lost in Goomburra.

Where will she go? Three of her school friends live within walking distance of the apartment but they're all away for the summer. It's always been the same. You hang out with them all year but come summer, everyone has somewhere better to be. And she doesn't have aunties and cousins like normal people. Her mother has no family and she's never met her father's family. How good would it be to have a big family instead of just a mother and a father?

She frowns, confused by the strange relationship between her parents — Mina Johnson and Jamie McKenzie. They don't act like they hate each other … yet they surely must.

A MAMIL — middle-aged-man-in-lycra — tings his bike bell and dodges around her. She turns right and begins to walk towards the Toowong Shopping Centre.

She thinks about being in the Goomburra forest with her father. It had felt so real. And good. Him and her. He'd been so great, the way he talked her into climbing up that cliff. By the time they'd walked back into the carpark together, she'd felt taller. Stronger. Almost invincible. And all those people had been there for them. For her.

Even Winter! She smiles, feeling unbelievably pleased that Winter had followed her to Goomburra and sorry that she hadn't gotten to say good-bye to her. She's probably home by now, and …

'I know where she lives,' Cass says out loud.

When she'd first got Winter's note, she'd Googled the address and discovered that Winter's house was just up the hill from the Vietnamese restaurant in Paddington — close enough for Cass to walk to.

Between calling Cass's friends, most of whom are away for the summer, Mina has been scratching at the skin on her wrists, leaving angry red streaks. She can feel her cheeks flaming red as well, flushed from the embarrassment of having to call people she doesn't know and admit that her daughter has run off, again, and begging them to contact her immediately should Cass turn up on their doorstep. Last time Cass had run off, she'd hidden out at her friend Sara's house and Mina had driven the streets for hours looking for her; then, when she'd been on the verge of calling the police, Cass had walked back into the apartment, cool as an ice princess, as though nothing was amiss. Now, she's taken flight again and her timing couldn't be worse. Shit! She's so mad she could strangle her.

Because she's been using Cass's phone, Mina almost misses the call that comes through on her own. *Lee Kelly National Bank*. It's the fake name she uses to hide Jamie McKenzie in her contacts.

'Hello?' she says cautiously in case Ray has Jamie's phone.

'Mina?'

'Jamie. I'm so sorry.'

'Are you okay? Is Cass alright?'

'Yes. No.' Tears immediately begin to flood her eyes. It's been so long since anyone asked if she was okay.

'You're okay?'

'Yes.'

'Cass isn't?'

'She … we had a fight and she's run off. I don't know where she is.'

Mina can hear him breathing as he thinks over the situation. Quietly, he says, 'It'll be okay. I'm sure she won't have gone too far. Have you tried calling her friends?'

'Yes … but … Jamie, you don't understand.'

'I might understand a little more than you think. Ray's been here with me. He's just left.'

'Oh Jamie, did he hurt you?'

'No. But I'm worried about you and Cass. I'm fairly certain the little bastard is headed your way and you've probably got little over an hour before he arrives on your doorstep. He seems pretty mad, so you might want to clear out before he gets there.'

'That's what I was trying to do … but Cass wouldn't hear of it. She thought I was trying to get her away from you.'

Jamie has always been the kind of person who thinks before he speaks, and Mina taps her nails against the coffee table while she waits for him to respond. It should feel odd talking to him like this — after all, he's virtually a stranger to her — but it's actually the opposite. She feels safe talking to him.

'We might need to call the police,' he says. 'Are you okay with that? You could be in danger. Both of you could be in danger.'

'Jamie … I … of course. But can you come and get Cass and take her back to Toowoomba with you. It's where she wants to be, and she'll be better off with you.'

'Even if I leave right away, Ray'll get to you first.'

'I can handle Ray. Just come and get Cass. Okay?'

'Okay. I'm on my way.'

She hangs up before he can say anything more about calling the police because she really doesn't want to go down that road. Imagine being *that* person on the news whose whole miserable life is laid out for everyone to discuss and examine and judge. Imagine having to stand up in court and try to get people to like you; and what if she ends up in jail because of what happened on Moonbroch all those years ago? What would happen to Cass if she was sent to jail?

If she talks to the police, the fallout could last for years and she can't risk that. With Ray, it'll all be over and done within a few days and he'll be gone again.

She's handled Ray before — she's been *handling* Ray most of her life. As soon as Cass calms down and decides to come home, she'll send her back to Toowoomba with Jamie; and she'll stay here with Ray. At first, he'll humiliate and belittle her and she'll agree that she really is a stupid dumb lying bitch and that's she's always been a stupid dumb lying bitch. Next, he'll point out his many virtues and she'll say how lucky she is to have him in her life and how grateful she is for all that he's done for her. Then, within a few days, he'll get bored and leave — just like he does every time. He'll disappear back into that slimy hole out of which he's crawled, and she and Cass will be left alone to get on with their lives.

Flat on her back, she stretches out along the plush sofa and pulls a silky, mustard-coloured cushion over her face. She closes her eyes and tries to concentrate on her breath. In and out. In and out. It's a technique a psychologist once suggested might help keep her anxiety in check.

Her thoughts are whirring in such fast circles, she feels as if she's just stepped off a high-speed cup-and-saucer ride. All her bodily systems are urging her to take some kind of action. But what is there to do? She has to stay in the apartment for when Cass comes back, and she's already humiliated herself by calling the parents of all of Cass's friends and telling them about the fight — but not that she has slapped Cass's face, of course. They already must think she's a useless single parent who doesn't know how to raise a child and she doesn't want anyone reporting her to the child protection people. That would be the last straw.

So, what else is there to do except wait for Ray? Waiting for Ray is so much easier than trying to run from him. She'd run from him in Goomburra and what had that got her? A shitload of anxiety, a heart rate that's too high to be healthy, *and* she's turned into a crazy mother who hits her own child.

At least she knows he's coming this time, unlike yesterday when she'd opened the door and found him right outside — the shock of seeing him on her doorstep had damn near killed her, especially since it had been two years since she'd last seen him.

She stretches her toes and thinks back to yesterday.

'Gonna invite me in?' he'd said, before pushing his way past her into the apartment. Fumbling in his pocket, he'd pulled out a flattened pack of Marlborough cigarettes and a lighter, flopped onto the sofa, put his boots up on the coffee table, and lit up. He'd taken one long drag, then blew the smoke in a long, continuous stream up towards the ceiling. She'd set a small ceramic pot next to his feet for the ash and sat down opposite him. He'd seemed to be in a good mood.

'Coffee would be nice,' he'd said after about fifteen minutes of chatting about his recent adventures in Bali.

While she was in the kitchen making the coffee, he'd started pacing the apartment, picking up her decorative little knickknacks and putting them down in a slightly different place than before. Closer to the edges so they had a greater chance of toppling off and breaking. That kind of thing.

Breathe, she'd counselled herself. In and out. It'll be okay. Concentrate on your breath.

Then he'd picked up the framed photo of Cass from the mantle — a beautiful black-and-white photo Mina had had professionally shot on Cass's twelfth birthday — and her breath had caught in her throat. She'd flinched. And, of course, Ray noticed the change — it was what he'd been looking for — and his malicious, mean little mouth had twisted upwards as if to say, 'Gotcha!'

'I want to get to know your daughter, Willy,' he'd said. 'It's time I started having a little more influence in her life.'

Despite her trembling knees, Mina had forced a weak smile. 'Don't be silly, Ray. You can't stand kids. You've said so heaps of times. Whenever you visit, I've always had to send her away to stay with a friend.'

He'd tipped the white frame slightly this way and that in order to minimise the glare off the glass and get a better view of the picture.

'She ain't a kid anymore though, is she?' he'd said, still staring at Cass's face. 'I think it might be best if she has a man about the place who can start giving her some discipline, now she's grown up. Girls her age need discipline, you know. You never got any and look how you turned out.' He'd made a sharp laughing sound, like a hyena.

'You need to leave,' she'd said.

Hugging the picture against his chest, he'd sat back on the sofa and flicked ash towards the bowl. Most of it had blown away across the table.

'Ray. You're not welcome here. If you don't leave, I'll call the police.'

'No, you won't.' He'd laughed and flicked more ash. 'Jeez. I'm only trying to help.'

'I don't need your help.' She'd gripped the edge of the kitchen bench so tightly that her knuckles had been white.

He'd shaken his head in mock weariness. 'Willy, Willy, Willy. You need all the help you can get. What the hell would you know about being a parent? Especially to a girl this good looking. No. It's decided. I'm gonna move to Brisbane and start taking a bit more interest.' He'd gazed around the apartment living room. 'Might even move in here with you.'

With his cigarette butt smouldering in the bowl, he'd then grasped the frame in both hands and studied the picture with sickening intensity. A crease of concentration had come across his brow. And despite her instincts warning her to remain calm, she'd raced out from behind the kitchen peninsula and made a grab for it. But he was too quick. He'd rolled to his feet and held it out of her reach, like a child teasing his sibling.

'No,' he'd laughed, studying the picture with his shoulder blocking her. 'I ain't finished looking yet.'

Then …

'Ho-ly shit!'

She'd frozen, her heart beating like a viper in her chest.

'I know who this looks like!' he'd said.

Beaming with delight, he'd spun back towards her, allowing a giant-sized whiff of his decaying mouth to slam full-on into her face.

'It's that dead girl,' he'd said, bouncy on his feet. 'The girl out west we did the séance for. We sat hand in hand with her picture on the floor between us. I remember that picture. And then that little kid got under the floorboards and pretended to be her ghost?' There was no humour in his laugh. 'Scared the shit out of me, he did.'

'Ray. Stop it. Give it back.'

'But, Willy, can't you see how weird this is? Your daughter looks like a dead girl.'

He'd held the picture in his left hand and waved his right around like it was helping him think. 'How old were you back then? Eighteen? I remember, 'cause I'd gotten you that pair of Docs for your eighteenth birthday, hey? The ones with the purple laces. So how does this kid of yours end up looking the spitting image of a girl who died when you were only eighteen?'

His eyes had widened then, as though the solution to a puzzle had finally been revealed to him.

'Holy fuck!' he'd said, shaking his head in amazement. 'You used the dead girl's brother to father your child, didn't you? That little shit is the father of your child? Which is a bloody miracle given that you haven't seen him since he was ten years old. Unless … unless you've been lying to me this whole time.'

Mina had turned away so he couldn't see how rattled she'd become. She'd gone back into the kitchen and started to shovel instant coffee into two mugs.

'Willy, you had a child with the kid you were babysitting. Don't you think that's kind of fucked up, even for you?'

She'd willed back her tears. She'd tried to hold her poker face. But it was too late. Not only had Ray caught her out in one of her greatest lies to him — that she'd not seen or talked to Jamie McKenzie since he was ten years old — but he'd also, unwittingly, uncovered her greatest vulnerability. Her daughter.

She'd known in that instant that she was in serious trouble. What she hadn't counted on was that Ray would track down Jamie McKenzie, because she'd always considered him a words-no-action kind of guy. But this time, Ray had gone out of character and acted. And he had found Jamie.

What must he have thought when he'd discovered that Cass was with him?

She shoves the mustard-coloured cushion angrily from her face and sits up. The stupid breathing technique isn't working. Her thoughts won't stop. Her anxiety is out of control.

If she only had to worry about herself, she'd be fine. She'd become a leaf in the stream and just go with whatever Ray wanted, and when it was over, she'd dust herself off and get on with her life.

But now, after showing no interest in Cass for the first twelve years of her life, Ray has turned his eyes in that direction.

If anything happens to Cass … if anything happens to Cass … well, that will be the end of everything.

I'll do whatever it takes, she thinks. So long as Cass is safe.

Robotically, she stands and goes to unlock her front door. She opens it and peers up and down the empty hallway outside, then leaves the door ajar and returns to the sofa.

This way, Ray can walk right in when he gets here.

CHAPTER 25

Winter's house stands out from the sleek, renovated homes around it. It's an original on stilts and in need of a coat of paint. The front garden is choked full of long cooch grass with two hibiscus trees either side of a broken concrete path. Along the driveway, Cass can see that the back garden is an overgrown jungle.

Because of the blisters across the tops of her feet, she carries her Havaianas on her hands like paddles as she makes her way barefooted up the rickety front stairs onto a wide, shady verandah. The front door is old wood with a stained-glass panel and because there is no doorbell, Cass reaches out to knock on the wood. The door swings wide, showing her an inviting, polished, hardwood hall.

'Hello?' she calls, then a little louder. 'Winter?'

Her head is starting to ache. She feels dizzy and clammy, and needs a drink of water. As she leans against the door-frame and her eyes become accustomed to the lower light inside the house, she can see, about half way along the hall-way, a row of hooks holding a few hats, a large yellow cotton shirt and … a school bag. Same as her own. With soundless grace, she steps inside and goes to check out the bag. On the back is Winter's name, written in large, neat letters with a black marker. She has the right house.

'Winter? It's me, Cass.'

She carries on through a lounge room and into a bright, farm-style kitchen with an industrial-sized refrigerator. She finds a glass in a cupboard, fills it from the tap and tips the water down her parched throat in three gulps. After another glass, she finds a bathroom, then Winter's bedroom. The bed is an antique, iron-framed double covered with a patch-work quilt and, to Cass, it looks like the most irresistible bed she has ever seen.

But before she can lie down, she needs to let her mother know she's okay. Last time she'd run off like this and gone to Sara's place, her mother had nearly had a fit. She's already worried enough about her mother's mental state and she doesn't want to make it worse if she can help it.

There's a phone on the kitchen bench next to the fridge and while she knows her mother's number off by heart, it takes a few attempts to make the call because she's never used a landline phone before. When she finally gets it right, her mother answers immediately. She says only what needs to be said — that she's staying at a friend's place, she's okay and not to worry. Then she hangs up.

Less than a minute later, she's curled up on Winter's bed, asleep.

Jamie calls Mina from the carpark to let her know when he arrives at the apartment block, but her phone is busy, so he goes upstairs in the lift. Her apartment door is ajar.

He pushes it open a little further and calls, 'Mina? It's Jamie. Can I come in?'

'Hello, Jamie.'

Willis! No. Her name is Mina now, he reminds himself. He feels as though the ground below his feet has become unsteady and presses his hand against the wall to steady himself. Other than a distant glimpse in Goomburra, it's been such a long time since he's seen her. Her hair is still strikingly blonde. Even though it's slipped loose from a clasp at the back of her head, it's smoother than it used to be. She's very thin and tired around the eyes. How old would she be now? Forty-three? Forty-four?

'Come in,' she says.

'Is Ray here?'

'Not yet.' She holds up her phone. 'Cass just called to say she's staying the night at a friend's place and I wasn't to worry about her.'

'Really? Okay. Good.'

He follows Mina through to her living room and indicates the Myer shopping bag he's carrying.

'Cass's things,' he says, 'from my place. In case …'

Mina points to the end of the white leather sofa. 'Put it down there. She'll be wanting them to take back to Toowoomba.'

He puts the bag down and sits next to it. Mina sinks onto the sofa opposite and pulls the mustard-coloured cushion onto her lap. They have so much to say to each other, but for a few moments, Jamie is not capable of using words. He needs time to adjust to being back inside her space.

And something is troubling him about her. He'd expected to be greeted by a feisty and vibrant person, someone similar to the person she'd been as a teenager, and to a certain extent, as a younger woman. His mind goes back to those few happy days in his childhood when it had been just him and her alone on Moonbroch. She'd been so alive then. What had really captured him about her, he remembers, was the way she had moved — like a dancer. She was all fluid movement and grace. The person before him now is nothing like that. She's completely listless, as if all the verve and fight has drained away; and he can see red welts on her wrists where she's been scratching herself.

'Did Cass say who she was staying with?' he says eventually, sitting forward and knotting his fingers together in his lap.

'No. When I asked her to put me onto the friend's parents, she hung up and I couldn't call her back because it was a private number.'

He frowns. 'Did she sound okay?'

'She sounded … tired, I guess. Like she needs about twenty-four hours sleep.'

'What's your gut feeling? Do you think she's in a safe place?'

Mina shakes her head and fidgets with a thread on the cushion. 'I honestly don't know. She's done this kind of thing before. Run off and gone to a friend's place. If only we could call her; but her phone is here.'

'You said you'd called all her friends? What about the girl who was in Goomburra with her grandfather? The girl called Winter. Did you call her?'

'I don't know anyone called Winter,' Mina says, sitting up straighter. She reaches for Cass's phone on the coffee table. 'I'm certain there's no-one by that name in her contacts.'

While Mina checks through Cass's contacts, Jamie begins to feel around inside the Myer bag that's on the sofa next to him, and he pulls out a folded slip of paper.

'I found this note in the bedroom where Cass has been staying and it has Winter's number on it,' he says. 'Why don't I give it a call and if we don't get an answer, I think we should call the police.'

Fear for Cass's wellbeing is twisting knots in his gut, but he's trying to appear calm for Mina's sake because he's worried about the apathy in her tone of voice and the restlessness of her hands. It's as if she's about to lose the plot. Or lose her mind!

He's still fumbling in his pocket for his phone when Mina's phone begins to vibrate on the coffee table between them.

'It's Ray,' she says, looking at the screen on her phone. Her entire body becomes deathly still. 'I'll put it on speaker so you can hear.'

'Willy.' Ray's voice blasts into the room. 'How the fuck are you?'

Both Jamie and Mina frown at the sound of his voice which makes a strange echo as he speaks, then both turn to look towards the entrance to the apartment. Ray is there.

Jamie slips the paper with Winter's number into his pocket.

'Don't antagonise him,' Mina says with low and rapid urgency. 'Do whatever he says, and it'll be okay.'

He thinks her warning is as much for herself as for him.

Ray pushes the heavy front door closed and from where he's sitting, Jamie hears the lock click. Then, with his phone still held against his ear and a smile plastered across his tooth-deficient, rat-like face, Ray is walking down the wide hallway towards them. Slung onto one shoulder, he has a small black backpack. And in his spare hand is a black revolver.

'Don't tell me you've gone and lost our girl, Willy,' he says, slipping his phone into his pocket. 'I always said you weren't cut out for motherhood, didn't I? But don't stress. I happen to know her friend Winter quite well, so when I'm done here, I'll shoot over to her place and collect the brat for you. Okay?'

With the remote, he switches the television on and runs the volume to 15 — not loud enough to attract the neighbours' attention but enough, perhaps, to drown out other noises coming from inside the apartment. Then he flicks through the channels until he finds a black-and-white Western movie with men on horseback yelping and yahooing and firing guns at each other. The irony is not lost on Jamie as he studies the revolver in Ray's hand. The only thing he's ever had to do with firearms was on the station when he was a boy, and that was rifles, not revolvers. He guesses the one in Ray's hand is a Colt that's fitted with some kind of silencer.

'Come on, mate,' Jamie says, half standing and looking at the gun. 'I hardly think this is necessary.'

With lightning speed, Ray grabs his arm and twists it behind his back in a painful hold, and before Jamie can even begin to struggle, the revolver is pressed against his temple.

'Don't you fucking tell me what's necessary and what's not,' he growls.

The man is much more dangerous than Jamie had thought and he has no choice but to swallow his rage, shut his mouth, and do whatever Ray wants — which is to take a roll of silver duct tape, a pair of large scissors, and some rope from the backpack and go ahead of him into Mina's bedroom. What Jamie really wants to do is slam his fist into the bastard's face, but Ray is agile and wily and doesn't give him the opportunity.

'Lie on the bed,' Ray says to Mina.

Mina crawls onto the bed, then lies on her side and curls inwards. Her movements are completely passive and she keeps her eyes down. Nothing like the girl who had once taken a beating from a man called Onfro. There is no defiance. No outrage. No contempt. It's as if she's an emotionless machine going through a routine that she's had years to perfect. Watching her, he feels his blood turn to ice.

'On your back, slut,' Ray barks. Then, while he swings the gun around at them, he tells Jamie to secure her ankles and wrists with tape and truss her to the head and foot board with rope.

'Do it,' Mina mutters.

Jamie concentrates on the task, taking pains to be gentle and keep the tape loose so that she can work her hands and feet free. But Ray is having none of it.

'Do it properly,' he says, and fires a shot towards Mina's foot. The bullet misses and goes into the mattress.

'Put some tape across her lying mouth as well,' he says. 'She can fucking stay here and think about all the fucking lies she's ever told me.'

Waving the pistol wildly in Jamie's direction, Ray says for him to back away into the corner of the bedroom and spread his arms wide with his palms facing out from the wall.

'Stay like that and don't move, or I'll fucking kill you both,' he says, stroking the side of Mina's head with the gun. Next, he begins to gently stroke her inner thigh for a few moments before roughly thrusting his fingers inside her underwear. Disgusted by what Ray is doing, Jamie turns his head away, but not before seeing the loathing in Mina's eyes and the way she cringes from his touch.

'I can see how badly you want it, Willy,' Ray says, 'but you're going to be disappointed, I'm afraid. My taste is for something a bit younger and sweeter than you these days.'

He withdraws his fingers and rubs them under her nose. A tear traces a lonely path across her pale cheek.

Back in the living area, Ray has Jamie sit with his palms spread flat on the distressed wooden surface of the dining table. He sits opposite.

'Don't worry about her. She loves being treated rough,' he says softly to Jamie, nodding towards the bedroom. 'I need you to do something for me. A small favour.'

Sickened by what has just taken place in the bedroom, Jamie remains silent and stares at his hands. In his peripheral vision, he's sizing up the smaller man across from him, thinking about what he needs to do to overpower him and take the gun. He's certainly not interested in engaging in conversation with him *or* doing him any favours.

Ray slams his fist against the tabletop. 'You listening?'

'Yes.'

'Good. Make sure you're listening. I need you to drive to Hervey Bay and pick up a package for me.' He lifts both hands up, shrugs and smiles, as if he's just made a perfectly reasonable request. 'That's all. Once you've delivered the package back here to me, we'll call it even and you can go. What d'ya reckon?'

'Why would I do anything for you?' Jamie says evenly.

'Because you owe me. I did you a favour helping out in Goomburra and driving you home, remember.'

The man is obviously completely deranged.

'Why not you and I go together to get the package?' Jamie says. 'I can do the driving.'

Ray scratches the side of his hand with the barrel of his gun. 'Nah. That wouldn't work. I need to stay here and give Willy her punishment.' He winks at Jamie. 'We wouldn't want to disappoint her now, would we?'

'Are you intending to hurt her?'

'Nah. Not really. No more than she deserves.' He gives Jamie a leery smile.

'Why do you think she deserves to be punished?'

'For all the lying she's done. If I don't deal with her, she'll never learn. She'll think she can do whatever she fucking well pleases.'

'Look, I —'

'Do this one little thing for me and I'll let her go unharmed. I promise. Or I could just go and fuck that pretty little daughter of yours until her eyeballs pop out the top of her head.'

Jamie feels as though a tsunami has slammed into him. Enraged, he's halfway to his feet before noticing that the black colt is aimed squarely between his eyes.

'Settle down,' Ray grins. 'Only joking. What sort of sick bastard do you think I am? So look, all I'm trying to do is help Willy sort herself out and stop her from going insane the way her mother did. I mean, it can't be easy for her given what she did as a girl.'

Despite his loathing, Jamie is intrigued to know what terrible thing Ray thinks Mina did as a girl. And Ray obviously want to tell him.

He sinks back onto the chair and sighs. 'What'd she do, Ray?'

Ray laughs. 'You should know. You were there. On Moonbroch.'

Jamie's eyes widen with surprise and his mind is suddenly filled with images he's spent most of his life trying to forget. Swirling brown water. The sound of branches cracking. The stench of mud. But Ray wasn't there. He can't possibly know what took place at that flooded creek all those years ago.

'What exactly is it you think Willis … Mina did on Moonbroch?' he asks.

'She committed murder.'

'No, she didn't.'

'Yeah. She did.'

Jamie shakes his head. 'No. She didn't. How would you know? You weren't even there.'

'Willy told me everything, including how she swung that lump of wood into the side of Onfro's head.'

Jamie looks down and gently shakes his head. He resists a smile of his own as he thinks about the irony of what is happening here — Ray has Mina trussed up in the bedroom as punishment for her lying to him and yet he still believes her biggest lie of all.

He closes his eyes and tries to force his exhausted brain to think rationally about his options. It's now obvious to him that there's a long history of abuse here. If he refuses to comply with what Ray wants, the outcome could be deadly. If he agrees to collect Ray's package, which he guesses is most likely a drug deal, he thinks Ray will wait in the apartment for his return, which means he won't be out looking for Cass. But can he walk away and leave a woman alone with her assailant? Could he ever do such a thing? Mina told him to do whatever Ray says — but can he really walk away and leave her behind? That seems impossible.

But he doesn't actually have to drive to Hervey Bay, does he? He can simply agree to Ray's request in order to get out of the apartment and call the police for help. And go find Cass.

'Promise you won't lay a finger on her,' Jamie says, locking eyes with Ray. He doubts Ray's promises are worth much but it's worth a try. After all, he seems to have a holier-than-thou attitude towards Mina's so-called shortcomings, so who knows? Maybe underneath all the obscenity is a tiny thread of integrity. 'Promise me you'll not go anywhere near her and you'll stay out here in the lounge until I get back. If you can promise me that, I'll go collect the package for you.'

Ray laughs out loud. A high-pitched sound. 'You're kind of forgetting that I'm the one with the gun,' he says. 'But, yeah. Sure. Why not? I don't want to go near the old slag anyway.' He wriggles on the chair. 'So, let's see. It's a three-

and-a-half-hour trip, seven hours there and back, but I'll give you eight so as you've got time to stop for fuel and allowing for the traffic on the Pacific Highway.'

He checks his phone for the time. Jamie takes the opportunity to check his watch and is staggered to see that it's already early evening — a lot has happened since he'd talked Cass up the cliff in Goomburra at daybreak.

'It's just before six now,' Ray says. Manipulating the pistol so that he can point at his fingers, he counts forward eight hours. 'Seven, eight, nine, ten, eleven, twelve, one, two. Two a.m. That's when I'll expect you back. Give me your phone so I can put the address into maps for you. You got hands free?'

Jamie nods and hands over his phone.

'Good, then Siri can do the navigating and all you'll have to do is drive. What's your password?'

Jamie watches as Ray deftly thumb types into his phone.

'I've put my number in your contacts under Ray, so give me a call once you've got the package and are headed home, in case we need to adjust the time. Oh good. I see you've already got the "Find My Friends" app.'

He has? Jamie had no idea. He uses the phone for calls, texts or directions, or to check his email or the weather. He isn't on social media and has no interest in the multitude of games and other apps that are available.

'There you go,' Ray says, passing him back the phone. 'I'll be tracking your progress, so I'll know if you're thinking about going rogue. And I'll know if you make any calls, too, so you don't wanna go callin' those boys in blue.'

Jamie had not counted on Ray being able to track him in such a way.

'Do as I say, and everything'll work out alright. I promise I won't hurt her. I'd never hurt Willy. You know that. She's like my oldest friend in the world and while what we do might seem weird to a person like you, it's all just a game to her. She's always loved playing games and, I promise you, she loves every minute of what I do to her. She loves the drama.' He sighs. 'But not me. I'm tired of putting up with her lies. As soon as I can get my hands on that package, I'm kissin' Australia's ass good-bye and moving overseas permanently. Too many shit people in this country now. Ruinin' the place. Muslims and chings and the like. Only reason I even made this trip to Queensland was to get that package; but then I thought, I might as well call over and see Willy one last time while I'm here.'

Jamie notices that Ray's tone is gentler. It's as if, for a moment, he's forgotten about the pistol in his hand, and about all the threats he's made towards both Jamie and Mina. Has he even forgotten that Mina is tied up in the next room or that he has digitally raped her?

'... So, I turn up here yesterday and discover she's been lying to me all along. Jeez. I hate it when she lies. You'd think she'd learn.' His voice has swung back once more to cold and menacing. 'I'm tellin' you, I've had it with her. I'm tempted to put a bullet right between those big blue eyes of hers. Really, I am. But I won't. Like I promised, I'll leave her alone if you'll do this one little thing for me.'

'Does the person I'm to collect the package from have a name?' Jamie asks, pushing away the image of a wet, smelly, glassy-eyed, beloved old dog lying in his arms in a rubbish dump with a bullet hole between *his* eyes.

'Yep. *She* does.'

'It's a woman?' Jamie had imagined he would be collecting the package from a seedy, middle-aged drug dealer with a goatee.

'Her name is Moira Tanning. You may remember her.'

CHAPTER 26

Outside, the evening is warm. Jamie stumbles to his car then drops his keys before he can manage to get them into the door.

'Damn.' He feels around on the darkened ground for them. He can't believe he's walked away. What the hell is he doing? Why has he left Mina alone in that apartment with Ray? A short while ago, he'd convinced himself that he simply needed to get outside long enough to call the police. That was before Ray had messed with his phone and talked about tracking everything he does. Talk about living in a big brother society. Shit! Does Ray really have a way of knowing what calls he makes? Is there an app that can do that?

He's afraid if he doesn't get into his car and start driving towards Hervey Bay immediately, Ray will shoot Mina dead. If only he wasn't so tired, he might be able to think it through more clearly, but he's beyond making even the simplest of plans.

A light shower of rain falls as he heads north — just enough to splay the lights from the oncoming vehicles in random directions and cause him to sit forward on his seat and grip the wheel a little tighter.

While he drives, he thinks about Mina. The mother of his child. A woman he barely knows. Except, he did know her once. When she was a girl called Willis. He'd once made her a pinkie promise to be her friend.

For twenty-five years, he's avoided thinking too much about that long-legged teenager whose life had once collided so violently with his own. Because it's always been too painful to remember. He missed her terribly when she left Moonbroch. He had been sick with worry that she had died and no-one had told him. It felt like everyone blamed her for what happened. For months, he checked every mail delivery for a letter from her. Every time the phone rang, his heart exploded with hope that it was her calling to speak to him. But there had been no letters. No phone calls. She had simply vanished from his life and eventually, he had pushed her from his mind and got on with life. But he never forgot her. Not really. He'd kept the knowledge of her existence deep inside his soul where no-one could touch it.

He yawns, plays musical fingers against the steering wheel and wonders if what Ray had said was true — that his mother had gone to the hospital and asked Willis not to contact him. He'd like to ask his mother, but these kinds of conversations had never been easy. It's was as though, after Sophie died, she had locked up a part of herself and thrown away the key.

He thinks of his mother now. Even though he's driving in darkness, it'll still be daylight out on the station and she's most likely outside talking to her chickens and watering her fruit trees.

It was strange that when he'd been home at Christmas time, she'd mentioned receiving a card from Moira Tanning. He'd been in the kitchen keeping her company while she baked, licking the cake mix from the bowl like he'd done as a boy, when the topic of 'old Mrs Tanning' had come up.

'You remember her, don't you Jamie?' she'd said. 'She used to be our bank manager when you were a boy. She gave you lollipops.'

'Why would *she* send you a card?' he'd asked.

'I guess she wants to keep her connection to the bush. Your father and I are still so terribly grateful to her for all she did for us, you know.'

'Mum,' he'd snapped, shocked by her words. 'You can't be serious?'

How could he even begin to explain to his mother the deep sense of fury he has always harboured towards 'old Mrs Tanning'? While the details of her involvement remain concealed behind the murky veil of his childhood, he has always believed that the trouble that followed so soon after Sophie's death had been entirely her fault — because she had wanted to steal their land.

'Jamie, whatever do you mean?' His mother had been surprised by his uncommon show of emotion.

'Don't worry about it, Mum,' he'd said. 'It isn't important.'

Then she'd surprised him even more by saying, 'I think it *is* important for us to talk about it.'

'But you're the one who has never wanted to talk about what happened back then.'

She had reached over and squeezed his shoulder. 'Well, I want to talk about it now. I want you to understand what went on back then.'

He'd stared blankly at her and waited for her to continue.

'In 1990,' she said, 'we had a million-dollar bank draft, one of the worst droughts in living history, no stock, and no income. We couldn't meet our repayments at the bank and the debt was tearing us apart. Moira was doing everything she could to help but it didn't seem like it would be enough. So, when her mother, Aggie, mentioned that she knew this fellow in Sydney who had a bit of money and was interested in getting a property out west, Moira thought it might be our chance to get a fair price, clear our debt and walk away. She couldn't see that we had any other choice.'

Her voice tightens. 'Your father and I ... our minds were on other matters. We were still dealing with the loss of Sophie and neither of us were thinking straight. Anyway, after Moira lost her mother in the floods, for some reason she changed her tune about us selling and decided she would help us stay on Moonbroch. The McKenzie family belongs on this land, she said, and, quite unexpectedly, we found ourselves with this gutsy little woman in our corner who was prepared to move heaven and earth to keep us here.'

After twenty-five years, Jamie had been stunned to get a different perspective on Mrs Tanning's involvement in their lives. A grown-up's perspective. Before talking to his mother at Christmas, his judgement had been based entirely on the opinions of Willis. But what if Willis had been wrong? What if Onfro and Aggie and Mrs Tanning were good people who had only ever wanted to help his family?

He shakes his head as if to clear it. That perspective doesn't fit. It doesn't explain Onfro and Aggie's cruelty towards Willis. It doesn't matter that they considered her an out-of-control teenager, no person deserves to be treated with such disdain. Someone with Willis's past surely needs kindness and understanding above all else.

Like a rising tide, hysteria ebbs and flows through his exhausted body and his mind returns to thinking about Mina, tied up and powerless back in the apartment. He applies his foot a little heavier on the accelerator and continues his way north along the highway.

The streets are wet from a recent shower of rain as Jamie enters the tidy coastal town of Hervey Bay around nine-thirty. He finds the units where Mrs Tanning lives without difficulty, parks, steps out of his car, stretches, and breathes the warm salty air deeply into his lungs. The neighbourhood is leafy and middle-class, and he can hear the rumble of voices, clatter of plates, and drone of televisions coming from inside the units. A crying baby is being soothed in an upstairs room. He walks up the driveway and knocks on Mrs Tanning's door.

She opens the door immediately and studies him through the security screen.

'Mrs Tanning? I'm sorry to call so late but I've come to collect a package for —'

'I know why you're here,' she says, her voice caustic. 'What's your name?'

'Um … I …'

'Cat got your tongue?'

'No, it's just …'

'I can't give you the package unless you tell me your name.'

He considers making something up, but she seems far too sharp to believe a lie.

'Jamie McKenzie,' he mumbles.

She nods her head slowly up and down, causing her wire-framed glasses to slide down her nose.

'You're mumbling, son. I'd have thought with a name like yours, you'd be proud to say it out loud.'

She makes him feel like a child being told off by a stern teacher.

'Sorry.'

'Don't "sorry" me,' she says. 'It's yourself you ought to be apologising to. What on earth are you doing running around with lowlifes like Ray?'

'Mrs Tanning, I'm sorry, but if you don't mind, I need that package. I need to be getting back.'

'Blah,' she says, waving her hand dismissively. 'Make him wait.'

'But you don't understand. I need to —'

She brushes away his request for urgency, unlocks the screen door, hustles him into her tiny living/dining/kitchen space, and directs him to sit in a well-worn velvety armchair.

'I'm going to make you a cup of coffee. Hopefully, it'll be enough to stop you falling to sleep and running off the road and killing someone.'

He watches her walk stiffly into the kitchen, as though she is in pain, turn on the kettle and begin spooning instant coffee into a mug. She's a stocky woman, deeply tanned with close cropped grey hair, but strangely, not much different from the woman he remembers giving him lollipops in the bank when he was a child.

Once she's set him up with a strong black coffee and three Anzac cookies on a plate, she says, 'I won't be long,' and leaves the room.

His phone vibrates. It's Ray checking that he has the package. Yes, Jamie says. And yes, he's about to head back to Brisbane, no problems, no police, and Ray says Mina is fine. She's sleeping. After the call is over, he sips the scalding coffee and eats a biscuit. The apartment smells like essential oils — frankincense and lavender. It reminds him of Sophie. A clock ticks. He hears a toilet flushing. And his eyes begin to droop and close. No! He can't go to sleep.

'I'm coming with you,' a voice says, and he opens his eyes to see Mrs Tanning back in the room with a large purple handbag draped across her forearm.

'Mrs Tanning. No,' he says, getting to his feet. 'That's not what's meant to happen.'

The old lady smiles. The skin around her mouth is a ghastly shade of green and he suspects her tan is hiding a ghostly pallor. Is she unwell?

'Jamie, I can't let you go out there in the state you're in. Whatever you've been up to, I can see that you're too tired to be driving and if you don't mind my saying so, you smell really bad as well. Like you haven't had a bath in a week. So, as an old family friend, I'm offering to drive you to wherever you need to go. Okay?'

'But ... I really only came for the package.'

She sticks her chin out and glares at him with stubborn eyes.

'I am the package,' she says. 'Come on. Give me your keys and let's get going.'

Her cautious driving makes him nervous at first but before long, he relaxes and stops paying attention, and despite his determination to the contrary, by the time they pass through Maryborough, he is asleep.

Jamie is dreaming of Moonbroch. He's immersed in the same sensory nightmare he's had a thousand times before — the pungent odour of mud, the deafening roar of flood water, Onfro's odd, staggering movements, sticky mud between his fingers, hard wood against his palm, swinging the club in a wide arc, a dull thud as it strikes the back of On-fro's skull. Then the chilling sound of the man's laughter.

His own moans wake him. He straightens and looks around, not immediately aware of where he is.

'Nightmare,' says a raspy voice. It's a statement, not a question.

Mrs Tanning is still cautiously sitting forward on her seat, squinting through her glasses at the oncoming cars as she guides his car down the dark highway to Brisbane. He checks his watch. Midnight. His limbs feel heavy and cramped.

'Want me to take over the driving?' he asks.

'No.'

'I'd like you to know how sorry I am that your mother drowned the way she did,' he says.

'Wasn't your fault.'

'She and Onfro went to the creek that morning because I'd run away.'

She glances across at where he's hunched in the passenger seat. 'You were upset. I understand that. Losing that old dog was too much for you to bear. I know how much you loved the old fellow because Mum would call me every day and tell me.'

Jamie swallows at the mention of Woofy and pushes away his impulse to think about that same dark-red bullet hole in the middle of Mina's forehead.

'I was never sure why Aggie and Onfro came to Moon-broch,' he says. 'Willis and I were doing fine on our own.'

He can tell by the tension in her shoulders that he's treading on delicate ground. 'Were they planning to take Moonbroch from my parents?'

'Yes. And no. Your parents were never going to claw their way out of all that debt, especially with the drought, and I genuinely thought they'd be better off if they could sell for a good price. Unfortunately, all my scheming went south because Onfro turned out to be not such a good person. And you're right to judge me harshly, if that's what you're doing. I broke the law. I should have gone to jail.'

They are passing through a built-up area and Jamie studies the woman's profile in the flicker of passing street lamps — the determined chin, the down-turned mouth.

'Why'd you pay Ray to come to Moonbroch?'

'I didn't pay him.'

'You offered to pay him though, didn't you? Why'd you want Willis gone so badly?'

'Onfro wanted her gone. And I needed his money for Moonbroch.'

'But she refused to leave.'

'Yes. And when Ray arrived back in town without her, I refused to pay him.' She pokes her chin even further. 'He went off his head, of course, and started demanding way more money than I'd ever promised in the first place. I ended up having to call the police.'

'What happened after that?'

'Well, by the time the police got to the bank, he'd skedaddled out of town and a few days later, Mum and Onfro were dead and I was somewhat preoccupied and forgot all about him. But once the dust had settled, he came back. Demanding the money. In the end, I gave it to him. A thousand dollars. Just to get rid of him.'

They sit in silence, each wrapped in their own thoughts.

'You never did get rid of him, did you?' Jamie says after several minutes.

She grips the wheel and shakes her head. 'I've been giving him money for twenty-five years. A little bit here. A little bit there. Never large amounts. I know you're probably thinking I should've put an end to it years ago, but it never seemed worth the battle. For one thing, he knew about my involvement in Moonbroch and if anyone had ever investigated, I'd have gone to jail for sure. I didn't only break the law by getting Onfro involved, I also did some rather creative book-keeping in order to save it for your parents.'

'And the other thing?'

She glances across at him, confused.

'You said, for one thing, which means there must have been another reason you kept him around.'

'Oh, that. It's embarrassing. You see, Ray has this uncanny way of making things appear different than they really are. He'd convinced himself that I actually wanted to give him the money — a lonely spinster in the company of a younger man and all that.'

'So the package I'm meant to have collected for him is money?'

She nods. 'Five grand.'

Jamie whistles. 'Why didn't he just come and collect it for himself?'

'I told him this was the last time he'd be getting a cent from me because ... well, I have pancreatic cancer. I'm not long for this world, Jamie.'

Jamie flinches at this revelation. 'Mrs Tanning, I'm so sorry to hear that.'

'Anyway, I guess he got spooked. Must have thought that if I was going to die, I'd have nothing to lose by going to the police. But ... as you can see, no police. I'm too old and sick to bother with all that. Instead, I've decided if he won't come to me, I'll deliver the damn package to him in person this one last time.'

'Mrs Tanning. Is there anything at all I can do for you?'

Any anger Jamie once had towards this tough little woman with terminal cancer has long since been dissipated by earnest conversation and understanding, and he feels overcome with a sense of wanting to make her remaining time on Earth as comfortable as possible.

'Just take me to Ray,' she says. 'That's all I want.'

Between thoughts of Ray, and how to safely get Mina away from him, Jamie dozes, but is brought back to full awareness by Mrs Tanning's angry tut tutting. An approaching truck is on high beam and she's flashing her lights at him.

'Idiot,' she hisses.

'For all we know,' Jamie says, speaking slowly and thoughtfully, 'Ray might have been robbing and tormenting women all over Australia his entire life … He's probably made a career out of this kind of thing. As you said, a little bit here. A little bit there. Never enough for them to want to do anything about it … He probably chooses his targets carefully. Anyone who has something to hide … Anyone who is in some way isolated from family or community.'

Mrs Tanning clears her throat.

'I'm well aware of that,' she snaps at him.

Jamie and Moira Tanning are on Sandgate Road when he gets a call from Mina.

'You're difficult to hear,' he shouts. 'Speak louder if that's possible.'

He imagines her tied up on the bed and holding the phone down between tied hands, or talking around the tape that he'd put across her mouth.

'… was asleep … woke up … tracking Mrs Tan … gone … Cass.'

Her words are too broken and disjointed to make sense.

'Has Ray gone to find Cass?' he says.

'Yes … yes …'

'How long ago did he leave?'

He doesn't understand her response and doesn't waste time having her repeat it. Knowing how much of a head start Ray has is probably not going to be useful information anyway.

'Are you okay?'

'Yes. Go … find …'

'Okay. Breathe, Mina. I'm not far away and I've got Winter's address and phone number here in my pocket.' He closes his eyes and makes a silent prayer that this is the friend Cass is staying with. 'I'll call the number now. And

I'll go straight to the house. You just hold on a little longer, alright. Just hold on.'

'Hurry,' she says.

CHAPTER 27

Cass wakes in darkness. Somewhere, a phone is ringing. She lies perfectly still and thinks — remembers that she's at Winter's house. In Winter's bed. There's no way of knowing how long she's been here, or what the time is, but outside, the street and the neighbours' houses are deathly quiet. So it must be late. Sometime in the middle of the night.

The yowl of fighting cats sends goose bumps up her arms. What if she's not alone? What if Winter's parents came home while she was sleeping, and they don't know she's here? What if they think she's an intruder and they've got a gun? She really needs to pee but is afraid to move. Then she remembers the unexpected warmth of her urine when she'd peed her pants in the crevice in Goomburra and blushes in the dark. She doesn't want to pee in Winter's bed. That would be way too embarrassing. So, she slips over the edge until her bare feet touch the smooth floorboards, then steps quickly away from the bed in case a bad man is hiding underneath waiting to grab her ankle.

Silently, she retraces her steps through the lounge room, the kitchen and into the toilet she'd used earlier, near the laundry. There's light seeping into the house from the street because none of the curtains have been drawn. Does this mean she's alone after all?

Without risking the noise of flushing or washing her hands, she begins to explore the house. In what she assumes is the master bedroom, she makes out the smooth outline of a neatly made bed and sighs with relief. After checking the other bedrooms, she remembers that she came into the house through an unlocked front door, so she goes back down the hallway, fumbles around with the latch and locks it. She also checks that the back door is locked.

Then she goes into the kitchen and is looking in the fridge for something to eat when the phone rings again. A loud and repetitive 'ting-a-ling' which nearly gives her a heart attack.

Who would be calling Winter's family in the middle of the night? She wriggles her toes against the cool floor and debates whether or not she should answer it. If someone like a robber or a rapist was in a house, they wouldn't answer the phone, would they? But she's not either of those things. She's Winter's friend. Only Winter doesn't know she's here. What if she doesn't answer and it turns out to be really important …?

She snatches the hand piece from the cradle on the eleventh ring.

'Hello?'

'Winter? Is that you?'

'Um … no. It's Cass. Dad? Is that you?'

'It's me. I'm about fifteen or twenty minutes away. Coming to get you. Are you okay?'

Well. Damn. After everything that's happened, she thinks she's going to cry.

'Dad. I'm … I'm at Winter's house. Except …' Her voice begins to crack.

'What is it, Cass? Is everything alright?'

'No-one else is here except me.'

'They've left you on your own?'

'They were never here. The house was empty when I arrived, and I was so tired that I just called Mum and went to bed.'

'You did the right thing calling your Mum.'

Cass sniffles. Tears start running down her cheeks and she angrily wipes them away.

'Cass? I need to hang up so I can …'

'No. Dad. Please. I'm really scared. Please don't hang up. Wait …'

What's that …? Just outside the back door? Light footsteps. The jangly sound of keys.

'Dad,' she stage-whispers. 'Someone's here.'

'Shit. Cass. You need to find somewhere to hide. Or better, if you can, get out of the house. Get out into the middle of the street and start screaming.'

But there isn't enough time to get out of the kitchen, down the hallway and out the front door. She delicately places the handpiece down on its side on the granite bench-top, slips around the enormous wooden table and into a small pantry that closes with two wooden, louvered doors — just as someone switches on the kitchen light.

Bands of light burst through the louvres and light up Cass's chest and legs with bright stripes. Without moving her feet and risking a creaky floorboard, she holds her breath, leans forward, and peeps through the gap between the pantry doors.

Then lets out her breath with relief and, grinning, she pushes open the louvered doors.

Winter nearly jumps out of her skin.

'Cass. Crap. You just scared the be-jingoes out of me.'

Cass laughs. 'Be-jingoes?'

Winter clutches her chest and staggers over to a kitchen chair. 'Can you think of a better word to describe someone who's about to die from a heart attack? What are you doing in my pantry?'

'Hiding out. I ran away from home.'

Winter pats a chair next to her and says, 'Sit. Tell all.'

Cass sits, her face once again gloomy. 'Not much to tell really. Only, I think my mother might have a mental illness. But it's okay. My Dad is coming to get me. He'll be here soon.'

Then she realises that Winter is alone. Where is *her* family?

'Did you run away too?' she asks.

Winter smiles and shakes her head. 'No. I've been staying out in Moggill with my Poppy while my parents are overseas, but he goes to the markets early on a Saturday and said I could hang out at home until he was done.'

'He lets you stay alone?'

'Sure. He knows I can look after myself.'

Cass is about to ask Winter about getting some food when the front doorbell rings.

'That'll be my Dad,' she says, rising up from the kitchen chair with the grace of a dancer and gliding effortlessly and happily down the long hallway.

'Wait,' Winter says, a small frown on her forehead as she hurries after Cass. Cass is already unlocking the front door and she doesn't notice Winter reach quickly into a recess to the left of the entrance and wrap her fingers around a small cylinder.

Cass flings the door wide. And both girls gasp. Because the man on the front verandah is definitely not Cass's father.

'Well, hello ladies,' says the evil-looking, smug man with bad teeth who is grinning maliciously at the girls and rubbing the palms of his hands together. 'Two for the price of one. Must be my lucky day.'

Quick as a flash, Winter uses her body in an attempt to ram the door closed but the man stops it with his foot.

'That's no way to treat a guest,' he says.

'You are not my guest, *Ray*,' Winter says, shoving forcefully against the door.

'You know him?' Cass whispers, her eyes widening with surprise.

'From Goomburra.'

The distraction of this exchange between Cass and Winter is all the man needs to force the door wide enough to get through. He uses the momentum of his forward motion to slam his open palm squarely against Winter's nose, causing a gush of blood to flow down over her lips. Then he shoves her sideways into the wall.

Ignoring the pain and the blood, Winter straightens herself. She positions her legs in a wide stance with her knees slightly bent, like a fighter getting ready to take on an opponent.

'Just do as he says,' Cass warns.

Winter ignores her friend and speaks directly to the man in a nasal but steady voice. 'You are not welcome here and if you don't leave, you *will* get hurt.'

Such is his surprise at being challenged by a little girl, he lets out a snorting laugh that lasts less than two seconds before Winter empties a canister of pepper spray into his eyes.

'Aw fucking jes—'

Cass scrambles out of the way as Winter spins sideways and brings her foot in a wide arc to collide with the man's groin. He curls forward in response to the pain and slumps, moaning, against the wall, but blocking their escape.

Winter yells at Cass. 'Run. Back door.'

Both girls scamper along the hallway to the laundry at the back of the house. Cass arrives first, but the door is locked, and she's frantically trying to figure out how the double lock works when she hears a dull boom and some wood splinters away from the door frame where a bullet has penetrated. Spinning around, she sees the man wiping at his face with one hand while swinging a gun wildly in their direction. If he fires another shot, he'll probably take out Winter who is standing in front of her, her shoulders squared as though she's not even scared. Cass lifts her hands in surrender.

'Get in there. Now.' He motions with the gun, indicating they should go into the kitchen.

'You obviously don't know who my parents are,' Winter says, using her hand to stop Cass getting past her and going into the kitchen.

'Who gives a fuck who your parents are, you little cunt. You'll regret what you did, you can be sure about that.'

'Ever heard of the Shēngcún Academy? My parents own it. We all have black belts.'

Winter's bravado is confusing the man.

He sneers. 'How do you suppose your black belt is going to protect you against my bullet?'

'I didn't say anything about protecting myself against your bullet,' she says. She has one hand twisted behind her back and is using it to gently restrain Cass, communicating her request to stay still and remain calm. 'You said you were my guest, didn't you? So I'm acting like a good host and making conversation.'

The man is half frowning, half grinning.

'I tell you a bit about myself,' she says, 'which I've done, and now it's your turn to say something about yourself.'

'Fuck. You're a piece of work.'

'We've already talked about me. Now it's your turn. What can you tell me about yourself, *Ray*? Why are you here and what do you want?'

He shakes his head. 'Fuck.'

'Thank you.'

'What?'

'Thank you for sharing.'

'I didn't say anything …'

'Yeah, you did. You said fuck. So now I've found out something about you.'

'Such as?'

'That you like to swear. You probably think it makes you look tough.'

He frowns. Confused. 'Are you making fun of me?'

He leans forward, his face red with confusion and anger and Winter tenses. Cass gasps. Then Winter holds up her hand.

'Wait. One more thing. My grandfather, the man everyone calls Poppy and who you've already met, well, he also has a black belt. And he's standing right behind you.'

Cass has been so focused on watching the intruder, she hasn't noticed the slight, older man who has appeared behind him. Winter's grandfather catches the man as he turns and the ensuing battle in the laundry doorway is short and one-sided. Before Cass can draw a breath, Winter's grandfather has him locked down on the floor, powerless to move without causing himself excruciating pain, and Winter has calmly removed the gun and placed it carefully on a laundry shelf. Next, grandfather and granddaughter work together to move the man into the kitchen where they tie him to a chair.

The man attempts to spit at Winter's grandfather, but the ball of saliva falls short and lands on his own thigh. He struggles and swears, then begs for mercy when they re-strain him. Winter and her grandfather ignore him com-pletely. Winter chats away as if they're doing something as mundane as gardening or cooking together and the older man nods from time to time to show that he's listening.

'It's the man who came in the van to Goomburra with us,' she says. 'I never did believe that story he said about being an old friend of Cass's dad and I can prove it too be-cause I wrote about him in my notebook. But I must say, I *was* surprised to see him turn up here. Sorry we opened the door. I know I'm not supposed to open the door to *anyone* but we thought it was Cass's dad and anyway, I'm pretty sure I could have taken him down if you hadn't come back, Poppy. I was ready to use my moves and was just waiting for him to step in so I could use his momentum against him. Sorry. I'm talking too much, hey?' She looks over at Cass who is leaning, wide-eyed and pale-faced, against the wall. 'It's how I handle stress.'

When they've finished securing the man with rope and have shoved a tea towel into his mouth to shut him up, the grandfather straightens and examines Winter's face.

'You okay?'

'Yes.'

'What about you, love?' he asks, turning towards Cass. 'Going okay?'

Cass nods.

'Your Dad called me just after I dropped Winter off,' he says, 'so I doubled back to check everything was alright. He should be here in a jiffy. He was going to call the police.'

Suddenly, an anxious voice calls from the open front door. 'Cass?'

'Dad?'

Cass runs out of the kitchen, down the hallway and into her father's open arms. She'd barely managed to hold herself together while Winter and her grandfather were dealing with the man and now, she's ready to fall apart. As her tears begin to fall and sobs wrack her body, her father's strong arms wrap around her and hold her tight.

CHAPTER 28

Jamie leads his hysterical daughter into the lounge room where they sit side-by-side on the couch. His arm is around her shoulders and he speaks to her in a low, calming voice. The old man and the other girl are in the bathroom cleaning blood off her face. Which means Ray is alone in the kitchen.

Moira Tanning has gathered from the snippets she's heard while standing in the front doorway to the old cottage that the police have been called and are expected to arrive at any moment. She'll need to act quickly if she's going to give Ray his package before they get here.

No-one notices her make her way painfully down the long hallway to the back of the house. She's skipped her medication and the long night has taken a toll on her poor, cancer-ravaged body. But it doesn't matter. There's only one thing left for her to do. Soon, it will be all over.

'Hello, Ray,' she says softly.

His head jerks up and she's amused to see such wild-eyed fear in the face of a man who has spent his life belittling others in order to appear strong.

'I hear you've been bested by a little girl.'

She gives a small, snorting laugh and pats his shoulder.

He flinches from her touch as though he's been burnt and begins grunting noises from deep in his throat, below the reach of the tea towel that has been taped into his mouth. Moira Tanning steps back and reaches into her oversized handbag.

'I've brought your package,' she says. 'It's rather small and probably not quite what you're expecting. But it's what you deserve.'

When her hand comes out of the bag, there is no hesitancy in her movement. She's already made up her mind. What will be, will be. She presses the cold steel of the pistol against his temple and pulls the trigger.

Before Jamie and Poppy can reach the kitchen, they hear a second gunshot and by the time they enter the room, both Ray and Mrs Tanning are dead.

While attempting to shield Cass from the horror that has taken place inside Winter's kitchen, Jamie answers questions directed at him by the police. Amongst the chaos, a green-eyed police officer with a steely expression informs him that a team of officers are at the apartment and that Mina is shaken but unharmed. His legs begin to wobble. He reaches for the wall to stop himself from tumbling over.

More and more people arrive. Whenever someone talks directly to him, he does his best to respond patiently and appropriately, but it's a relief when he and Cass are eventually given the all clear to leave. They're both anxious to get back to the apartment and check on Mina.

Outside, the sky has begun to lighten and a new day is beginning. The street is filled with flashing lights and bustling, purposeful people. Someone who appears to be from the media calls out to them from behind an orange barricade, asking if they'd be prepared to make a statement. A small gathering of onlookers chat nervously to each other, curious to find out about the dreadful crime that has disrupted their usually quiet neighbourhood.

Before he can get into his car, Jamie needs to adjust the position of the seat which is still set forward to accommodate Moira Tanning's shorter legs. Reaching for the lever, he notices that an envelope has been left on the seat. He turns it over.

'What is it?' Cass asks, clicking her seatbelt in place.

He holds the envelope up for her to see. Written across the front is *Wilhelmina Johnson*.

Back at the apartment, Cass hands the envelope to her mother, curious about its contents and impatient for her to open it immediately.

'Mrs Tanning must have left it for you,' Jamie says.

Frowning, Mina takes the envelope between two fingers and crinkles her nose at the musty smell coming from the old paper. She slides a finger under the sticky strip, gently teases apart the flap and extracts a hand-written note from within. Without expression or comment, she reads the note in silence and when she's finished, she allows it to drift from her fingers and float to the floor. Then she curls under a blanket at the end of her sofa and closes her eyes.

When it's obvious she's not intending to comment, or communicate in any way further, Cass snatches the note from the floor, sits opposite her mother and reads it out loud to Jamie, stumbling over some of the unfamiliar words.

Wilhelmina

I have decided to return to Brisbane with Jamie and put an end to all this. (Jamie doesn't know yet. He's waiting next door, expecting me to bring him a package. Actually, I think he might have dropped off to sleep.) When you find out what I'm planning to do, I hope that you will understand my actions.

For a long while, I thought you and Ray were a team, working together to extort money from me. It has only been in recent years that I've begun to suspect that you, too, might have been his victim. But I was never sure until a few days ago when he called me up and said some things that finally led me to the truth — that you are most definitely a victim and not an accomplice. For what it's worth, I want to apologise for misjudging you. I'm truly sorry.

I also want to apologise to you for my interference on Moonbroch all those years ago. When I first took you to the station, my instincts were that you were a reliable, trustworthy person who would be good company for young Jamie. And I'm sure my instincts were right. However, I allowed myself to become persuaded by my poor, misguided mother, and I got Ray involved. And after it was all over and you were lying in that hospital bed, I allowed the McKenzies to think badly of you.

I've never forgotten the day you arrived on Moonbroch. It was as if you had stepped into a new world and I could see that you instantly fell in love with the place. Sadly, because of my poor judgement and interference, nothing turned out the way you had hoped, and you've been paying the price ever since. It might not make a difference, but I wanted you to know that I have written a letter to John and Sue McKenzie and attempted to set the record straight.

Hold your head high, girl. I know it is hard when you've been dealing with a shitty little weasel like Ray for so long but, with any luck, by the time you get this, he'll be out of the picture and you'll finally be free to start living your best life.

Yours
Moira Tanning.

One week later, Jamie is looking forward to escaping the brutal humidity of Brisbane and heading back up the range to Toowoomba. It'll be dark before he gets home, he realises, especially since he has to collect Cass and Winter from Winter's grandfather's place on his way. He'd been surprised and delighted when Mina said Cass could stay with him for the remainder of the school holidays and is happy to have her friend tag along as well.

Before heading out, he calls at the apartment to see Mina. She'd texted him earlier to say she had something to give him.

She wears a pale t-shirt, bone-coloured pants and gold canvas sneakers; and her damp hair has been tied back into a ponytail. In her hands is a white plastic shopping bag.

He stares at her wan, waif-like appearance, struggling to know what to say to her. There's so much he *wants* to say, about how sorry he is that Ray got away with hurting her for so long, and for leaving her alone with him to go to Hervey Bay; about the role he wants to play in her and Cass's lives, about Mrs Tanning's suicide note … but since that morning in Winter's kitchen, he hasn't had the chance. They've not had a single moment alone together. And even if they had, it feels as if she's retreated from him, and everyone else. Even Cass. She's become impossible to reach.

'I wanted to give you this,' she says, holding out the bag. 'I should have given it to you sooner, but I never got the chance.'

He'd been expecting something of Cass's, some extra clothes perhaps, but ... it isn't clothes. It feels like a book.

He looks inside ...

CHAPTER 29

For some time after they pulled him from the flooded creek, Jamie was too out-of-it to wonder about the sudden arrival of his parents back on Moonbroch and it wasn't until years later that he asked Dad about it.

'It was your mother,' Dad had said. 'She insisted we move hell and high water to get home when we did. I guess you could call it a mother's instinct.'

At the time, however, with the roar of the flood water still confusing his senses, Jamie had simply snuggled against Mum's chest, breathed in her scent, and accepted the trembling rhythm of her sobs.

Later, back at the homestead, Mum tried to keep him inside because she didn't want him to see what was happening with Willis. She tried to persuade him to take a bath, to eat and drink at the kitchen table, to sit on her lap so she could stroke his hair and put kisses on top of his head like she used to do — anything to stop him participating in the drama going on outside.

'Stay inside and let the grown-ups handle it,' she said.

He didn't want to upset her or make her sad — he wanted her to be happy — but he couldn't stay inside. Still wearing his wet shorts and boots, with an old beach towel draped about his shoulders, he pulled free from her and went out the screen door.

'Jamie. Wait,' she called.

'I need to see her,' he said.

Willis was on a stretcher covered by a white sheet. The brilliance of the sheet stood out against the muted background. It was as if the rain had washed all the colour from the landscape and bleached the sky, and the only point of brightness left in the whole world was the white sheet that covered her.

As he approached, he saw a bag hanging on a long silver pole. Clear fluid was flowing down a tube and entering her body at the crook of her elbow. A plastic collar was fitted around her neck. She didn't look *too* badly hurt, he thought — but then he remembered that the parts of her body where the ute had smashed into her were underneath the sheet and he wondered what those parts might be like — shattered bones and torn organs. Blood pooling.

He rested his small boy hand that smelt of wet dog and had dirt in the creases onto the white sheet … and her eyes popped open.

He looked around to see if anyone noticed that her eyes were open. But except for the nurse, everyone was standing back a few paces. The pilot was talking to Dad about the best way to take-off in the heavy conditions.

'Can I talk to her?' he asked the nurse.

The nurse gently stroked a few strands of white-blonde hair from Willis's forehead and said, 'Sure. But be quick. We need to get Willy to the hospital.'

And … his brain had snapped.

'Her name is Willis,' he said.

And even though he put all his remaining energy into screaming at the woman who was using the wrong name, very little noise came out his mouth. But it was enough for Mum to rush forward, ready to rescue the poor nurse from his anger. The nurse raised her hand and stopped her.

'It's okay,' she said to Mum. 'Just give him a minute to say good-bye to his friend.'

He turned his attention back to Willis and realised she was trying to say something, so he leaned in close in order to hear her words.

'Everything will be okay,' she said, her voice hoarse and scratchy.

A swell of tears threatened to unhinge him.

'It will. I promise,' she said.

He squinted his eyes against the sting of tears and glare of the sun.

'But what if you die?' he said.

'I won't die.'

'What if you do?'

'Jamie. I promise I won't die.'

He stared into her unfathomable blue eyes, willing her to be telling the truth. But how could he be certain? Sophie had thought she would live. And she hadn't …

Willis's eyes drifted closed for a moment, as if she could no longer fight the pull of the drugs flowing through her bloodstream; and he glanced to where Mum and the nurse were waiting.

Then Willis was looking at him again.

'Friends forever?' she said.

He cleared his own scratchy throat and nodded. 'Yes.'

Then he reached down and gently tangled his little finger with hers.

'Pinkie promise,' he said.

Her face lit up with the most beautiful of smiles. Then, the nurse and doctor were by her side indicating that it was time for him to step away so they could take her to the plane.

'Will I see you?' he asked, gripping the stretcher's side rail and walking with her.

'I'll write to you. Lots and lots of letters. I promise.'

The nurse had had to fold open his fingers in order to get him to let go. Then his father had gathered him into his arms and carried him a good way back before setting his feet back onto the ground.

The door to the plane was closed. He could see the doctor up front in the cockpit speaking on the radio. Then the plane taxied down the wet runway, turned, gained speed, lifted heavily into the sky and swerved southward towards the flooded creek.

He watched the sky until he could no longer hear the drone of the plane's engines; then he turned and walked back to the house.

Even though the roads in and out of Moonbroch were impassable for nearly two weeks after the flood, the station was like a small, bustling township with people coming and going via the air. Mum and Dad were flat out managing everything but, for the first time since Sophie got sick, they seemed to be pulling together rather than apart. Mum arranged for groceries to be sent from town with whoever was coming, and she prepared meals, cleaned out the mess at the shearing shed, and put the mattresses back in the quarters for extra accommodation. Dad transported people between the homestead and the creek on an old trailer attached to the back of the dozer and helped with the search for Aggie and Onfro.

Then he helped with the removal of their bodies.

Whenever Jamie went out to investigate what was happening, people would pat him on the head and make comments like, *glad you're okay, buddy,* so mostly he stayed out of the way. His anxiety that someone might figure out he was a murderer was relentless and he had no way of sharing how he felt. He could never speak of what had happened. His parents wouldn't survive losing both their children. Moonbroch wouldn't survive.

His dreams were filled with images of being taken away in handcuffs and sometimes in the middle of the night, when he woke from a nightmare, he wanted nothing more than Mum's comforting arms. But he never called for her.

Mrs Tanning, the bank manager, arrived in a helicopter. Her eyes were weary and bloodshot and every time she looked at Jamie, there was a little crease in the centre of her forehead. He did his best to avoid her. Whenever she was at the house, he would hide under the oleander bush with Hebe, who had somehow managed to take Woofy's place as house dog, even though she was the youngest of the dogs.

One day, a policeman arrived at the house wanting to ask some questions. Until then, no-one, including Mum and

Dad, had pushed him to talk about what happened because they were too scared of upsetting him. The policeman was different. His job was to ask questions. In the lounge room, he and Dad sat in armchairs while Jamie sat on the couch with Mum.

'How are you, Jamie?' the policeman said, leaning forward.

'Good.'

'Do you know why we're here?'

He nodded.

'We're just trying to figure out everything that happened. Okay?'

Jamie studied the bulge in the side of the policeman's trousers wondering if he had a gun or handcuffs. Or both.

'Jamie?'

'Yes.'

The policeman's questions were relentless. How did he get along with Wilhelmina? Did they ever have a fight? Did he know the name of the young man who had visited? Why was there a photo of Sophie in the shearing shed? Why were there candles? At the end of each question, Jamie had locked eyes with the policeman and responded with either yes, no, don't know or don't remember.

Can you tell me how Woofy died?

Jamie stared at the policeman's feet when asked about Woofy. Like everyone else, the policeman's boots had been left at the kitchen door and the man's socks didn't match. Both were grey but the weave was different.

He could feel Mum's body shaking and knew that she had started to cry.

'Jamie?'

'I don't remember.'

Then Mum stood up.

'Stop,' she said. 'Jamie's been through enough. I want you to leave.'

Eventually, the policeman did leave.

All the other people left as well.

And it went back to being he, Mum, and Dad.

Bit by bit, life returned to normal — a new normal that no longer included Sophie. The black hole left by his sister was still there. That never went away. But somehow, they learnt to live around the edges.

The story about the deaths of Aggie and Onfro made the news for a few days. The story about the little boy who lifted a car took longer to gain momentum but also lasted longer and travelled further — from the outback to the cities, across Bass Strait to Tasmania, over the Nullarbor to Perth. He heard that there was even a story written about it in the 'Athens Times' in Greece.

Being called *Australia's Littlest Superhero* didn't make him feel any particular sense of achievement because, by then, having a superpower no longer mattered. Sophie was dead and nothing, not even a superpower, was ever going to bring her back.

One day, Mum decided it was time to clear out Sophie's room and she told him to go in and see if there was anything of Sophie's that he might like to keep.

'Take your time,' she said.

He sat on her ballerina bed cover for a while, chewing his bottom lip and gazing around at all her dusty little possessions. Then he started to search for the glossy pink notebook with white dots and a spiral down one side. He looked high and low for it. Checked every draw and under the mattress. But it was nowhere to be found.

In the end, he chose the tiny, porcelain ballerina that hung on the outside of her door.

The following year, Mum and Dad took Jamie to the city where, for the next five years, he was to attend boarding school during the school term and would only go home to

Moonbroch for the holidays. It was a place of old stone and brick buildings many stories high, stain-glass windows, emerald green ovals, massive trees, boys in uniforms, teachers wearing ties, plaques and tradition. At boarding school, he would learn rugby and cricket, algebra and physics, Dad had told him.

Deep down, he sensed that going away to boarding school was to be the start of a new life for him — a life that would eventually lead him away from Moonbroch and into a future that was different to the one he had once imagined. But by choosing to move away from Moonbroch, he would also be choosing to move away from Sophie. Every memory he had of her was there.

'Excited?' Mum asked as they stood out the front of the boarding house with his oversized suitcase.

'Yes,' he said.

And he gave her his biggest, bravest smile.

CHAPTER 30

In a quiet corner of the Regatta Hotel, Jamie swallows a mouthful of beer, then sets his glass carefully to one side and stares at the plastic shopping bag that Mina has given him. With unsteady hands, he slides away the plastic and lifts out the glossy pink notebook with white dots and a spiral down one side.

It's been twenty-five years. The girl who wrote inside these pages with a feathered pencil would be thirty-seven now, had she lived. She'd probably have children of her own and he'd be their Uncle Jamie.

Running his fingers across the smooth surface of the notebook, he's surprised at the raggedness of his breathing. The sharp poignancy of his memories. He remembers the day he'd gone into her ballerina bedroom with his big idea and her suggesting they write down a list of possible superpowers in her notebook. He remembers the quick, neat way she wrote the words and how each superpower had seemed funnier than the one before, until they were both laughing so hard they were nearly wetting themselves.

It was the last time they'd been happy together. Brother and sister.

He takes two more mouthfuls of beer, dries his moist fingers on the front of his shirt and opens the notebook. His fingertips sweep whisper-light across the smooth paper seeking the slight indentations made by Sophie's pencil. These were amongst the last words his sister would ever write. Soon after, she became too lethargic to bother. Too ill. And then she was gone.

He gazes at the writing. Tiny words written by the hand of a child. Row after straight row. The forty superpowers are lined up neatly, one after the other — healing people, flying, dancing like Anna Pavlova (crossed out), seeing in the dark, being very, very strong, seeing through walls, walking through walls, teleportation — his eyes flick down to befuddlement and he smiles, remembering how clever and funny he'd thought that was.

Rubbing his hand over his face in an effort to control his emotions, he begins to think about Cass and about a love so intense, it makes his heart ache. He wonders if his powerful feelings are, in some small way, connected to the fact that his daughter looks so much like his sister once did.

Then, he begins to wonder about the notebook. And Mina.

How did it come to be in her possession? Why had she kept it all these years? Maybe she *had* taken it from Sophie's room. Maybe she lied that day in the chook yard when she said she'd found it in her own room under some magazines. Ray had said that she was a pathological liar. Could he have been right? With his elbows on the table, he sinks his head wearily down into his hands. He just doesn't know how to feel about her. Or how she fits into his life. She confuses him.

He recalls the strange apathy that seems to have defined her over the past few days. Once, when she had been a girl called Willis, she had stood out because of her strength and verve. Because of the sparkle in her eye and the way her smile could light up a room. Because of the way she stood up to people like Aggie and Onfro and refused to be put into a box. But all that is gone now. Life seems to have finally beaten her into submission. And it's no wonder. She's been a victim of domestic violence, she's driven, terrified, to Goomburra in the middle of the night in a gallant attempt to save her daughter, who subsequently ran away, she's been tied to a bed … and raped. The list of rotten things that has happened to her goes on and on. He could write at least forty of them in the notebook on the table, right next to his and Sophie's list of superpowers.

And who is looking out for her? Who is putting their arms around her and telling her that everything will be okay?

Something Ray said is needling at the back of his mind ... something about how her mother had topped herself — killed herself — and how he'd been the one who went to her pauper's funeral. Maybe Mina's mother had been the same as Mina — isolated and taken advantage of. The continuing cycle and all that.

And she had killed herself.

'Shit.'

He snaps the notebook closed, gulps down the remainder of his beer and scrambles to his feet.

He's doubled over trying to catch his breath after running back to the apartment from the pub and taking the fire stairs two at a time. When he reaches out to knock on Mina's door, it swings wide.

You'd think she'd have learned to lock up tight, he thinks, as he calls her name. But only silence greets him as he wanders through the empty apartment. Her keys and phone are still in their usual place on the kitchen peninsula. Her wallet is on her bedside table. Her running shoes sit untouched inside her walk-in robe.

Shit.

He sits on the sofa, takes a long settling breath and calls Cass.

'Dad? Is everything okay?' she says.

'Sure. Just running a bit late, love, that's all. Your mum asked me to call over to the apartment and pick something up and I'm here now but there's no sign of her. I'm just wondering. Do you have any idea where she might be? Does she have some special place she likes to go ... to chill out?'

'Dad,' Cass says. 'No-one says chill out anymore.'

'They don't? Goodness. You'll have to give your poor old Dad some lessons in how to be a modern human when we get home.'

She laughs.

'So, any ideas where your Mum might be?'

'Um ... well, sometimes, when she has some processing to do, she goes up to the roof.'

'Okay. Good. Thanks, love,' he says.

'Take as long as you like, Dad. Winter and I are helping Poppy make ratatouille and we're making extra so we can take some home.' Her voice drops to a whisper. 'It looks pretty gross.'

The door leading to the roof is unlocked and beyond the door is a rooftop terrace. Jamie sweeps his eyes around the neglected space. The ceramic floor tiles are covered with dust and grime. Two plastic chairs lie on their sides and a chipped coffee mug is filled with a slurry of cigarette butts and rain water. Someone once tried to grow tomatoes in pots up here, but the bushes are now dead and the leaves scattered.

Dark storm clouds have begun to gather across the afternoon sky. Jamie shades his eyes against the glaring light and studies the many structures that occupy the roof beyond the terrace.

No-one is up here.

Disappointed, he's about to go back downstairs when his eye is caught by some marks on the tiles — slight smudges, running one-way across the terrace to the barricade fence. They appear to have been made by bare feet, not shoes; and he quickly finds a pair of gold canvas sneakers tucked behind a large, concrete garden pot.

His mind begins to create images — Mina's broken and bloodied body lying on the asphalt in the carpark below, the look on Cass's face when she finds out that Mina is dead. Pushing such thoughts away, he begins to examine the rooftop more closely, looking for clues as to which section she may have jumped from. The largest structure on the roof is an enormous, box-shaped air-conditioning unit. It sits above an atrium that runs the full height of the older-style building. If a person were to crawl behind the unit, she would not be visible from the terrace or the ground. What if Mina is there? Behind that unit? What if she hasn't jumped yet?

He grips the top of the fence, pulls himself up by his arms until he can lift his right leg over the metal bar at the top, then balances a moment to give his nerves a chance to settle before lowering himself carefully down the other side. Intermittent cloud flashes light up a bruised, stormy sky as he drops two metres from the bottom of the fence to a lower section of roof.

He assumes a low crouch as he approaches the air-conditioning unit. Despite the rolling waves of nausea that always seem to accompany him whenever he's high up, he can't seem to help a small smile as he remembers coaching Cass up that cliff in Goomburra. An odd thought comes into his mind. In Goomburra, he and Cass had been creating their own story. Crawling shaky-kneed across this grimy rooftop is part of his story with Mina — a story that began twenty-five years ago in a distant place at the far reaches of the universe. A beautiful story about the friendship between a small, grieving boy and a lonely girl.

There's more to this story, he realises.

He's not ready for it to end.

His only option for getting behind the air-conditioning unit and checking if Mina is there is to sit on the very edge of the roof with his legs dangling and side-shuffle his way along. About half way, he realises that the unit is hollowed out to form a small recess.

Inside that recess is Mina.

CHAPTER 31

Most of the internal filter pads inside the disused air-conditioning unit have been removed and there's adequate space inside for both he and Mina to sit comfortably.

'Mind if I join you?' he asks.

When she doesn't answer, he carefully pushes himself backwards until he's leaning against the back of the recess with his legs stretched out in front, the same as her. From this position, he can see the stormy sky and distant city high-rises.

'It's like your own little cubby house,' he says. 'Do you come here often?'

'Often enough.'

'But why?'

'It reminds me of Moonbroch.'

The only way he can respond to such a surprising statement is with humour, so he gazes at the corroded, aluminium walls and remaining air filter pads and says, 'I see what you mean.'

She doesn't even smile. 'It's away from people, most of the city noise is filtered out and it smells like first rain on dry earth.'

'Oh.'

He inhales deeply.

After several minutes spent silently watching the sky, he says, 'I was worried about you.'

She glances across at him.

'You were worried I might harm myself?'

'The thought did cross my mind.'

'Well, you don't have to worry. I have no intention of killing myself. I'm not my mother.'

He's shocked by her sharp tone.

'Are you mad at me, Mina?' he says, looking sideways at her. 'Have I done something to upset you?'

Then he notices her glassy eyes and tight mouth and realises that her sharpness is because she's struggling to hold
her emotions in check.

'You're like everyone else, Jamie,' she says, eyes glistening. 'You judge before you know the facts. My mother killed
herself, so you assume I'm going to kill myself too. Ray says
I'm a liar, and you start to wonder — could it be true? Is
she a liar? Did she lie to me all those years ago?'

He squirms. 'Mina ... I ...'

'And, yes, I did lie to Ray,' she says, cutting him off. 'I
lied to Ray all the time, for my own protection. But I never
lied to you.'

'I never said you did.'

'I saw the look in your eyes when you opened that bag,'
she says. 'But, like I explained at the time, that notebook
wasn't in Sophie's room when I was at Moonbroch; it was
in the spare room where I was meant to be sleeping. And it
was Aggie who packed up my things, remember, because
she thought I was going to leave with Ray, and she must
have put it into my bag.'

A few seconds tick by, then she continues to speak. 'But
the fact that I never lied, and I never stole, is irrelevant because my place in the universe seems to have been prede-
termined. I was born worthless little Willy Johnson with the
crazy mother and that's who people are always going to assume I am. People are never going to make the effort to get
to know the real me because it's so much easier for them to
assume I am who they think I am, based on my past.'

Jamie wipes his palms against the fabric of his shorts.
He's nervous about opening up to her but knows if he
doesn't, he might lose her for good this time.

'Sometimes, assumptions are all a person has to go by,
Mina,' he says quietly. 'When they're not given the chance
to get to know the real person.'

He clears his throat. 'When I was a boy, I thought we'd
be friends forever. After you left Moonbroch, I waited and
waited for a letter or a phone call and when none came, I

… I guess that's when I began to make assumptions about you. I assumed you didn't care. I assumed you didn't want to be friends with a murderer. I assumed you hated me because I threatened to tell everyone it was your fault. Or that you blamed me for your accident. Or because I was just a stupid kid.'

'Jamie. None of those things are true.'

'I found out that my mother prevented you from contacting me. I'm sorry.'

Mina sighs. 'Her instincts were to be to protect her child. I understand that now.'

'I've also made assumptions about why you didn't want me to be part of your life. And about why you've always been so unpredictable when it comes to my seeing Cass.'

She begins to scratch her wrists.

'But now, I think it was because of Ray that you did these things.'

She nods. A tear traces a path across her flushed cheek.

'You'll never have to worry about him again,' he says softly.

'I'll never be free of him,' she says, pulling up her knees and hugging them to her chest.

He feels his heart rate increase. 'Why?'

'Because I once told him that I hit Onfro in the head with a lump of wood. What if he told someone else? What if, one day, my dirty little secret comes out and I'm charged with murder?'

Jamie shrugs. 'If and when that happens, I'll speak the truth. I'll say it was me who swung that club.'

He feels Mina stiffen beside him. She makes a small gurgling sound in her throat.

'What?' he asks, uncertain if she's laughing or about to cry.

'You think what happened to Onfro was entirely your fault, don't you? But you're wrong. It was as much my fault as yours.'

'It was me who hit him. Not you.'

'Yeah. But he was also high on drugs,' she says.

Jamie shudders as he remembers the man's chilling laughter just before he fell into the water.

'He was stoned?'

She nods. 'The first night Ray was on Moonbroch, he gave me these two pills — ecstasy or something like that — but I didn't swallow them. I spat them out when he wasn't looking and put them in the pocket of my shorts. Then, after you ran away, I was convinced Onfro was planning to kill you. He was so mad. So I crushed the pills in his coffee. I thought it might calm him down.'

'You drugged him?'

She nods. 'I was terrified he would notice the taste, but he just gulped the coffee down in three mouthfuls and went back outside with the rifle. So, you see, we both had some responsibility for what happened.'

Outside, the sky has darkened to a deep plum colour and rain begins to fall, pinging against the aluminium frame of the air-conditioning unit. Side-by-side, they watch the spectacle of the evening storm over the city landscape. He feels no compulsion to respond to Mina's startling revelation about the drugs. It is what it is. It happened. It's in the past.

After many minutes of silence, Mina speaks again, and he leans his head towards her to hear over the rain.

'Growing up,' she says, 'I was always being told I was stupid and dumb, and I was well on my way to turning into exactly the person everyone thought I would be. But when I went to Moonbroch, it was like, for a few days at least, I got to be someone different. I got to be me. I can't even begin to describe how much I loved Moonbroch. It was like a new world to me.'

Jamie nods. 'I remember. You noticed everything. The tiniest creatures. It was as if your senses were on steroids.'

She continues, her voice uncertain and introspective. 'You thought I was a better person than I actually was back then, you know. But because of it, I found myself wanting to be that amazing person you'd created in your head. Someone who stuck to her word and kept her promises.'

'I didn't create anything,' he says, softly. 'You might not have realised it, but you were already an amazing person long before I ever met you.'

She blushes. Her lips turn upwards. 'Maybe so. But once I went to Moonbroch and met you, I started to believe in myself. He — Ray — knew I had changed too, and he didn't like it one bit. He did everything he could to squash that little kernel of self-belief I had found out there. It made him crazy to know that, whatever he did, there was always going to be a part of me he could never reach.' She gives a nervous chuckle. 'Which probably explains my addiction to Moonbroch. And the reason I come up here and sit inside of this old air-conditioning unit like a crazy person. It feels as if there's this tiny thread that still connects my heart to that wild place out in the desert. It helps to keep me sane.'

Jamie shuffles around so he's facing her. 'What if you could go back to Moonbroch, Mina? And what if we could become forever friends again?' He blushes and gives her a shy smile. 'I mean … I don't see why those things are not possible. It might stop me making assumptions about you if I could get to know the real you. The fabulous you.'

As he talks, tears begin to flow unimpeded from her eyes. She doesn't attempt to wipe them away and she doesn't attempt to avert her eyes from the raw intensity in his face. The urge to look away and hide her emotions must be enormous, he knows, and the fact that she holds steady shows him her immense courage.

'Moonbroch is still there,' he says. 'If you want, I can take you back. First, I'll talk to my parents and set the record straight. I'll explain that you are a good person. And I'll tell them you were not responsible for what happened all those years ago. I'll tell them that you brought me nothing but friendship and hope at a time when my life had been hollowed out by grief. *And* I'll tell them how you came to be the mother of our beautiful daughter. And then, if you want, I'll take you home to Moonbroch.'

Through her tears, her mouth twists upwards. She crooks her little finger and lifts it up for him to see.

He gently entwines his own finger with hers.

'Pinkie promise,' he says.

'Friends forever?' she asks.

'Friends forever.'

EPILOGUE

On the first day of the summer school holidays, Wilhelmina wakes early in a state of anxious excitement. All morning, even though Jamie, Cass, and Winter are not expected to arrive on the station until late afternoon, she finds herself gazing down the dusty track towards the crossing, checking her watch and pacing ineffectively from job to job. Around four in the afternoon, unable to bear the waiting any longer, she decides to take the Cessna out of the hangar and escape to the skies.

High above the ground, she can see the wide land spread out in miniature below. It never ceases to take her breath away — the stony hills to the south, tree-lined creeks, red-sand and mulga country, the flats, the sheepyards, the shearing shed and homestead.

Her own little cottage arrived on the back of a truck last summer and is now nestled amongst a small grove of trees, not far from the gravestone of Mary Withers and the memorial plaques of Sophie McKenzie and Moira Tanning. Mary, Sophie, and Moira. At rest amongst the gidgee trees.

She gazes down at the curved roof of the hangar with its familiar giant letters on the roof — M.O.O.N.B.R.O.C.H. Repainting those letters had been the first job Jamie's parents, John and Sue, had given her after employing her as a station hand two and a half years ago. One look at her manicured hands had them convinced she wouldn't cope with stock work, but she had proven them wrong. Within months, she had begun to hear John McKenzie boasting about her talents to anyone who would listen — *best damn cocky I've ever seen, born for a life on the land, a real instinct for breeding sheep, a quick learner.* After he'd sent her away to get her pilot's license, she also became *the best bloody pilot* he'd ever seen. Sue McKenzie had been more circumspect about

Mina's place in their lives, and the warm friendship she now shares with Jamie's mother has built slowly over time.

She sighs. It feels good to have finally found her place in the world.

She takes the small aircraft out towards the rugged jump-ups on the Walls of China, loops away to the west and swoops over the channels and flood plains of the Paroo River before turning once again towards home.

She flies low over the homestead and her heart leaps at the sight of Jamie's old Landcruiser parked by the back gate. They're here. Finally. Arcing to the left, she studies the ground around the homestead, the hangar, across towards the end of the airstrip ... and finally sees what she's searching for. The people. They're coming to greet her.

John is already there, sitting astride his Yamaha motorbike, happily shooing the flies with a small leafy branch. Jamie is pushing his grandmother, Linley, across from the house in her four-wheel-drive wheelchair. He waves enthusiastically towards the Cessna as she swoops overhead.

Fifteen-year-old Winter, who will return to the city with Jamie in a week's time, is doing hands-free cartwheels along the track, much to the delight of the three dogs who run about her in excited circles. Mina's heart swells with affection and gratitude for the girl who has been such a wonderful friend to her daughter. Winter is brave, fiercely loyal, hilariously funny, and if she decides to do cartwheels, she does cartwheels. And she doesn't apologise to anyone about it.

Her stomach spasms with nervous anticipation as she searches for Cass, who she hasn't seen since the September school holidays. Once, she would never have believed she'd willingly live apart from her daughter for such a large part of each year. But it works. Jamie has a good job in the city and lives in the apartment with Cass during the school term; and every school holidays, he drives her, and often Winter, out to the station. Mina is immensely proud of her extraordinary daughter who moves with such ease between these two worlds — the city life she shares with her father and the country life she shares with her mother.

In the heavier shade of a large box tree, she spies Cass, one arm waving at her while the other rests casually across her grandmother's shoulders — Cass is already taller than Sue McKenzie. From the very first moment Sue and Cass met, Sue's sharp edges had softened and melted away; and the two now share an ineffable bond — the kind of bond Wilhelmina would love to have shared with an older woman when she was fifteen.

Watching the people on the ground below — John, Jamie, Linley, Winter, Sue and Cass — Mina feels the inexplicable sense of panic that always takes hold when she is overwhelmed with happiness. She's got people in her life who love and respect her. She's got a family. She's got a home and a job she loves. This kind of happiness must surely be a fragile thing that can shatter in an instant. She never wants to wake and discover it was all a dream. But what if those people on the ground change their mind about her? What if they decide she doesn't fit with them, after all? What if, one day, the façade of Wilhelmina shatters and everyone realises that she's still just worthless little Willy Johnson from the slums?

With her head filled with nauseating doubt, she loses her nerve about joining the family, pushes forward on the throttle and climbs back up towards the endless blue sky. Circling around again, she sees that Jamie has parked Linley's wheelchair next to Cass and Sue and is now standing by his father's motorbike, messing with the radio that sits over the handlebars. Moments later, his voice fills the plane's tiny cockpit.

'Hurry up and get your arse down here, Princess Wilhelmina of the Wide Blue Sky, and quit showing off.'

Despite her misgivings, her lips part into the widest grin. Maybe, just maybe, the dream will last.

She lines the plane up with the airstrip. Just before reaching the ground, she raises the nose slightly, closes the throttle and holds back the control yoke.

Then she gently touches down.

ACKNOWLEDGEMENTS

Thanks to everyone who believed in the possibility of me being a writer; to those who lavished me with their enthusiasm; and to those who challenged my thinking and shaped my thoughts. Thanks to those who shared their wisdom. And to those who listened with an open heart and a critical mind. I hope you know who you are because you are my inspiration.

To my beta readers — Judy Rafferty, Fay Cooney, Ellie O'Connell, Melissa Huestis, Jennifer Fordyce, Angela Banning and Anna Neumann — who agreed to read an unpolished story from an unknown writer and who provided me with such generous feedback and insight about my story and characters. And to Vincent Hall who instructed me in the art of flying small aircraft.

To the team at Black Phoenix Publishing Collective — to Dallas Baker for seeing the potential in my story and helping me get from being a dabbling creative to a published author; to my editor, Jessica Stewart, whose brilliance and kindness were second to none; to Shay for holding my hand and leading me through the awkward world of marketing; and to Alix Kwan, Christopher Magor, and Saira Manns.

Commissioning Editor: Dallas John Baker
Editor: Jessica Stewart
Copyeditor: Alix Kwan
Proofreader: Christopher Magor
Layout: Saira Manns
Marketing: Shayla Olsen and Lauren McKechnie
Cover Design: Wordsmiths Studio

Made in the USA
Middletown, DE
09 November 2019